The Magician's Accomplice

The Magician's Accomplice

Michael Genelin

Published by
Soho Press, Inc.
853 Broadway
New York, NY 10003

Library of Congress Cataloging-in-Publication Data
Genelin, Michael.
The magician's accomplice / Michael Genelin.
p. cm.
ISBN 978-1-56947-626-0
1. Matinova, Jana (Fictitious character)—Fiction. 2. Women police
chiefs—Fiction. 3. Police—Slovakia—Fiction. 4. College
students—Crimes against—Fiction. 5. Magicians—Fiction.
6. Europol—Fiction. I. Title.
PS3607.E53M34 2010
813'.6—dc22
2010008170

10 9 8 7 6 5 4 3 2 1

For the ladies in my life, Susy and Nora, who keep me involved and focused on what's truly important, and Noah, who always shows me the need for loving humor in the world.

Acknowledgments

I would like to continue to thank all of my friends in Slovakia for their inspiration and interest. And their fellow countrymen and women in the United States who helped me celebrate the release of my first Jana Matinova novel. Needless to say, Laura Huska, has outdone herself with this book: She has the sure red pencil that every author needs. I'd also like to acknowledge my family, who urged me on . . . and leave one last large thanks to the Muses. I tried to listen.

The Magician's Accomplice

The Savoy Hotel, once known as the Imperial Hotel or the Grand Hotel when the Hapsburgs reigned in Slovakia, was now the Carleton Savoy, part of a worldwide chain. The new owners had retained its classic façade so it still maintained its old majesty, satisfying the local city officials that they had not destroyed the "spirit of Bratislava." This, in turn, placated most of the old residents of the city, allowing them to continue telling their stories about the happenings during the Hapsburg reign. Of course, the owners of the hotel had gutted the interior and filled it with the new amenities foreign travelers now demand. Most of the Savoy's aristocratic ambience had been lost in the process.

Denis would have been happier with the old building. Even though he was young, he was a traditionalist: unlike other traditionalists, he accepted change as the way of the world, particularly today. On this Friday he was looking forward to the Royal Breakfast the Carleton Savoy provided for its guests. The breakfast buffet, set out in the dining room, was truly scrumptious, arrayed on a multiplicity of tables that occupied the whole center of a huge area, the platters of food encompassing everything the heart could possibly desire for breakfast.

Denis was not a guest of the hotel. He could never have

afforded a room here, even for one night. Like so many students in Slovakia and the rest of the world, Denis had very little money. He scrimped and scrounged his way through life, but today he was going to have a special treat. This weekend his belt would not pinch his backbone through a screamingly empty stomach, courtesy of the Carleton Savoy's Royal Breakfast.

To accomplish his mission without being discovered, Denis had dressed up in his only suit, put on a white shirt and tie, brushed his shoes, not forgetting to put a little fireplace soot on the leather to conceal the scuffs. To complete his image, he carried a large briefcase. Once at the entrance to the hotel, Denis took on the slightly bored look of a guest and walked through the front doors into the lobby as if he belonged. Today, as he passed the desk, the pretty young receptionist with the enormous brown eyes nodded at him. Denis nodded back with a slight smile, picking up a Slovak daily newspaper provided for guests on one of the large, ornate lobby tables, then walked to a corner chair next to a massive urn filled with newly cut flowers and unfolded the paper. Denis scanned the front page. The major headlines revealed that a loan firm had been burglarized and two hundred thousand euros had been stolen; the president had condemned a contract with the foreign oil company that was to exploit the new field found in the low Tatras; Finland's minister of economics had been killed in an apparent robbery; and the Communist Party legislators were making noises about delaying the enforcement of the new penal code. More of the same garbage, Denis thought. He managed a chuckle at the editorial cartoon with the U.S. pictured as an infant giant, a baby bottle labeled with a dollar sign in one hand, the other wiping his backside on little Slovakia.

Denis took a quick look at his watch. Mr. Fico was due in two minutes.

Every morning, Fico, as prompt as the clock over the desk, would hurry through the lobby, pass though the front doors, and walk out to the sedan that was waiting to take him to his business appointments. Fico did not generally have breakfast, which was the reason for Denis's interest in him. Although the man didn't know it, he was the key to filling Denis's stomach. This morning, Denis would identify himself to the maitre d' servicing the dining area as guest Miroslav Fico, Room 321. Denis merely needed to be sure that the real Fico had left before he commandeered the man's identity.

The elevator door beeped as it arrived on the ground floor, and right on time, Fico, leafing through a sheaf of papers he was carrying, bolted out and, looking neither right nor left, went through the front doors, entered a vehicle, and was driven out of the parking area. That was Denis's cue.

Denis folded his paper, picked up his briefcase, and, looking for all the world as if he belonged, casually strolled into the dining room.

"Good morning," he nodded to the maitre d', making sure to articulate clearly, "Room 321, Fico." The maitre d' checked off the number and name on his guest list and paid no further attention to Denis. The young man selected a window table, placed his briefcase on it, sauntered back to the multiplicity of tables laden with food, and, picking up a plate, strolled down the row. There was all kinds of cheeses, sausages, timbales of hot meats, Oeufs Benedictine, Oeufs Diablo, and Oeufs Bordelaise in hot trays, cold loin of pork with citrus fruit, baked ham, honey-roasted bacon with peaches, three types of quiche, tomato clafoutis, chevre infused with cognac on toasted walnut bread, melon, berries, and exotic fruits.

Denis viewed them all, just to be sure he didn't miss anything, then walked to the other side of the tables. He eyed the stewed chicken with chestnuts and ginger, buckwheat pancakes, gravlax, all types of rolls overflowing their bins, four types of fresh-baked muffins, and maple pecan waffles. It went on and on, truly a royal banquet. For a simple student, the array was mind-boggling. He decided to ignore most of it and focus on what he liked.

Denis decided his first course was to be simple. Initially, eggs, scrambled. Then fruit. Then a side dish of cereal, bacon, of course, and fresh rolls, and maybe just a bit of sweet cake to treat his palate. At the last minute, he decided to also have a few slices of sheep's milk cheese and a pair of sausages. His second and third trips would entail very little eating but a lot of filling his briefcase with food enough to take him through the next few days.

Denis sauntered to the window table where he had left his case and seated himself facing out the picture window looking toward the greenery and fountains, and an almost 180-degree panoramic view of Hviezodoslavovo Square. He set his dishes on the table, placed his napkin on his lap, then took his first forkful of eggs. They were delicious, mixed with some ingredient that Denis couldn't identify which made them smoother and moister than normal scrambled eggs.

As he ate, Denis watched the pedestrians outside the building. Beyond the hotel, people were scurrying to work, many coming from the direction of the Nový Most bridge, others from that of the baroque National Theater on the opposite side of the square, all busy ants going about their morning activities in Bratislava's Old Town.

Denis felt wonderful, momentarily the lord of all he surveyed, pretending to wealth he didn't have, eating a leisurely breakfast while everyone raced to jobs. If it weren't for the final exams at the university next week, it would be a perfect moment to be alive.

Outside, a man approached the window. The figure in a bulky black overcoat filled Denis's vision. The man's eyes were hidden by dark glasses, but there was no doubt that he was looking directly at Denis, examining him as if he were some type of small caged animal. For a moment, Denis felt a surge of anxiety, wondering if his fraud had been detected, then decided that it must be something else; the man was not dressed as a member of the hotel staff. Denis smiled, trying to appear friendly, wondering why the man continued to stare at him through the window.

Make him happy, Denis thought. It was morning and all was right with the world, Denis told himself. Today, inside the restaurant, he was a star. And, this morning, he even had an audience. It was a good time for him to perform a little sleight of hand.

Denis pulled a coin out of his jacket pocket, an American quarter. He picked up his napkin with his left hand, waved it in the air, and then covered the twenty-five-cent piece with the napkin, holding it so that the quarter was visible under the white cloth. Denis then bit through the cloth, into the quarter, twisting the coin with his teeth. Under the cloth the coin looked as if it had been bent in half. Denis went through the process again, this time reducing the coin obscured by the cloth to one-fourth of its size. He then whipped the napkin off the cloth, showing that the coin had indeed been bent in half, then half again. After a quick pause, Denis whisked the napkin over the coin, furiously rubbed the coin beneath the cloth, and then took the coin out. It had been restored to its original shape.

Denis looked cheerfully at the man outside the window for a response. The man was scanning what appeared to be a photograph through his dark glasses. The magic-coin act had not interested him. Denis felt like a failure; he told himself that some people are hard to entertain.

The man pulled a small automatic from his pocket and pointed it at Denis. Denis got out one word, "No!," when the man began firing. Five bullets pierced the window. The thick glass did not shatter, but the bullets left holes in the window, each surrounded by the slightest spidering. All of the bullets hit Denis. He was dead after the second slug hit him. The other shots had been fired as insurance.

The coin and napkin that Denis had used for his magic act slipped to the floor. The murderer pocketed his gun and quickly walked away, mixing with the passersby. People outside the hotel who'd heard the shots milled around anxiously; but in the huge space fronting the hotel, the gunshots had reverberated and it was not clear where they had come from.

The murder, and the murderer's escape, were over before anyone noticed that Denis, still sitting at breakfast, was dead. Aside from a few forkfuls of eggs, the young man had not eaten his royal meal.

Chapter 2

Jana Matinova was sound asleep after a night of investigating a barroom brawl that had resulted in the deaths of two men and one dog. The bar's manager had ordered the dog's owner to remove his dog. The man refused. The manager tried to pull the dog out by his collar. The dog bit him. The manager lost his temper and hit the dog over the head with a bottle, killing it. With that, the dog's owner attacked the manager with a knife, the manager used a broken bottle as a weapon, and before long both men were dead, one from stomach and lung wounds and the other from a severed artery.

Jana considered not answering the phone when it rang, but commanders of the Slovakian police are required to pay attention to their phone calls, so she eventually picked it up. "Be quick with whatever it is you have to tell me," she said. She had been dreaming of her lover, Peter Saris, and resented the interruption.

"Commander Matinova, it's Warrant Officer Seges."

She did not like to hear from her warrant officer during office hours, much less when she was in a deep sleep. She checked her alarm clock; she'd managed to get exactly an hour and a half of sleep. Jana was about to launch into a diatribe when she realized that Seges was aware she'd worked all night. One thing he knew, under these circumstances, was not to call unless it was urgent.

"The prime minister has been assassinated, I take it," she suggested.

"No, but there's been a murder."

"So, assign two of the senior men." There was a procedure for such events. Jana was still in the grip of sleep and could not remember who was on duty at the moment. "There's a duty roster. You should know who to assign."

"Commander, Colonel Trokan asked me to call you."

She sat up in bed. It couldn't be a simple murder if Trokan wanted her on the case.

"Who was killed?"

"From what our patrol people said, a student."

"From a well-known family?" She swung her legs from under the covers and sat on the edge of the bed.

"No, Commander."

"One student killing another?"

"I don't think so, Commander. I was told it looks like a professional assassination."

That jolted her awake.

"Where did it happen?"

"At the Carleton Savoy."

A professional killing at the Carleton. Now it made sense. The colonel was a canny man who carefully watched his back; he would want her to supervise this case. It would make the news. And whenever there was big money involved, as there was with this hotel, the management would want assurance that the police thought enough of the seriousness of the situation to attach a senior officer to lead the investigation.

"Send a team to the site."

"They're already there."

It wasn't like her warrant officer to be this efficient. He

was too lazy and inept. But, she guessed, even Seges recognized the need to appear competent on a case like this.

"I'll be there," she growled into the phone, then hung up.

Thirty minutes later she walked through the front door of the hotel.

The dining-room staff huddled at two tables in the corner, as far away from the murder victim as they could get and still be in the room. Several guests occupied another corner. They were being selected and questioned one by one in the atrium area by the investigators from Jana's division.

Jana nodded to her men. One of them, Benco, began to approach her. Jana gestured him back to the witness he was questioning. She surveyed the room, the table at the window where the body was still being examined and photographed, then focused through the windows on the area fronting the restaurant.

A perimeter of barriers had been set up outside to keep the gawkers away. Canvas, quickly supplied courtesy of the hotel, had been stretched high enough to block both the window in front of the body and the immediate area around it. They didn't want people to see a corpse inside the dining room. Bad for business.

Jana walked to a table next to the body, where Elias, another of Jana's investigators, was seated listing the contents of the dead man's briefcase as well as the items that had been taken from his pockets.

"Commander," he nodded at her. "The kid's name was Denis Macek, a student at the Polytechnic University." He slid the decedent's student ID over to her. Jana studied the picture of the young man in the left-hand corner of the laminated card, then put it down. Not much else, not even a book in the briefcase. Just waxed paper peeping out, apparently lining the case. She fingered the paper. "This is the first time I've seen a male student who took such a thing as cleanliness at all seriously." She sighed. "I guess I have to go pay my respects to the dead."

"Good morning, Denis," she murmured to the body as she started examining it. "I'm truly sorry you find yourself in this position. I grieve for you. If you'd lived, you might have gone on to raise a family and do great things." She glanced around and saw their photographer sitting in a chair, munching on a celery stick he had purloined from the food tables, which were still set up. "Have you got all the photographs you need?"

He wiped his mouth. "Yes, Commander."

Jana looked at the holes in the window next to the dead student. "Did you get close-ups of the area in the window penetrated by the bullets?"

"Of course, Commander."

She checked the floor under the dead youth. A napkin and what looked like a coin barely protruded from beneath the decedent's shoe.

"These items as well," she instructed the photographer.

Jana moved the victim's foot slightly to reveal the coin. She signaled the photographer to take a few more photos and then picked up both the coin and the napkin.

She moved around to the other side of the table to face the dead youth. For a student, he was all dressed up. It was neither Sunday nor a holiday. Students were rarely attired the way he was unless forced to by their parents or by other pressing circumstances. Jana slipped on a pair of plastic gloves and looked closely at the bullet holes in the window, checking the angle of the shots as well as she could, even feeling the holes to check their paths through the glass. A close pattern, which meant an individual who knew how to handle a pistol. A professional.

Jana gestured for the photographer to move back, then stood behind the dead youth. "I'm about to pull him erect in the chair. I want you to take full photos with him in the upright position, then closeup shots of the wounds both with the jacket open and the jacket closed."

Jana took a fistful of the dead youth's hair with one hand and seized his shoulder with the other, easing him erect, propping him up in the chair so he would not fall, walked around to look at him, then straightened his jacket. All the bullets had hit him in the chest. Yes, the assassin had been a good shot. As the photographer began to take the new set of photos, she went back to Elias and sat opposite him as he began placing the belongings of the dead youth into a large evidence envelope. Jana stopped him.

"I want a quick look."

She examined each personal item: the boy's student ID card, a comb, a ballpoint pen, tissues, a wallet with no cash, only a driver's license. There were also a few coins of no real interest. Except for the driver's license, which she kept, Jana indicated that Elias could now bag the rest of the items.

"Did you move the body to get these items?"

"No. I reached around inside his jacket pocket and pulled them out. I patted the pants pockets. Nothing in there."

"You missed two items on the floor at his feet." She held up the napkin and the coin. "You're getting careless."

"Sorry, Commander."

"That's why we have at least two people on the scene: four eyes are better than two." She gave him the napkin and examined the quarter herself. "An American coin. Something odd about it." She held it up to the light, running her fingers around the rim. "Slightly uneven." She began to press around its edge, and was able to bend the coin, then bend it again.

"You're a magician, Commander."

"A trick coin." She paused, thinking. "What was an American coin for a magic act doing on the floor?"

"Perhaps we should see if there is an American magician registered at the hotel."

"Perhaps. Most likely not," she concluded. "Magicians keep close tabs on their props. Their livelihood depends on them. Log it on the manifest of items. I'll keep it for a while." She slipped it into her pocket. "What time was the decedent shot?"

"Give or take a few minutes, just about 7:45."

"Did anyone see the actual killing?" She sighed, knowing her question was probably futile. Unless they were professionals, themselves in the business of killing people, or police officers, everyone else would have been too excited or too frightened to remember what happened, much less give an accurate description of the murderer.

"No one inside or outside that we could find," Elias responded. "Patrol officers are still walking around the square trying to locate anyone who can give us a description. So far, zero. One of the staff here saw a man wearing an overcoat, dark glasses, and a hat walking away from the window, but he's not sure the man was the shooter and so far has not been able to give us anything except a build and a height that changes every time our witness thinks about it."

Jana checked the name on the driver's license. "Hello again, Denis Macek." She looked up at Elias. "Is he a guest at the hotel?"

"The manager of the hotel says he's not registered. She

assumes the dead kid was just walk-in traffic having the Royal Breakfast."

"Couldn't be: no money in his wallet and no credit cards."

"Maybe he was waiting for someone else to join him and pay for the meal?"

"The food was on the plate in front of him. The fork had bits of egg on it. He was already eating, so he wasn't waiting for anyone." She nodded, in the direction of the staff tables. "That the staff in the corner?" Without waiting for an answer, she walked over to them.

"Hello, everyone. I am Commander Jana Matinova." The employees were seated at two tables separated by a gap of about three feet. "Let's move the tables together. That way we can all talk, like one big family."

She pulled up a chair and sat. "I'd like you all to know that I've heard such great things about the staff at this hotel that I consider it an honor to sit here with you."

There were a few nods, sheepish smiles, and murmurs of "thank you" from the group.

"However, there is one thing that I don't understand— besides, of course, the question of who killed the victim. How could this man," she consulted the driver's license of the decedent, "Denis Macek, a student at Polytechnic University, breakfast here today?"

"We were serving it," murmured one of the waiters, not understanding what she meant.

"I know you were serving." She smiled at the maitre d'. "You were working the front of the restaurant today, I assume?"

"I'm the host for the restaurant," he conceded.

"Then you would have approved Mr. Macek's arrival for breakfast."

He nodded, with a worried look. "I don't know a Mr. Macek. I know we have a guest named Miroslav Fico. The man who was killed told me he was Mr. Fico, so I allowed him in."

"And Fico is actually staying in the hotel?"

"I have a guest list. He's on it."

"Do you know what Mr. Fico looks like?"

"He's the dead man."

"I don't think so, sir." She stood.

"Can we leave?" asked a waiter.

"Only when the other officers tell you that you're free to go. That may be a while yet. Thank you all." Jana walked back to Elias, who was watching the photographer complete his pictures.

"Anything?" he asked Jana.

"They thought the dead student was a guest, a man named Miroslav Fico. The front desk is our next stop."

Elias fell in step with her. Jana waved the decedent's license at her investigator. "I think our dead student was scheming to get himself a free breakfast. He knew Fico was a guest. He used Fico's name to get seated. I have to believe our student didn't want to be caught stealing a breakfast. So, how did our dead young man know there was a guest registered by the name of Fico, and how did he know Fico was not having breakfast so he could successfully impersonate him?"

They walked out of the dining area and over to the registration desk. A woman wearing a severe business suit bearing a nameplate that identified her as the hotel manager stood next to the desk fidgeting with her hands. She walked a few steps toward them, her lips pursed with stress.

"I understand the job the police have to do, but can you tell me how long you must keep the corpse in there? We have guests who will not appreciate seeing a dead man in the dining area."

"Just a while longer. Perhaps another half hour." Jana assured her. "Are the desk staff members who were on duty at the time of the killing still here?"

"Their shifts aren't over yet."

"I'd like to talk to them," Jana said.

"We have a hotel to run. They can't be occupied for very long."

"Just a short conversation."

A man and two women were huddled at the rear of the counter. The manager beckoned to them, nodded, then stationed herself behind the desk to serve guests as the three desk employees somewhat anxiously walked over.

"I'm Commander Matinova; this is Investigator Elias."

The three desk people nodded at the two police officers. Jana held out the dead youth's driver's license for them to examine.

"Tell us if you recognize either the young man in the photo or the name on the license."

The man and the older of the women looked at the license, both of them murmuring a quick "no." The younger woman hesitated. She stared at the photo silently. When she finally lifted her head, a solitary tear trickled down her face.

"Thank you both." Jana dismissed the other two desk clerks. The young woman's ID tag read "Maria." "Maria, I'd like you to stay for a few more minutes," Jana said. "I think you knew the victim," Jana suggested.

As soon as the other two clerks returned to the counter, the manager darted over to Jana. "Why are you detaining Maria?" She stared into the young woman's face. "What have you done?" she demanded.

Jana put her hand on the manager's shoulder. "She hasn't done anything. Absolutely nothing! It's just that we want to clarify a few points. We need to speak privately with Maria. Procedure, you know."

The manager hesitated, darting a last suspicious glance at Maria, reluctantly acquiescing. After a last quick warning glance at Maria, she moved away from them.

"Perhaps we can sit over here," Jana suggested, leading the young woman to a configuration of easy chairs and couches that had been set up in the lobby for guests and their visitors. "It's always best to be comfortable." Jana spoke softly, trying to assure Maria that she was not someone to be afraid of. Jana gestured at one of the couches, easing herself down next to Maria. Elias took one of the chairs across from them.

"Let me promise you that anything you say to me or my associate will be kept from the manager and anyone else at the hotel," Jana began. "Only police officers will have access to what you say. So you have nothing to fear from the manager or anyone else at the hotel, or in your private life. Everything you tell us will be confidential. I hope that eases any fears you might have about talking to us."

Maria thought, then nodded.

"Good. Please tell me your full name."

"Maria Anikova."

"May I call you Maria?"

"Yes."

"Good. My name is Jana."

"Jana." Maria tried to smile. "Pleased to meet you."

"Not too pleased, under these circumstances, though?"

Another tear trickled down Maria's face.

"How well did you know the young man who was killed?"

"We grew up together. I knew his mother and father before they died. I know his Uncle Denis."

Jana glanced at the dead youth's license, then looked up at Maria. "The same name as your friend?"

"Yes. Denis was named after his uncle."

Elias made a note of the fact.

"Your friend didn't have much money, did he?"

"No."

"Am I correct: he was not a guest at the hotel?"

"Yes, that's correct."

"So, you were trying to help him. That's what friends are for, to help each other."

"We'd been friends for a long time."

Jana nodded approvingly. "Old friends are the best."

"He didn't eat regularly. He had to go days without meals." The tears flowed more freely down Maria's face. "I couldn't stand to see him wasting away."

"And that's how he came to eat breakfast here?"

"This was the first time. I thought it would be wonderful if he could have the Royal Breakfast." She added, "They prepare so much food in the kitchen for today. Too much! What isn't eaten is thrown away. Wasted! How could it hurt to give some of it to Denis? Kindness is everything."

"I can understand that," Jana nodded. "Arranging for him to have breakfast even once a week was very thoughtful. You jeopardized your job to keep him from starving. You were a true pal." Jana paused, trying to think of a diplomatic way to ask the young woman her next question. There was no other way except to directly put it to her. "Were you having a sexual relationship with Mr. Macek?"

Maria stared at her, embarrassed. "We were friends. We grew up together. We were never . . . lovers!"

"I see, just friends." Jana thought for a moment. "Let me make sure I understand how you worked it. You give him the name of a guest and a room number, a guest who had checked out early that morning without breakfast, or one you knew wouldn't eat breakfast. At a certain time your friend came into the hotel dressed in his best clothes, perhaps idled around until the guest left, and then walked into the dining room, simply telling the maitre d' that he was that guest and giving the suite or room number corresponding to the actual guest's. The maitre d' checked him against his guest list. Your friend would then eat a meal without having to pay for it."

"Yes."

"Did your friend have any enemies? People who might want to kill him?"

"He was a lovely person. Everyone liked him. He never did any harm to anyone."

"So, no enemies. Anything else you can think of which might be helpful?"

Maria shook her head. "Nothing."

Jana nodded, again trying to be reassuring. "Thank you for your cooperation, Maria. You can go now." They stood, the young woman looked at her with pleading eyes. "Not to worry," Jana assured her. "Your job is safe. I won't tell the manager."

Maria hurried back to her work. Almost immediately, the manager approached the two detectives.

"What did she have to say?" she demanded.

"Nothing of any importance, except how much she liked working here."

The manager's face registered surprise.

"Then why did you have to talk to her alone?"

"We cross-check every statement. We often get something

by talking to people separately. Unfortunately, she had no information for us. I understand your concern, though. This business is bad for the reputation of the hotel. But don't be troubled. Your staff doesn't seem to be involved. Relax. In a little while, everything will return to normal."

Jana and Elias left the hotel.

Once outside, past the revolving doors, Jana paused before she went to her car. "Why would anyone want to execute a starving student?"

"No reason I can see."

"Was Fico, the man whom the victim impersonated, the real target of the murder?"

"A mistake killing? The killer thought the student was Fico?"

"A possibility. You checked Fico's room?"

"I searched it."

"There was nothing worth a second look?"

"Nothing there worth a second or even a first look. We're trying to locate Fico. I've left word we want to see him."

"If possible, I want to be at the interview."

"Yes, Commander."

Jana looked at the screen that prevented the crowd of spectators from gazing into the restaurant's window. They all knew by now that someone had been killed. Many would stay at their vantage points until the body was removed. Jana saw it all the time at crime scenes: there is nothing like a murder to stir up morbid curiosity.

Jana went to her car and began to drive to headquarters. After traveling a short distance, she abruptly realized that she didn't have to go to her office. Elias would write up the preliminary reports and continue the investigation. The reports would be on her desk the next morning. She still had a chance to get at least a few hours of sleep before reviewing the summary of the initial police investigation. No, she was no longer sleepy, but she still had the time to spare. On a romantic whim, Jana decided to pay a quick visit to Peter Saris at work.

Peter was a prosecutor in the attorney general's department. He was currently so tied up in pulling together a corruption case that he often slept at his office. He'd been doing so for the last three days. Jana understood, but she hated this routine because it kept him away from her. If she went there now, she would manage to kiss him once or twice before he shooed her out.

They had been going together for slightly less than a year. Their only problem was that since he was a prosecutor and she was a police commander, they had to keep up an appearance of formality to prevent the gossipmongers from wreaking havoc on their careers.

Recently, they had decided to stop sneaking around and to announce their engagement as soon as he was finished with his current case. It would be a relief to finally have everything out in the open, although, as she reminded herself, everyone in both of their departments seemed to know about it; but aside from the jokes that her men privately told each other about her affair with Peter, they had kept out of the public eye. Soon even the veiled sexual innuendos and back-office gossip would end.

Jana pulled into the parking lot at the side of the Ministry of Justice and eased her car into the last space available, still dreaming of the future with Peter, got out of her car, and walked to the front of the building. It wasn't until she began climbing the steps to the entrance that she saw the fire trucks on Palissady Ulica, with police vehicles lined up behind them. Officers were redirecting traffic away from the front of the building, and several officers, one of them wearing the gear of the bomb disposal unit, were just leaving the building. The men saluted her as they walked past.

A bomb scare, Jana thought.

"What's happening?" she called after them.

"A bomb," one of them called back.

He'd said a bomb, not a bomb scare. It was real.

Jana hurried through the front door. The guards nodded in recognition as she angled around the table to avoid the metal detectors, then turned left, going toward the stairs leading up to the floor where Peter had his office. There was a small cluster of people at the bottom of the stairs, a few judges, police officers, and Trokan, who saw her as soon as she strode in. He was in full uniform, which was unusual for him. Trokan came toward her, deliberately blocking her way.

"Let's walk over there and talk." He took her arm, which was also unusual. From the look on his face, something was dreadfully wrong.

"Sit down." He pointed to a wall bench.

She looked at his face. He was going to tell her something terrible.

"I'll stand."

"I'm ordering you to sit."

She continued looking at his face.

"It's Peter Saris?"

"Yes."

She could feel the tremors going though her body, one wave following another, traveling down to her legs, her knees starting to go, her body beginning to sway. She managed to lock her knees and braced herself with a straight arm against the wall. She willed herself to stay erect.

"He's dead?"

Trokan nodded, concerned, watching her. "You should sit down."

"What happened?"

"A phone bomb. There was a call on his office phone, his secretary picked it up, transferred it to Peter, and when he answered, the device was triggered. He died immediately. No pain," he tried to assure her.

"Where is he?"

"They're taking him out now."

She turned toward the stairs. Trokan put his hand on her shoulder, trying to slow her down. She shrugged him off.

"At the moment it would be better to stay away from me, Colonel."

"You want to look at him, I know. He's much damaged. If you insist on seeing him, then wait until he's been . . . made to look a little better."

They were bringing the body down the steps on a wheeled stretcher. Jana started toward the stairs, Trokan walking with her.

"Jana, he wouldn't like you to see him this way. Allow us to take him away. Let it go for now. Then we can begin to deal with this thing as police should." He tried to grab her arm, to stop her. She shook him off again, reaching the gurney just as they wheeled it onto the marble floor.

"Stop!" she ordered the attendants. "Unzip the bag. I want to see him."

They looked at her in confusion. Trokan quickly stepped forward. "Open it so she can see the face."

One of the attendants unzippered the body bag so the head was visible. Part of the skull was gone; the face that remained was almost completely shredded.

It was Peter; it also wasn't Peter. Nothing was left of the Peter she loved. He had died and left her. She fought back the urge to scream, to shout her grief and anger and sorrow at everyone here. Instead, she did what so many police officers have to do: she screamed inside herself. Then silently screamed again. She took deep breaths to calm herself, and then held the air in her lungs for a long moment.

The bag was empty. The opening of the zipper merely revealed that the rest of the sack was vacant. Her lover was somewhere else. He wasn't on the gurney. Not her Peter. Not her laughing, loving Peter.

She zipped the bag closed.

They rolled the gurney out of the building.

Using the banister for support, Jana slowly lowered herself to a sitting position on a step. Trokan eased himself down next to her.

They sat there for two hours before Trokan finally persuaded her to go home.

Chapter 3

Jana couldn't bear to attend the funeral. The air would be filled with empty phrases and condolences which would never ease her grief. She could not face all the people who would be there, the attorney general impotently promising to exact vengeance; the prime minister's turning it to his own advantage by urging that the national assembly pass the pending program of criminal law reforms; and everyone eyeing her, wondering about her relationship with Peter. The only thing in common would be their thanks that they hadn't been the one who'd answered the exploding phone.

Instead, she went to the cemetery two days later, bringing a small bouquet of flowers which she laid on the ground near the grave. She couldn't get very close because of the heaps of bouquets placed there by Peter's friends, family, and colleagues, as well as the politicians who hoped to impress constituents with the large condolence cards with their names prominently displayed affixed to the flowers. Jana could only stand there, mute, hoping Peter would miraculously appear next to her, laughing, to tell Jana it was an elaborate hoax to gain some advantage in a case he was investigating. Only it was no hoax; Peter did not appear and Jana went back to her house, unable to vent her grief except in the privacy of her home.

She cried on and off for days; everything she did around the house was done mechanically. She managed to get up in the morning, brush her teeth, make breakfast, and perform all daily tasks by rote. There was no other way she could have survived. Trokan called her every day, and she managed to say a few words, but intense feelings of loss came at her in waves, pulses varied by anger and disbelief. Slowly, eventually, she had a gradual perception that she needed her normal life back. At the beginning of the following week, she got up very early one morning and decided she had to go to work. Jana went directly to her office that Monday, arriving before anyone else on that shift. She sat at her desk, unable to remember anything she'd been working on. She panicked for a moment, wondering if she'd had a stroke and was now unable to think.

Jana struggled to focus, to take herself back to the period immediately before Peter's death. But Peter's image kept conjuring itself up and she began once again to drown in a sea of disparate emotions.

She ultimately pulled herself together by forcing herself to look intently at the pieces of furniture in her office, describing each item aloud in the most minute detail she could, noticing the grain in the chairs in front of her desk, the nicks and scratches on her cabinets, the very thin layer of dust on the top of a wall table, another wall table holding the remnants of a few flowers that had, in the week she had been away, withered into desiccation.

It finally came to her: she had gone to the Carleton Savoy on her last day at work. As soon as she remembered going to the Carleton she recalled the investigation she had participated in and began to make notes of what she remembered. When she got to the end of the crime-scene investigation, she remembered driving to see Peter. Jana felt her emotions welling up. She forced herself to think again about the murder of the student.

The victim was studying geological engineering; something she had no knowledge of. Evidently he'd been a bright young man, but one with so little money that he was hungry enough to try to "steal" breakfast. Jana amended the thought slightly She recalled the briefcase with the wax paper lining. Denis Macek was planning to steal more food than he could eat for breakfast. He was going to stuff food inside the briefcase after he had filled himself up that morning, and he was trying to ensure that the food he put in the briefcase to eat over the next few days would not cling to the inside of the case and, subsequently, get grease on his school textbooks and papers.

Jana heard people moving around the outer offices. The staff was starting to arrive for work. What was she supposed to say to her officers? That she had taken a short vacation and now wanted them to brief her on the current status of their cases? "Yes" to the briefing; no, she would be open and straightforward about her sorrow. She had been mourning and had needed the time off. They knew about Peter. They would understand.

She forced herself to focus again on the killing at the hotel. A motive was out there, just hanging out of reach, begging Jana to find it. Could there be a connection between the student's murder and Peter's death? Bratislava was not a town where professional killings occurred daily. These had both been carefully orchestrated assassinations. Jana had to look at the possibility. She went on with her analysis. Several people must have been involved. Yes, she agreed with herself: multiple killers, a minimum of two: the professional shooter and at least one other person who had paid for and ordered the shooting. As for Peter's murder, if his killer had not shot the student, then at least three people were involved: two "hit men" and at least one "customer" who had paid for the gunman. If the killings were not related, then . . . a second "customer."

Jana thought over the false use of the hotel guest's name in the student murder. Had the killer actually made a mistake when he shot the young man? Was he supposed to kill the man whose identity the student had appropriated? And, if so, how could he have known that "Fico" was supposed to be in that particular place at that particular time?

Jana heard more people arriving in the outer offices, cheerful, drinking tea or coffee, exchanging pleasantries. She toyed with the idea of joining them, and then realized that she would be a dead weight on their spirits. Instead, she dialed Elias to get an update on the investigation. A recorded message referred her to another number where Elias could be reached. She called, Elias answered. "Anti-Corruption Division, Investigator Elias. Can I help you?"

"Matinova here. What are you doing up in the Anti-Corruption Division?"

"I've been transferred, Commander. Just a temporary seconding."

"Why the transfer?"

There was a momentary silence. She could hear his breathing get louder, as if he were under stress.

"They wanted an experienced homicide investigator."

"What case, Elias?" As soon as Jana asked the question, she knew the answer. Because of his experience, they had assigned Elias to investigate Peter's killing. That was bad. Anti-Corruption would lock up all information. Any evidence they found, and progress or lack of progress about the investigation, would be buried in the sealed files of the very secretive personnel of that division. That way, they would also keep control of, and silence about, the cases Peter had been looking into. Yet one case or another under their jurisdiction was almost assuredly the basis for Peter's murder.

"I asked you a question, Elias."

"I'm not allowed to discuss any of the cases I've been assigned to here, Commander."

"Understand this, I didn't just ask you a question: it was an order. Are you working on the telephone murder of the prosecutor?"

"Commander, I'm under other orders that supersede yours. To repeat, I can't answer any of your questions. Good-bye, Commander." He hung up.

Jana stared at the receiver as if it had betrayed her and then slowly placed it on its cradle. She had been walled off from the investigation of Peter's death. She had also not received any progress reports on the killing of the student. Elias's answer was the key: someone in the higher echelons of command had approved Elias's transfer and set up the roadblock to her participation in either investigation.

It took a few seconds for Jana to realize that her phone was ringing. She grudgingly answered it. "Matinova here."

"That's not the approved way to answer the phone, Commander."

"Colonel?"

"Yes, I heard you had signed in."

Jana *hadn't* signed the roster when she came in.

"I assume Elias told you."

Trokan was not the slightest degree nonplussed about being caught in a fabrication. "He seemed a little worried on the phone. He's a good man." There was a moment of silence. "You feel okay?"

"Never better."

"That's a lie."

"Yes, it's a lie."

"Do you feel well enough to come into my office? I need to talk to you."

He didn't wait for her answer.

She walked toward Trokan's office, passing a number of her men. Each nodded in a simple greeting. Everyone was pretending that she had never been away and this was just another day at police headquarters. It was better this way. She silently thanked them all, glad they were making it easy for her. Trokan's door was open; Jana walked in without knocking.

The colonel looked up from a set of reports he was studying, nodded her to a chair, then walked to his office door and closed it. He came over, hunkered down near her, and took her hand, patting it in consolation.

"I'm glad you're back."

"Elias was assigned to Anti-Corruption. You had to be the one who assigned him. Why remove him from my unit, Colonel?"

"As I said, he's a good man. It seemed like a good idea."

"He's taken the hotel case with him?"

"He's the one who carried out the initial phase of the investigation, so it seemed appropriate."

"And the killing of . . . the prosecutor?"

"We've decided to conduct a discreet investigation. There are lots of possibilities as to where it will go, and prudence is advisable. We don't want any of the cases that Peter was working on to be compromised. You, of all people, should realize that. Your involvement would also present the appearance of a conflict of interest. We don't want to taint any case we develop." He eased himself erect, then walked back to his desk, sighing as he sat down. "I find I like softer chairs as I age." He leaned back , gazing at Jana, waiting for her to speak.

"That means I'm to sit on my hands." She held her hands up for him to see. "These hands don't like people to sit on them, even if it's me. They complain. They're only happy when they have work to do."

"I would never have my very best investigator sit on her hands. That'd be a waste of her considerable resources and the state's money, and I'm very careful with the state's money."

"You're asking Elias to do a lot."

"At one time or other, we each have to shoulder the burden. Which also means you. We have a special assignment for you."

Jana was surprised by this unexpected announcement. Everything was taking a turn for the worse.

"I want to continue with the work I've been doing."

Trokan went on as if he hadn't heard her, finding a black loose-leaf book marked CONFIDENTIAL on its cover. "This is the protocol for Europol. Slovakia is required to send another representative to The Hague to work on the cases which are generated through the program. Europol has cross-country jurisdiction, which means, as an investigative body, it has enormous power. We've selected you as the new representative of our country."

He placed the book on the desk in front of her and waited for her to take it. Jana did not move.

"You want to stay here, I know," Trokan growled. Then he softened his voice. "Your man is dead, and there is nothing that can be done about that."

"I can do at least one thing about it."

"No, you can't find the killer. Because you're not working the case. You are officially relieved of your duties in this division. You have one responsibility left: to go to The Hague. No one, I repeat, no one does what *they* feel *they* want to do in our police force. If, for a second, you think I'm going to allow you to go off on your own because of our close relationship over the years, you're mistaken."

"I'll find out why he was killed; I'll find out who killed him. It's all very simple."

"Yes, it's simple: you won't remain on the police force if you begin an illegal investigation of your own. Rogue police officers don't stay on the force." He exhaled noisily, then tried another tack. "We have known each other for half-of-forever. I've done you favors; you've done me favors. Do me one last favor: don't make me have to begin a disciplinary proceeding which you can't win. Go to Europol. Then, if we don't succeed in our investigation here, I will bring you back in a bit and you can take it over. I promise you, my word of honor as your friend and colonel, I'll do that.

"Realize, this new assignment has been cleared all the way through to the minister. He has spoken, and he won't like it if you disobey him. And, since I'm charged with having my subordinates do what he wants, he won't like *me* if you disobey the order. And I would become very cranky and be forced to do things to you which I will hate myself for afterward. So, go, Jana. Please go!

Jana wanted to get up and pound on his desk, to shriek at Trokan until he could no longer stand it and had to agree with her, then run to the minister's office and put a gun to his head to force him into letting her stay to work on the case. In the end, after flirting with these fantasies, Jana looked at the reality of the situation. If they kept the case files away from her, refusing to let her work as a police officer with access to all the resources that the department had, she would be stymied. She had no option.

Jana nodded her assent. "Okay."

"Good. Be well, Jana."

Jana went home. She had been given three days to prepare to leave the country.

But after an hour of sitting, looking at the walls of her kitchen, Jana decided to take action. She had three days. She had to take advantage of them. Jana also knew the first place she would start: Peter's apartment.

Chapter 4

It did not take her long to get to the apartment. However, she sat in her car outside for a while to steel herself to return to Peter's space. Being inside would conjure up all the memories she had of the two of them together: holding hands with him, the brush of a kiss on her neck, an exchange of looks that told them both how connected they were to each other, making love in his bed. She would remember everything that the relationship meant, and everything that was now irretrievably lost. Jana tried to repress her feelings, to compel herself to ignore memories, to exist only in the present. She would always have Peter in her mind. He would go with her wherever she went. But, at the moment, Jana had little time to waste. At the moment, recalling memories was not the way to spend her time, for her or for him.

She slid out of her car and walked into the building and climbed the stairs to the third floor where Peter had lived, all the while wondering what she would look for. The answer was simple: Peter's murder had to be connected to his investigations. She had no access to his office files, but he brought work home, and maybe she would find case files, notes, photographs, potential exhibits, anything and everything that a trial lawyer would use.

When she reached the door, Jana pushed the remaining stray thoughts of her lover away and, as a precaution, knocked on the door. Almost immediately, it opened. A bird-beaked, heavy-set old woman stood in the doorway. Jana recognized her as the landlady, a harridan who would howl if you were even a half-day late with the rent or committed some imagined infraction of the house rules. The landlady looked at Jana, not recognizing her. Then she frowned, a glint of recognition arriving in her eyes.

"You're the police officer Saris was having a fling with."

Jana had to stop herself from acting on her impulse to slap the woman.

"We planned to be married."

"If he was planning to marry you, why did he have the other woman stay here?"

This question drove Jana back a step.

"Surprised you, no?" The woman's face had a malevolent glow. "Women should know better when it comes to men. None of them are faithful."

Jana took a breath, remembering what the woman was: a troll posing as a human being. She contained her anger.

"I'm here to look over the apartment."

"It's not your apartment. Why should I let you in?"

"Because I'm here as a police commander on an official investigation. So get out of my way."

"A whole bunch of them already investigated."

"Then one more won't matter. In case you didn't understand, I said get out of my way."

The woman tried to outstare Jana, finally realizing that Jana was going to come in whether she liked it or not, and grudgingly stepped aside.

"You're not going to move the furniture around again? I've spent all day putting everything back where it belonged, and I won't stand for you making another mess."

The woman droned on, whining about the inconvenience

and the extra work that she'd had to endure over the last week because that "man" had gotten himself killed. Except for an occasional twinge, Jana went about her business, managing to block out most of the woman's litany of complaints.

The rooms had changed. Nothing personal was left; everything had been boxed up and taken away by Peter's relatives or the police. It was as if Peter had never lived there.

The landlady could sense what Jana was thinking.

"They took all there was of his to take. I don't know what you expect to find. They carted every last piece they could out of here."

"I see," Jana murmured.

"Every drawer in the place was pulled out. Cushions had been yanked off the couch and chairs and sloppily piled in a corner. All the silverware was dumped in the sink. They took the paper I lined the cabinets with and crumpled it up when they didn't find what they were searching for, simply tossing it on the floor as if this were a garbage dump. All police are the same. They don't care that we have to get on with our own lives. We work, too, you know."

"The police try to make people's lives safer. Unfortunately, searches are often part of the process. Unfortunately, it's a shoddy business"

The woman glared at her. "How much more time do you plan to spend here? I need to finish my business." She pointed to a broom in the corner near a small pile of dust devils culled from under the couch mixed with scattered pieces of detritus picked up from the corners of the rooms. "One more thing: who is going to pay me for back rent? He was three days into the new month. I tried to get him to pay me, but he was never home. And then the police closed the apartment down until they were finished, so more days passed before I could lease to a new renter, and I am out of pocket." A sly smile suffused her face. "I can make a deal, if you want."

"What kind of deal?"

"My rent for the picture in the silver frame of you and him. It would be a shame to throw it away."

Jana had remembered the photograph on her way over to the apartment. She and Peter had picnicked on a bench along the Danube, brown-bag lunches they pretended were a feast. They'd bought both a small bottle of wine and a camera. The wine had made them both slightly giddy. Peter had asked a passerby to take their picture, rewarding the man with a plastic glass of the wine. The photograph was not a professional one, but it had captured the magnificent mood the two had been in as they toasted the camera with their raised plastic wine glasses.

She looked the landlady over; now she had something to work with. There was only one way the woman could have come by the photograph. She must have taken things from the apartment before the police came, including the photo. It was in a silver picture frame. The woman thought it was costly, so she'd stolen it, along with any other items of value she could get her hands on.

"How much do you want for the rent?" Jana could see the landlady doing a quick calculation of how much she could ask for. "Be careful; I won't stand for being taken," Jana warned the woman.

The landlady rubbed her large nose. "All I want is what's just. That's all!"

"Three days' rent," Jana suggested.

"They kept me out of here for a full week. I couldn't

even clean up," the woman said. "How could I rent it if they wouldn't let me in?"

"Three days," Jana repeated. "I was not a member of the group that searched the apartment. I can't be held responsible for that. I'm paying Mr. Saris's debt, nothing else."

"I could make more selling the frame."

"I told you to be careful. Now I'm angry, and my offer has gone down. The price is presently fixed at two days' rent."

"What?" yelped the woman.

"You heard me. In a second, it will be down to one day."

The woman's eyes enlarged as she found her possibility of gain diminishing.

"No more time left," said Jana.

"I'll take it," the woman blurted out.

"Good."

The woman led Jana down to her own apartment on the ground floor, complaining all the way that she was being cheated, that the state was taking advantage of a poor widow, that the world was unfair, that she had gone out of her way to be a good landlady to Peter, and he would want her reimbursed for everything she'd lost. She kept walking, opened the door to her own apartment, and, after a brief hesitation about letting Jana in, both of them entered.

The landlady trotted into her bedroom, coming out almost immediately with the photograph in the silver frame. Jana examined it, touching Peter's face in the photo, then looked up at the landlady.

"You took other things."

"How dare you!" The words popped out of the woman's mouth. "I would never steal."

"But you did. That's why you took this photo: for the silver frame."

The woman's voice became faint. "Are you going to arrest me?"

"What else did you take?"

"I would never—"

Jana interrupted her by raising a hand. "We've already settled that you did. Now, I want to know what else you took. I hope you will tell me. If you don't, or I find out you're lying, you go to jail. Do you understand?"

The woman nodded, fear written on her face.

"You have one minute." Jana looked at her watch, counting the seconds. Finally, she looked up. "Everything you took. Now!"

The woman nodded, her head bobbing up and down. "Just the frame, and the toaster, and a small radio that was by his bed. Also his old camera. And a picture of that woman I saw with him."

"There were other items," Jana insisted. She forced herself not to change expression at the mention of this other woman.

There was a long pause, the woman's eyes searching Jana's face.

"Another small item."

"What?"

"His electric razor. . . . And a food mixer." She stopped, waiting for Jana to speak. Then, "I swear that was all. Everything. I haven't held anything back, I promise you. Nothing."

"He always kept cash in his drawer."

The woman blanched, her voice pleading. "I swear there was not anything in his drawers. No money. I promise, not a cent."

Jana watched her for a long moment. The woman was

trembling, her breath coming in gasps. She thought she
was going to jail.

"I want the razor and the camera. They were personal
things of his. Also the photograph of the woman you said
you'd seen him here with. The rest will be enough to pay
you for any rent that was owed, and I'm being generous."

The landlady scurried to do her bidding.

Jana walked out of the building with the photograph
still in its silver frame and the razor and camera in a
plastic bag she had acquired from the landlady. She also
had the photograph of the unknown woman. When Jana
got to her car, she checked the items. The only object she
was concerned with now was the photo of the woman. It
had been taken by some type of digital camera, and on its
lower right-hand corner was a date, one month earlier.
Peter's camera did not log dates on photographs. She
checked it; it was a cheap simple instrument that had only
one purpose: taking candid photographs. No photographs
remained in it.

She looked at the photo of the woman again, a plain
enough woman with nothing about her face or hair or dress
to distinguish her. She wore simple clothes. There were no
marks or moles on her face. She stared at the camera, waiting to get a chore over with. As for the photographic paper,
it appeared to be plain word-processor paper. The photo
had been printed from a computer. It was not a photograph
like the one that she and Peter had had the passerby take,
the one in the silver frame. There was the dreariness of
necessity about the posture of the woman, an absence of joy
in her expression, none of the cheeriness that most people
adopt for pictures, and the shot itself was straight on, no
attempt at creating anything but an image for identification

purposes.

Why would Peter have this photograph? And why did Peter interview this woman in his apartment? Jana felt that she knew Peter well enough to know that he would not have had a secret love affair which he was concealing from her.

She hoped.

Jana drove back to her home.

Perhaps she was ready to report to Europol after all.

Chapter 5

Jana sat in her living room, staring at the walls. Just before she placed the silver frame atop her living room mantel, she checked behind the photograph itself on the off chance Peter had written a note there, left some token, or perhaps hidden something between the photo and the frame. There was nothing.

She decided she'd have to resign from the police force and continue her investigation of Peter's death. Jana retrieved a scratch pad from her desk and began to write a resignation letter. What she wrote was all very civilized. She did not argue about the injustice of the restrictions placed on her, or the fact that she had been given an assignment that would take her away from Slovakia. Rather, she wrote a paragraph about how much she had enjoyed the work, her comrades' dedication, and public service, segueing into an explanation: "circumstances" dictated that it was time she changed the direction of her life.

Jana didn't finish. She crumpled the letter, dropping it to the floor, and then stamped on it in frustration. She could not leave the police force. It was her life, what she had trained for, and what she was good at. There still might be something that she could do before she was forced to leave for The Hague. Although what that might be was beyond her present ability to reason.

Jana still had Peter's electric razor and camera sitting

next to her in a bag. She had given Peter a small closet near the kitchen in which to store garments and other personal items. That way he could come and go as he pleased and still have fresh clothes without having to go home if he wanted to spend the night with her. Jana carried the two items to the closet.

She opened the door with some trepidation, not knowing what her reaction to seeing Peter's clothes might be. The shock she got was greater than she anticipated: there was nothing inside the closet. All of Peter's belongings had been taken. Someone had come into her house when she was away and cleaned it out. She looked again, just to assure herself that the closet was empty, then looked through the house to verify that everything else that should be there was in its place.

Nothing else was missing. Nothing was out of place, the windows were not broken, the locks had not been tampered with. Jana had a habit of leaving the front door unlocked. After all, who breaks into a police commander's house unless they have a suicide wish? So they had had easy access, not needing to force entry. One thing Jana could conclude was that the burglary had been a targeted event. Whoever had entered had come only for Peter's things, not Jana's. What had they been looking for? Not just his clothes. That wouldn't make sense. Perhaps Trokan had sent officers to find any effects Peter had stored with her?

Jana had been so startled by finding the closet empty that she realized she was still carrying the bag with the razor and camera. She went back to the closet that had held Peter's things, turned on the closet light, then placed the bag on the top shelf. She had begun to back out when she realized there was a gap in the side panel immediately adjacent to the inside of the doorjamb. Jana knew her home. It had been her mother and father's house before they'd died. She had been brought up here. In all those years, she had never noticed this gap. She knelt next to the space, barely able to get the tips of her fingers inside, realizing she would have to use additional force if she wanted to pry it from the wall.

She retrieved a hammer from under her sink, then went back to the closet. She was in no mood for finesse. She smashed the panel over and over again until it was just shards of plaster and wood barely clinging to the wall, then quickly slipped her hand inside the space.

Jana almost missed the envelope. It was a standard business size, blank on the front, containing several sheets of folded paper. She took it back into the living room, sat next to a lamp and went through the pages one by one. They were not good copies. Apparently, they had been made using old carbon paper and were barely legible enough for her to make out the text. The writing was in a language Jana was not familiar with. It was not a Slavic tongue nor a western European one Nor was it written in the Cyrillic alphabet. Interspersed with the narrative in the report were also two very small faded diagrams, marked with symbols, numbers, and alphabetic designations which, along with the words, held no significance for Jana.

She would have to get someone to translate it. Who could she get? Not someone with the police department, at least not right now. Who could she trust?

The doorbell rang. Jana put the report behind the couch cushions and went to the door. Surprisingly, Colonel Trokan was standing on the steps.

"Jana, how are you?"

"You just saw me this morning, so you know how I am."

"Can I come in for a moment?"

She stood aside to let the colonel enter. She gestured toward one of the overstuffed chairs.

Trokan shook his head. Standing in the middle of the room, he said, "Jana, I clearly informed you that you were off the case involving the murder of your special friend."

"I heard you."

"Apparently not. You went over to his apartment."

Jana hesitated before she answered. "I was getting a few personal things from the landlady."

"Jana, you and I know you were not there just to get personal things from a thieving landlady. Please, no lies to me, Janka."

"She called you?"

"After you left, she was afraid she would be arrested for having some other items still in her possession, so she called and told us about them, explaining she had only kept them to pay the overdue rent. She also told us you had been there."

"Have you come for the electric razor, the camera, or the picture in the silver frame?"

"I came for none of them. Instead, I came to give you something." He was holding a bulging manila folder, which he handed to her. "Here is an itinerary, initial instructions, the hotel where you are booked for the next few days until you can find a satisfactory apartment, and an airplane ticket to The Hague. When you've digested it all and spent a day or two acclimating in your new job, you are to call me for a further briefing. The minister and I have accelerated your departure date. The plane leaves at eight hundred hours tomorrow morning. If you are not on it, Janka, the minister and I have also agreed that you are no longer on the Slovak police force."

He saw the shock in her eyes and reached over to hug

her. "I told you, Janka. At times it is all or nothing. Make the right choice. Be on the plane."

He affectionately kissed her good-bye on the cheek. Jana tried once more to change his mind. Her words came out as a complaint rather than a persuasive argument.

"Martin Kroslak is already stationed at Europol for us. He has all the experience necessary for a police officer in that position. What's the use of two of us being there? I will be like a third shoe: worthless."

"Ah, I almost forgot. Kroslak disappeared four days ago. Vanished into space without telling anybody. The director of Europol called the minister, who called me, and now I'm informing you. Take over his duties, but most of all find out what happened to him. His file is in the papers I've given you. You now know all we know."

"Did you have a crew take Peter's clothes from my closet?"

"Jana, I would not invade your privacy in that way."

"So who did?"

She eyed Trokan. He had no answer. The question came back to her: who could she trust?

"This is all crazy, Colonel."

"True. I congratulate you on your perceptions. You have just discovered a small part of an important fact: the whole world is insane. Good luck, Janka." Just before he left the house, he turned and winked at her. "I'll send you the Slovak newspapers so you don't get too lonely."

He walked out.

Early the following morning she was on the plane to the Netherlands.

Chapter 6

The plane, which had been booked from Vienna's *flughafen*, was due to arrive in Amsterdam's Schiphol airport in two hours. The flight was full. Jana's seat on the aisle gave her a little leg room and space to move her papers around. She began examining the briefing papers that Trokan had left with her. The first described the city of The Hague itself; most of its information Jana already knew. The Hague—Den Haag—was the actual seat of government of the Netherlands, containing all the government ministries one would expect. It was also the site of the International Court of Justice, the International Criminal Court, and a myriad of other national and international agencies. Most pertinent to Jana, it was the home of Europol, her new but unwanted assignment that took her away from her real work.

Jana's new "home" had its own section in the folder. The explanation of the organization's purpose, and particularly its cross-border rights of investigation, piqued Jana's interest. Europe was a web of competing law-enforcement agencies, all of them jealous of their own national prerogatives. Those prerogatives collided on a regular basis, preventing timely cooperation. Anything that could put an end to that would be an improvement, Jana thought. Except, to be successful, competing agencies also had to be politic, and police officers were far from politic. Not a good portent for success.

Jana looked up from her reading. The man immediately across the aisle from her was watching her. He was an older man, perhaps in his seventies, with a white, bushy moustache and a head of wildly rampant gray hair. He smiled at Jana.

"Lots of papers to read." The man spoke in Slovak.

Jana nodded, trying to be neighborly. The man nodded back. He pulled out a miniature deck of cards, shuffled them, and suddenly one of the cards popped out and flipped to the floor.

"I always have trouble with the three of clubs. It won't behave. You're a bad boy," he scolded the card, waving his finger at it in warning. "You will be lonely there. Come back to the other cards."

The card picked itself up, stood on its edge, swaying, then floated back up to the man, who, with an elaborate gesture, showed it to Jana, then slipped it back in the deck. As advertised, it had been the three of clubs.

"What are you supposed to do with a bad-boy card? You can't spank it. I know he'll run away again. One can never tell just what he'll do." The man abruptly coughed, put his hands to his throat as if he was choking, made a gagging sound, then reached into his mouth and slowly pulled out the three of clubs. With a sly look on his face, he showed it to Jana.

"I told you we couldn't trust the three of clubs."

Jana laughed and applauded. "A wonderful performance."

"Thank you, madam. I am grateful for your appreciation. At this stage in my act, if I were on the street, I would pass the hat around and urge the audience to make a small contribution." He held up his hand to stop her from giving him anything in case she was of a mind to. "No money, thank you. The applause was sufficient. I'm in semi-retirement, so I don't have to make that effort any more. I try not to even read the newspapers these days. You read them, the next day there are more to read, and the day after that. It never stops. I've determined, from the lofty position I occupy as a senior citizen, that from now on I'll only read on Monday, Wednesday, and Friday. This means, if I haven't finished what I've received by Tuesday, Thursday, and Saturday, I merely chuck what's left into the garbage bin. Besides, for the last few years I've realized reading newspapers doesn't make me any better informed. It just gives me eyestrain." The man smiled. "You may call me Professor. I'm used to that title by now. If anyone were to call me by my given name, I'd think they were talking to another person."

"You're a teacher?"

He laughed. "No one would ever confuse me with a teacher. But over the years I grew into the title. And what's your name?"

"Jana Matinova."

He looked surprised. "The famous Jana Matinova?"

Jana's eyebrows went up. "There's nothing famous about me. Infamous, perhaps," she joked.

He studied her more closely. "But I know the name. I have a remarkable memory for names. No, you're not an actress." He thought for a second, then smiled again. "Yes, now I remember. The police officer. You're forever in the news."

"Only sometimes," Jana admitted, a little embarrassed. "It's not good for a policeman to be in the news. Public visibility can hinder you from doing your job."

He looked at the papers she had been studying. "Important work?"

Jana shrugged. "Just briefing materials."

"And here I was hoping to get the inside story of a famous case."

"Sorry to disappoint you."

"Just a minor disappointment."

Their conversation brought to Jana's mind a childhood event. "When I was a very little girl, I thought I wanted to be a magician."

"Instead, you became a police officer."

"I found out that magic isn't real." She thought about Peter. "It's an illusion."

"It's always real if you trust in it."

"I'm a realist, Professor. I have very little trust left."

"Apprentice to a good magician, and you would accept it."

"Apprentice? Accomplice is a better word. I'd be aiding and abetting a lie."

"Giving pleasure to people isn't a lie." He yawned. "Goodness, plane rides always make me sleepy." He looked contrite. "I'm sorry I interrupted your reading. I once read in those newspapers that I've just disparaged that older men always look for ways to meet younger women. Now that I'm older, I find out that it's true."

Jana smiled. "I liked the conversation. It isn't a problem."

"Nevertheless, I am penitent about my conduct. My advice is to ignore me. Besides, I need a nap. Please, go back to your vital work."

He smiled again, then tilted his seat further back, adjusted a pillow, closed his eyes and seemed to fall asleep almost immediately. Jana returned to her papers, the most important of which was the file on Martin Kroslak, the officer who had disappeared.

She knew Kroslak, having dealt with him on a number of occasions. He'd been very voluble when they'd worked together in Slovakia, chattering all the time, generally getting on Jana's nerves if she was in his company for very long. But Jana had also found him to be fairly competent, so she'd made the effort to ignore her irritation at his garrulousness. His other bad habit had been poking about in people's private lives. Some years back, he'd been reprimanded for electronically eavesdropping on employee personnel files. The man's special interest was information retrieval systems, and when he was caught tuning in on other people's electronic lives, he'd claimed he was just trying to perfect his skills. Kroslak had been contrite, apologizing to everyone he'd intruded on. After he was disciplined, he had stopped.

When he'd been selected as Slovakia's representative for Europol, Jana had thought that despite his prior problem, he was a decent choice. He'd never be more than an average investigator, but he'd developed a specialty which would be of use in an organization that focused on criminal information networking, one of Europol's prime missions. Except now he had gone missing.

Martin Kroslak's personnel file gave her some minor bits of information. No siblings. Not married. He loved fooling with electronics as a hobby; his other primary amusement was biking, and other than the one event when he'd been caught snooping he'd received good personnel evaluations. But for the commentary about his occasionally talking too much, and his excellent work with the Slovak Police on developing their own criminal information system, there wasn't much to distinguish him from any other cop. He'd given up his flat in Bratislava when he'd been sent to Europol; its address was crossed out and an apartment in a building in The Hague inked in. There was also a cell-phone number.

Jana closed the folder. There was nothing there that would explain his disappearance. Hopefully, the people at Europol might have some more current information that could lead her to him. Enough for now, she decided. Jana put the rest of the briefing papers aside and began her own nap. The next thing she knew, they had landed at Schiphol.

Before she claimed her baggage, Jana went to the airline's main counter, showed them her credentials, told them that she was now with Europol, and requested a passenger list from the flight she'd just been on. The content of the list confirmed her suspicion. She went to the baggage pick-up area and got her suitcases off the ramp. The professor waved at her from across the moving conveyer belt as she walked toward the exit and tried to determine how to get to the hotel room that had been reserved for her. She scanned the area for a bus, which would be substantially cheaper than a taxi. The home office always questioned cab fares when she turned in her expense report. Unexpectedly, she found the professor at her shoulder, panting a little as he pushed his bags on an airport trolley cart.

"I hope you don't think this is too forward of me, but I have a suspicion that you are going to The Hague. Getting there is much pleasanter by taxi, so I was going to suggest that you and I might split the cab fare and go together. Faster, more comfortable, and actually less expensive. It will take us maybe thirty minutes to get there if we go by cab. How about it?"

The suggestion made sense. "Why not?"

They stepped into the waiting line for taxis.

"A nice airport, don't you think? It used to be much less busy, but they keep stuffing international offices, businesses, and large high-rises into Amsterdam and The Hague. There are more and more visitors. Most of them go on to Amsterdam proper, but The Hague gets its share."

"You come here often, Professor?"

"Once in a while. The European Patent Office is in The Hague. I come to complain. This is not the first time. They have been slow in approving a patent application of mine. I've invented a few devices. And I sometimes do work for other people who have designs, and such. Things they've invented for their acts. European bureaucracy has to be pushed, you know."

"All bureaucracy has to be pushed." She reflected on what the professor had just said. It didn't quite jibe with one of the facts in the briefing papers she'd been reading. "The EPO is in Rijswijk, not The Hague."

The professor looked slightly nonplussed, then nodded vigorously. "Rijswijk it is. But Rijswijk is adjacent to The Hague, and I prefer to stay in The Hague because it's so much more active." His voice took on a confidential tone. "No one in his right mind would spend the evening in Rijswijk. It doesn't even have a good movie house."

They reached the head of the line. A cab drove into the pick-up area; the cab driver got out of the car, opened the trunk, and loaded their baggage. Very gallantly, the professor held the passenger-side door of the vehicle open for Jana, then trotted around the rear of the car and got into the seat behind the driver.

"What's your hotel?" he asked.

"The Novotel at City Centre," Jana told the professor, who in turn relayed the information to the driver in English. "All the Dutch speak English. I've heard one confess that he speaks so much English, he's forgetting how to speak Dutch." He giggled. "Can you imagine forgetting how to speak your native tongue?"

"Disgraceful," agreed the cab driver, pulling away from the terminal. "Everyone is forgetting their heritage." The driver was Indonesian.

They drove through flat country, country like some pleasant rural area in any part of Europe just outside some large city, with the addition of a great deal of water slowly moving through canals—and if the water wasn't in canals, it was in ponds or small lakes. Jana could feel the soft touch of moisture on her face.

The light was also different, a delicate light without glare, as if a diaphanous veil filtered all the harsh qualities from the air. Perhaps it was because of the closeness of the sea, perhaps just a bit of mist in the air blurred the light. Every place, no matter where, thought Jana, had its own atmosphere. This one gave the countryside an ephemeral feel, making the passage through the area the Dutch had recovered from the sea a little otherworldly. It felt like they were passing through an imaginary landscape.

The professor fell silent after they had gone a few kilometers, withdrawing into himself, his face and body posture sagging, as if he had suddenly remembered some sadness. Jana watched him, wondering what experience he was remembering, what event he was reliving, which threatened to engulf him with depression. Jana had a strong feeling that she knew part of it: the plane's passenger list had the professor's true name listed. It was the same as that of the student murdered at the Carleton Savoy; he had to be the dead student's uncle, the one Maria had told her about.

The professor didn't communicate with Jana until they were well within the outskirts of The Hague.

"We're here," he announced.

The city center, at first glance, seemed like a place in transition with tall buildings going up, as well as a number of high-rises already looming over downtown. However, it was sparkling clean, unlike other urban areas, and there was still a feeling of comfort in the city, a sedate, calm prosperity that pervaded the streets despite the many construction projects in progress.

As promised, they reached the hotel in less than thirty minutes. As soon as they arrived, the professor seemed to completely recover his former good cheer, offering to get together while they were both still there, perhaps for dinner or to visit a museum. Jana tried to pay half the fare, but the professor refused, telling the driver to go on; then he waved madly out of the car window to Jana as the vehicle drove off.

Jana waved back, amused by the man, all the while knowing he was really in The Hague to see her. Jana walked into the Novotel.

It was a well-kept hotel, rating four stars according to the brochures. Jana was impressed. Given the cheap daily rate that Jana was informed of when she checked in, the Slovaks had made a very good deal. It was positively luxurious in comparison to the usual frugal lodgings Jana had to endure whenever she was sent anywhere by the government. Unfortunately, Jana was also aware that she wasn't going to be spending many nights here. Europol was supposed to help her find permanent accommodations which, if she knew the way bureaucracies worked, was going to be old, creaky, and barely habitable.

The deskman went into his usual patter for a first-time

guest. He gave Jana a map of the city, informed her that the hotel was in the huge Haagse Passage shopping arcade, and if she wanted anything, toiletries, clothing, gifts, it would only be a few short steps to the arcade proper. For any other matters, all she had to do was consult the concierge or the desk and they would be glad to assist her. And, he joked, if she had any inclination to take part in parliamentary debates, across the street was the Dutch parliament. Jana dutifully smiled at his attempt at humor, then followed the bellman to the elevator.

Her room was well furnished, with a touch, here and there, of the luxurious. There was even a welcoming basket of cheese, fruit, and crackers and a small bottle of wine. Perhaps the ministry had decided to be nice to her since they had hustled her out of Slovakia in such a rush. The bellman opened a window, turned on the air conditioning to FAN, and then paused long enough for Jana to give him a euro for his work. As he left, Jana began munching on an apple she plucked from the basket, settled in an easy chair, and wondered if she would have time to acclimate herself to the area by taking a walk before she had to report to Europol. The decision was made for her when the phone rang.

An hour later, she was standing outside the building housing Europol. It was an older structure, three stories high at street level, displaying the architecture of an earlier century, without any touch of flamboyance, although much of its brick work had been covered with ivy in an effort to soften its appearance. Despite the touch of greenery, the building, like so many other buildings housing police, had a hulking look, as if it were a live, brooding creature.

After passing security clearance, within a short ten minutes, Jana was sitting on a chair outside the Department of Serious Crime's deputy director's office.

Chapter 7

Jana would have to wait, the secretary informed her in a tone of self-importance. The woman's expression and posture had become militant, a martinet enjoying her power. Europol was hosting a conference for senior law-enforcement and immigration officials, she explained, to combat illegal immigration, and the assistant director was giving the welcoming speech. The woman peremptorily nodded Jana to a seat along the wall, then went back to her work with a finality that brooked no further intrusion. Jana sat for thirty minutes but finally became impatient.

"I haven't had a chance to unpack. I'm going back to my hotel. Have him call when he's ready to see me."

The secretary looked shocked, gabbled something about the assistant director wanting to interview her, and insisted that she wait. Jana opened the door to the outer corridor just as Assistant Director Mazur came through it. He looked flustered when he almost ran into her.

"I assume you're Commander Matinova?" His secretary handed him telephone message slips. "Come in, please." He gestured a welcome to Jana while he checked the messages, then opened the door to his inner office, pausing to make sure she followed him.

"I'm happy to see you, Commander. Sorry I had to step away from my desk. My schedule is more appropriate for a man who competes in track and field events. I have to run from one place to the next without the help of periodic doses of oxygen." He focused on Jana. "There's been no one from Slovakia to fill the vacancy left by your compatriot when he walked off the job." He gestured her to a seat. "Not very professional of him."

"I assume you've investigated to determine if Kroslak informed anyone he was leaving?"

"I certainly did. No one had the vaguest idea that he was going, or where he is."

"Kroslak was not the type to run off without telling anyone. Normally, if he'd planned to go somewhere, he would have volunteered his destination to anyone within earshot, and beyond."

"He didn't, at least not to our people."

"Where did he work?"

"The same area you'll be assigned to. We have a total of 581 people on our staff," he boasted; then his voice took on a peevish tone. "Originally, Slovakia was supposed to supply four. Now we just have you." He paused to surmount his frustration. "Work, work, work. There are seven criminal investigation teams under my supervision. You've been assigned, naturally, to this department, and to. . . ." He consulted a desk schedule, ". . . to SC 4, Financial and Property Crime."

The news of this assignment jolted Jana.

"Assistant Director, I think a mistake has been made." She felt annoyance build inside her. "I'm not a specialist in that area. That section needs investigators who are experts in accounting, property records, stock and bond transfers, insider trading. I'm a homicide investigator."

He looked at her, then scratched his head. "The person we asked your government for was to be a replacement for the man who has gone missing. They sent you. I assumed they knew what they were doing. However, because we do have intergovernmental problems, the language barriers, the differences in systems, it's possible they may have made a mistake. I'll check on it. In the meantime, you are assigned to Financial and Property Crime." He pulled out a large loose-leaf volume bearing the Europol and European Union logos from a credenza behind him, then slid it over to her.

"Please familiarize yourself with everything that's in here: your obligations to this office, the do's and don'ts, procedures, the limits of your authority, our rules and regulations, chain of command, and, of course, the powers vested in us through mutual treaties with all the signatory countries."

"I'd like to repeat, I'm not a specialist in the area you are assigning me to."

"I heard you the first time," he said with asperity. "Let's see how your office responds when I fax them." He paused, as if trying to remember what he had to do next. "I think that's it. Please check in with your section. My secretary will direct you. You can probably use your ex-colleague's desk. Perhaps even his apartment. I understand the rent is paid through next month." His eyes lit up as if he were now about to do her a favor and was pleased with his own generosity. "Take the rest of the day off after you've checked in with your section. Work can wait until tomorrow." Mazur held his hand out for Jana to shake. "Welcome to Europol."

The secretary described how Jana could get to SC 4. As Jana followed the woman's directions, she passed a row of vacant offices, some of them no more than just cubicles. A receptionist told Jana that most of the investigators were probably at a conference on illegal immigration. No, the woman replied to her questioning look: none of the officers from that section were involved in illegal immigration, but they were encouraged by Europol to participate in order to broaden their expertise.

A short, older woman, with dyed-blonde hair at odds with her dark complexion and eyes, stepped in from the corridor. She glanced at Jana, then entered a cubicle. Jana knocked on the door frame. The woman looked up.

"Can I help you?"

"My name is Jana Matinova. I've been assigned to the section."

The woman nodded, closing a drawer; then sat back in her chair. "You're the Slav we were expecting."

"I'm also a Slav, but I think you mean 'Slovak'."

"Slovak, Slav, all the same. I'm Paola Rossi."

"Italian?"

"Yes. A southern Italian, but trying to look like I'm from Northern Italy. Lots of Austrian and German intermarriage there. So, behold, a blonde Italian." Rossi seemed to relish the fact that her hair was obviously dyed. She leaned even further back, putting her feet on the desk.

"They told us you would be taking the other guy's desk. It's the room next door." She cast a thumb in that direction. "I cleaned out what was left in his desk. You want the stuff?" Without waiting for an answer, she sat up far enough to be able to reach into a bottom drawer and pull out a clear plastic bag. "All his papers were gone; nothing personal was left. Just the junk that we all collect in our jobs." Paola dumped the contents of the bag onto her desk, then sifted through the small pile of bits and pieces. "One stapler, a box of plastic paperclips, three pencils, a fountain pen, several half-used packets of tissues, and a small pocket notebook." She stuffed them back into the plastic bag. "Take it, it's yours. It's easier than trying to requisition items from this organization. They make you account for everything in triplicate."

"Did you know Kroslak?"

"Sure. A decent sort. Polite enough. Sometimes too polite. Kind of secretive. Kept to himself."

That didn't sound like the talkative Kroslak that Jana knew.

"He wasn't always trying to talk your ear off?"

"Nope. A hard worker, though. Always sifting through papers and printouts."

"So I can use it, do you have the password for his office computer?"

"He used his name spelled backward. K-a-l-s-o-r-k."

"How do you know the password he used?"

"The ass who's our assistant director gave it to me so I could search the data on it. He wanted me to see if it held material which would clue us into where he'd gone. There was absolutely nothing in the computer. We even had to re-program it. Data gone, wiped. No," she corrected herself. "Just clean."

"What do you mean, 'just clean'?"

"If you know how to do it, data can always be pulled up even if you erase it from a drive. We tried to pull it up. The computer's hard drive had been replaced with a new one. So, no data at all. We figured Kroslak had replaced the drive himself so that no one could ever access it."

"Maybe someone else replaced the drive?"

"Could be. Easy enough to do if you have access." She reached inside her pocket. "I forgot something." Paola tossed a key ring with a pair of keys onto the desk. "His apartment keys. After he didn't come in for a second day without calling I went over there. His clothes, all gone, nothing of a personal nature left. Everything was spick and span. Nothing even in the wastebasket."

Jana picked up the keys, examined the contents of the bag containing Kroslak's desk remnants, then pulled the pen out of the bag. "A fountain pen." Jana uncapped it, testing the nib with her thumb. "Not many people use these things any more." She screwed the cap back on. "A Mont Blanc. They're expensive." She waved the pen at Paola. "See, he left a personal belonging after all." Jana tapped the pen on the desk. "I wonder why he would leave this kind of pen behind."

Paola shrugged. "Maybe, in his hurry to get out, he overlooked it."

"He was meticulous about his personal things."

Paola shrugged again, dismissing the issue.

Jana nodded. "Thank you, Paola." She turned to go. "I've been given the rest of the day off. See you tomorrow."

"My pleasure. Good to have another woman in the section."

Jana walked out carrying the plastic bag without bothering to enter her new office. She would be here tomorrow. Time enough to get settled. There was another destination in her mind for the moment. Nobody ever succeeded in completely cleaning up a location. There was always something left behind. She walked a block before she could catch a taxi to take her back to her hotel. After she finished unpacking, she'd head for Kroslak's apartment.

Chapter 8

B etween the plane ride and her visit to Europol, Jana had developed cramps in her joints. She needed exercise. Inspired by the large number of bicycle riders on the streets, she decided to rent one. Changing into slacks, windbreaker, and walking shoes, she went to the lobby. The concierge was polite and drew a route on her map in red pencil which would take her to the *Statenkwartier* neighborhood near Kroslak's apartment. Then he directed her to a bike rental shop where, knowing she was never going to qualify as a professional cyclist, she selected a basic three-speed with a large sideview mirror and pedaled out into the light traffic.

She stretched her leg muscles as the exercise worked some of the kinks out of her body, becoming more and more adroit as she weaved in and out of the traffic. The trip was fairly quick; it took her a little over fifteen minutes to get to her destination, a neighborhood located between the city center and the dunes facing the North Sea.

When she reached Frederik Hendriklaan, the main street in the area, Jana stopped at a small café, the Kaffé Hayden, sat at a table, and relaxed. She drank a café filter and watched a small but steady stream of people pass her by. Another cyclist, a man dressed in a business suit, stopped almost as soon as Jana did, parked his bike next to hers, and took a seat at an adjacent table. He ordered a small pilsner, sipped at it when it arrived, then looked over at her, raising his glass in a half-toast.

"Nothing like a cold beer, is there, Commander?"

Jana had already made her evaluation of him before he sat down. Some people can't help revealing what they are, she reflected. The man had first assessed his surroundings, including the patrons in the café; then taken his seat and continued measuring everyone who passed on the sidewalk. He had what most professionals in her line of work called "cop's eyes." The man was a police officer.

"I take it that you've been following me?" Jana couldn't help the irritated tone in her voice. "You did a good job."

He nodded, pleased she hadn't observed him tracking her. "Not your fault for missing me," he assured her. "You were too busy weaving through traffic. You were better than some, but the combination of sightseeing and caution set you apart. Easy for me to track you; hard for you to see me."

"It's always flattering to have a man follow you, even though he's just an officer doing his job. Please join me." The man shifted to her table. Jana watched him as he moved. He was her age, a few centimeters taller than she was, blond hair receding slightly, slim waist indicating that he kept himself in condition. "And your name is?" she asked, as he put his beer down.

"Jan Leiden, Commander."

"Why would an investigator with the Dutch police follow me?"

"We were told by Europol you were arriving. I went to registration at your hotel and they pointed you out just as you were leaving the concierge's desk. I decided to see where you were going, watched you rent a bike, and followed you."

"If you wanted to talk to me, you had the opportunity at the hotel. Why not then?"

"It's too beautiful a day not to get some exercise out-doors. And I didn't want you to miss it."

"That's not why you followed me."

Jana was not angry, merely stating a fact.

"I like tailing women." Leiden grinned at her. "However, you're right, that's not why I followed you."

"Then please answer my question."

"Are you aware that all police who work for Europol are totally immune from prosecution, except for minor offenses: traffic tickets in England, for example? Can you imagine, immune from criminal acts but they have to pay traffic citations? The British have always been odd."

"I haven't had the opportunity to commit any crime yet, Investigator Leiden. Not even traffic violations."

"And we don't want you to, Commander."

"I don't need to be advised of that, Leiden."

"We always try to vet people who come into the country and work with Europol, particularly when there has been trouble. We also want to make sure they're protected."

"I don't need security, Investigator Leiden." She thought about his "offer" of protection. "You're talking about my predecessor, Kroslak. Was his disappearance linked to a crime? Was he killed? Kidnapped? Dumped in a Dutch canal, perhaps?"

"Perhaps all of the above. We don't know."

"Nothing at all?"

"Nothing. No girlfriend we could find; no bank accounts; no signs of violence. He walked away, or someone walked him away. Police officers simply don't leave a job without telling anyone."

"Unless it's planned."

"Why would he plan it?"

"Investigator Leiden, you would have to tell me. I just arrived in The Hague."

He sat silently, then finished his beer, laying money on the table. "I've bought your coffee." He winked at her. "Welcome to Holland."

"Thank you, Jan Leiden."

"You're in this neighborhood for a reason: to see Kroslak's apartment." He hesitated for a moment. "Unless I've not been informed correctly, Europol has not taken jurisdiction to investigate Kroslak's vanishing act, correct?"

"Investigator Leiden, I have permission to live at the hotel for only a limited time. I'm just going to look over the neighborhood and Kroslak's apartment to see if I might like it enough to take it, considering that Kroslak doesn't seem to want it."

Leiden laid a business card on the table. "If you need a guide in the near future, please feel free to give me a jingle. And, if you find anything, well, you know, the same number." He walked to his bike and rode away without looking back.

Jana finished her coffee, then remounted her bike.

The apartment was just two blocks away from the Kaffé Hayden. Jana made a circuit of the building before she entered it. It was apparently a nineteenth-century house that had been converted into four apartments; the façade had been left intact so it would not jar with the style of the neighboring houses. Jana checked the mailboxes at the front door. Kroslak's name was still displayed. There were a few fliers inside the box but no personal mail. She keyed herself into the building, then went to the stairs. Kroslak's apartment was on the second floor. Jana ascended the red-carpeted steps to his door. Even the welcome mat was still in place.

Inside, the apartment was decently furnished. A living room led to a small dining area, with a kitchen off the dining area. There was also a bedroom with a connecting bathroom, and a second bedroom on the opposite side of the bathroom. It was immaculately clean but for a slight patina of dust which had accumulated, Jana concluded, since Kroslak had left the place. She began, methodically, to search, starting with the master bedroom, carefully working each wall from the top to the bottom, making sure that the baseboards had nothing concealed in them. Then Jana stripped the beds, checking all the seams of the mattresses to determine if they had been pulled apart and re-sewn. Then the closets, top to bottom, paying special attention to the floors. Finally she checked the dressers, behind the mirrors, beneath the drawers. Again, nothing.

The bathroom was next, the shower first, then the drainage pipe as far as she could determine without tools, then the sink and medicine cabinet. Nothing. The dining room followed, then the living-room area. Every piece of furniture was explored, even the fringes of the rugs examined and the large couch stripped of its slipcover so she could finger every inch of the cushions. Again, nothing. By the time she was through, two hours had passed, the place was a mess, and Jana was tired.

There was a hesitant knock at the door. Jana did not have her sidearm and considered not opening the door. After all, the prior tenant of the apartment had disappeared. Jana didn't want whatever had happened to Kroslak to happen to her. She went to the door and, to surprise whoever was outside, quickly pulled it open. The young woman who was standing outside jumped back, letting out a squeak of fear.

Her eyes wide with shock, the woman backed away as if

she was going to turn and run. Jana quickly stepped outside, touching her on the arm to reassure her.

"Sorry. My fault. Everything is all right. No need to be afraid," she said in English.

The young woman nodded, unable to find her voice.

"Why did you knock?" Jana asked.

"I heard you inside," the woman answered slowly. Her English was good enough, but halting.

"So?"

"Well, I wanted to know if you'd changed your mind and wanted the place cleaned. Except, you're not him."

"Mr. Kroslak?"

"The man who was here before. I met him when he rented the place."

"He told you he didn't want the place cleaned?"

"It was in the lease, a service as part of the rent. He said he didn't want to be disturbed, ever. So, no cleaning."

"You haven't been in the apartment since then?"

"No." She looked concerned. "It wasn't my fault he didn't want it cleaned."

"Clearly it wasn't your fault."

"So, do you want it cleaned?"

Jana considered her request. She had searched the place thoroughly. There was nothing more to be found. She gave the woman a friendly smile.

"I think the apartment could stand tidying up a bit."

She stood aside so that the cleaning woman could see the mess Jana had made.

"I guess it does need . . . tidying," the young woman stammered.

"Good. And thank you."

Jana picked up her shoulder bag and walked down the stairs and outside. As she got back on her bike, she looked up at the second floor. The maid was looking down at her, hesitantly lifting a hand in "good-bye." The friendly Dutch, Jana thought, returning the gesture.

Jana reflected on Kroslak's apartment. There was no shaving equipment in the bathroom, no soap in the shower, no shampoo. There were no cleaners under the sink in the kitchen. The plates were neatly stacked in place in the cupboards, as if standing at attention hoping someone would reach in and use them. There was nothing of any personal nature except Kroslak's name on the empty mailbox. The sheets and pillow cases on the beds were clean, the corners of the sheets evenly tucked in. If he had left his apartment suddenly, as he had left Europol, he would not have taken the sponges, the mop, the vacuum cleaner, the detergents. Everything would not have been that neat. And, finally, Kroslak had not wanted anyone to enter the apartment, not even the cleaning lady.

The more Jana thought about it, the more convinced she became. No one had been living at the apartment. Certainly not Kroslak. It had been a blind, a front, an address to put on his records at Europol and nothing else. Kroslak had been living somewhere else. He hadn't wanted anyone to know where that place was. Whatever it was Kroslak had been doing, he had gone to great lengths to keep it hidden.

And now Kroslak was gone.

Jana checked her watch and then got back on her bike. She had a few hours of daylight left, and going back to the hotel after arriving in a new city was distasteful and ultimately wasteful. Besides, Jana told herself, she'd be working hard enough in the next few days simply to absorb the information in the loose-leaf binders she'd been given by the assistant director. Jana remembered Jan Leiden, the

Dutch police investigator, and his excuse for following her. "It's just too beautiful a day not to take advantage of the opportunity to ride a bike." Jana didn't believe that was his reason for following her, but decided his observation was correct. She would spend the rest of the day biking through the streets, taking in the sights.

Jana pedaled in the direction of the Kaffé Hayden, quickly reached Frederik Hendriklaan, then fell into line with the other bike riders, swinging through the city's districts, taking the longest possible route to bring her back to the hotel. Every once in a while she consulted her map. She followed an arc from the North Sea area of Scheveningen into Segbroek and then turned southeast through Rustenburg/Oosbroek, then through the Transvaal neighborhood and into The Hague Center. She could have stopped anywhere along the way to examine the art deco buildings or the museums or any of two dozen other sights, but instead she let her mind clear as the wind blew through her hair, as she tried to forget Peter, her *exile* to The Hague, as she thought of it, and even the riddle of Kroslak's disappearance.

Suddenly, Jana was brought back to reality. Her police training, triggered by the recollection that Jan Leiden had been able to follow her without her knowledge, made her check her sideview mirror. A gray car fifty meters back appeared to occupy more of the bikers' lane than that reserved for automobiles. A man occupied the driver's seat; another figure, perhaps a woman, sat next to him. There was nothing to prove they were following her, but they appeared to Jana to be "lurking" behind her.

A major intersection was coming up. Jana decided to find out if they were trailing her. She watched the light at the intersection, then slowed to wait for it to turn yellow.

As soon as the warning light appeared, Jana surged ahead, crossing the intersection as the light turned red. She watched the car in her mirror. It picked up speed as she increased her pace, then went through the red light, almost colliding with intersecting traffic. Cars and bicyclists had to brake, swerving; several of the bike riders went down. Jana's instinct at that moment told her that the car behind her was being driven by a man who wanted to kill her.

The car picked up more speed. In ten seconds the car was going to hit her and, if it did, it was going to put her in the hospital, or worse. She scanned the street. Even if she could turn off, she was going too fast to do so safely.

Driving in the lane to her left was a canvas-covered open-back truck. Jana swung toward it, pedaling as furiously as she could, then hoisted herself so that her feet were momentarily balanced on the seat of the bike, and jumped for the back of the truck. There was a moment when she thought she was going to fall; she reached out frantically to grab a loose piece of the canvas, managing to steady herself, then slid into the rear of the truck, tumbling against a stack of boxes.

As she slid, she caught a quick glimpse of the gray car. It slammed into her abandoned bike, sending it flying onto the sidewalk, narrowly missing several pedestrians, then crashing through the plate-glass front window of a pharmacy. The driver of the car didn't pause to see what damage the bike had caused. The vehicle sped out of sight.

Jana waited while the truck passed through several intersections to make sure the gray car was gone, then got out when it stopped for another traffic signal. She was only a short distance from her hotel. She went to the bike shop to tell them that their bike had been smashed by a hit-and-run driver, signed a form, then went back to her hotel and had the desk call the traffic police for her. She arranged with the police to contact the bike shop for the damage report. They informed her that they would interview her as well within the next few days.

Jana went up to her room, took a quick shower, then lay on her bed trying to make sense of what had happened. There was no question that someone had tried to kill her, or at least put her out of action. It was one more event in the horrible two weeks she had gone through. And she was tired.

She faded into sleep pretending that Peter was holding her in his arms.

Chapter 9

Jana slept deeply through the night. When the light woke her, she was not quite sure where she was. It was still early, the sun rising, when Jana heard a rustling noise at the door to her room. She shifted in her bed and watched two newspapers slide over the lintel. After she retrieved them, she sat on the edge of the bed to peruse the headlines. One was the *International Herald Tribune*, a newspaper the hotel supplied to all its guests; the other, *Sme*, a Slovak publication. Trokan had kept his promise: he was having one of the Slovak national newspapers supplied to her.

Jana skim-read *Sme*. She felt a sudden pang of depression. An investigative panel had been established to look into the facts of Peter's death. There was also a squib, on the fourth page, asserting that the police were following leads in the killing of Denis Macek at the Carleton Savoy hotel. Jana felt another pang, this time of disappointment. Articles which declared that police were following leads almost invariably meant that they had no leads.

The rest of the paper was filled with the usual reports of turmoil: a minister was under fire for having committed Slovakia to an American company to develop the newly discovered oil field in the Low Tatras; the communists in Parliament were making noise about protecting workers being fired from government jobs; there were letters to the editor complaining about everything from plumbing to the cost of bread. As for the *Herald Tribune*, it had its own share of stories: Japanese voters had tossed out a number of Liberal Democrats; the Middle East was mired in the usual attacks and counterattacks; there had been a breakthrough on treating multiple sclerosis; and a story related to the one in *Sme*, about an American oil company having to increase oil exploration activities to obtain new reserves around the world. It was the same old same-old.

Irritated, Jana tossed both papers in the trash, feeling like she had been deliberately put out to pasture in a corner of the world removed from relevant events . . . until she thought about what had happened yesterday. Maybe The Hague was not a backwater far off the beaten path after all.

She took a quick shower, mulling over the previous day's events. Perhaps a perceived traffic slight had caused an already-deranged man to target her? Not likely. What had happened did not suggest she had done something on her bike which had propelled a driver into an episode of road rage. Jana dressed, reviewing the cases she had left pending in Slovakia, the two murders she had begun investigating: the hotel killing and Peter's murder. There was nothing in the little she had done to indicate that she would be targeted next.

Perhaps the cause lay in one of the cases she had investigated in the past? All police officers make dangerous enemies, but would one of them have known she was coming to the Netherlands and followed her while she rode through the city until they determined the right spot to kill her? An outside possibility; not probable. And, as far as she could tell, she hadn't done anything yet in The Hague to attract anyone's malevolent interest.

Jana went down to the dining-area buffet and took a breakfast roll and coffee. The professor came hurrying over.

"Hello, hello, hello," he chortled. "I hope you remember me from the plane and the drive over here?"

Jana was surprised. "Of course I do, Professor."

As she started to rise, the professor lightly placed his hand on her shoulder. "Finish your breakfast. I thought you might be here, so I stopped by to suggest we have dinner tonight. I know a few places on the beach in Scheveningen. Indonesian. Indonesian food in Holland is better Indonesian food than in Indonesia. I felt it would be nice for the two Slovaks to have dinner, and I wanted to be the first to introduce you to this cuisine."

Jana began to refuse, but the professor made a further plea before she could finish. "Yes, I know, you think a handsome Dutchman is hulking in the shadows preparing to sweep you away. If he's 'hulking'—or is the word 'lusting?'—he will do it tomorrow. Meanwhile, cater to the whims of a countryman, old but still captivating, and join me tonight."

Jana started to refuse again. The professor put his finger to his lips. "Shhhh, not a single 'no' will be accepted. I will whisk you away from the front door of the hotel at 19:30. A good time?"

Jana couldn't help smiling at the playful insistence of the old man. He wasn't aware that she knew who he was. She decided she would let him play out the game he was engaged in, and she nodded.

He clapped his hands. "Wonderful. I will be here, without a chariot, but with great expectations."

Mission accomplished, the professor danced off and out of the dining area, blowing kisses all the way.

Jana caught a taxi for the short drive to the Europol building; the cab driver, a stocky, bristle-faced Dutchman with a very red face, insisted on playing the radio and occasionally singing along with the music as they drove through the traffic. The trip was brief. The driver let her off at the building and, as she was paying him, asked her if she knew anything about the structure she was about to enter. He cheerfully told her that it had been Gestapo headquarters during the Second World War. "They used to bring people in the front door and truck their bodies out the back. I'm sure it's different now," the man assured her, then drove off singing even more loudly.

Jana concluded that the day was starting off more bizarrely than she could have imagined.

The sedate Netherlands were not so sedate.

Chapter 10

The detectives on the SC 4 team began meandering into their offices. Paola, the first to arrive, offered to introduce Jana to her new associates.

Gabi Laszlo, a Hungarian from Gyor, a town near the Slovak border, had been the first to arrive after Paola. When he was introduced to Jana, he kept kneading his shoulders as if they were stiff and he needed to loosen them. Worse, he wouldn't look directly at Jana, almost as if he was afraid to see rejection on her face. Then he surprised Jana by handing her a small box of marzipan cookies. A friend in Budapest, an investigator-supervisor who had worked with Jana on a case, had learned she was coming to Europol. He'd ordered Gabi to buy the cookies for her.

Still kneading his trapezius muscles, but now chewing on one of the marzipan cookies, Laszlo walked away. *Sotto voce*, Paola told Jana that Laszlo was still recovering from a failed love affair with a visiting Chinese student. Gabi had proposed marriage, but the woman had told him he was too old for her, which had gone down badly with Gabi. That's when his body had started aching and he began the business of massaging his shoulders.

"Finding the weakness in a man seems to come easier to young women," Jana suggested.

"Older women forget how to do it, or they're too afraid

to try," growled Paola. "They should do it more often. It keeps the men coming back."

Hans Zimmer, a very tall, almost-emaciated blond man with a slightly protruding mouth and a dour look on his face, trotted in. Paola tried to signal him to come over, but he only favored her with a brief nod and then vanished very quickly into his office.

Paola snorted. "Forgive the man. He can't help himself. He's Prussian." She dropped her voice. "Zimmer doesn't make small talk with anyone. Besides, the man has a habit of covering his mouth with his hands as if he's afraid people will notice his crooked teeth, which makes for difficult conversation because you have to strain to hear him."

Rushing in, almost on Zimmer's heels, was Camille Grosjean. He immediately walked over, introducing himself as a police officer from Antwerp.

"Have you ever worked with the Belgian police?" he asked. "Well-trained investigators," he told her without waiting for an answer. He snapped his fingers, as if he'd just remembered a task he'd forgotten. He gave Jana a wide, insincere smile. "Got to go." He darted off, hurrying.

Paola shrugged. "The man is a 'kiss-ass.' He brown-noses the supervisors. The bastard plays down everyone else's work while pumping his own 'accomplishments.' Piss on him."

Jana held out the box of marzipan cookies to Paola, who took one, and then she selected one herself. The strong almond flavor came through while she chewed. Between bites, she noticed the arrival of a solidly built man, now going a little to flab, his erect posture doing its best to conceal his midriff bulge. A slight man, wearing a Tyrolean hat with a red feather, tufts of contrasting jet black hair showing underneath the hat, entered in his wake. Paola beckoned to both of them.

"Right there, Paola darlin'." The big man sauntered to the coffee table, poured himself an oversized cup of coffee, then ladled a huge amount of sugar into the cup.

"He's Aidan Walsh, not a man to be rushed," Paola informed Jana.

"A man who takes coffee with his sugar."

Gyorgi Ilica, the man with the Tyrolean hat, cheerfully walked over to them. He swept his hat off with the ease of a professional flirt, gave Jana a head-bow, said something in Romanian, and then, in barely passable English peppered with odd expressions and extravagant gestures, tried to make her feel at home.

"Welcome to the beautiful city of The Hague. It mean the 'hedge,' which is why they still have greenery in this city, but do not in Amsterdam, which is why I never go to Amsterdam. You see what we mean?"

"I certainly do," said Jana, not knowing what he was talking about.

"You need learn The Hague before you go the city of sin."

"Amsterdam is the city of sin?"

"Why, sure. Big sex section. Narcotics. Robberies. The Hague is clean."

"Glad to hear it."

Aidan Walsh finally sauntered over, sipping his coffee. Ilica continued chattering, taking Jana's hand in his, stroking it. Jana pulled her hand away; Ilica went on as if he hadn't noticed.

"I am suggesting it always hard starting in new place and that it is perfectly right if you come to me to inform any questions about procedures."

"I'll remember to do that," Jana assured him.

"Good, good. You see I help you."

Ilica put his hat back on and walked to his office looking smug. As soon as he was out of sight, Paola and Walsh exchanged glances, smothering laughter.

"He's generally a decent sort," Walsh said. "It's just that he likes to brush his hands against any portion of the female anatomy that's near him. If you can keep a chair or a desk between you, and if you manage to understand his English, he isn't a bad man to go to for advice." He held out his own hand. "My name is Aidan Walsh."

Jana focused her attention on Walsh. He was a prototypical Irishman with a fair, almost milky complexion, and the air of a man open to everyone. Jana offered him one of the marzipan cookies. He took two.

"Trying to get me fatter, eh?" He patted his stomach. "You like to eat?" he asked.

"Only good food." She smiled.

Walsh launched into a brief commentary on local food, commending those restaurants within walking distance that served edible fare, telling her to avoid most of the *Dutch* restaurants as if they carried the plague. "The Dutch," he confided, "don't even know how to cook their native dishes."

With the arrival of Walsh, Assistant Director Mazur popped his head into their offices to remind everyone of the meeting, insisting upon leading a parade into their small conference room, prattling on and on about the need for team play and cooperative behavior, which was essential to solving cases. He didn't notice the distaste written across the faces of most of "his" team.

Mazur apologized to Jana for the investigators who were missing, on vacation, or in the field, as he explained it; then required all those sitting around the table to relate their disparate backgrounds in law enforcement, ostensibly so Jana would become aware of their particular skills. Once that was over, Mazur distributed several new Europol regulations and procedures and then abruptly launched into a semi-tirade which was directed, without using her name, at Jana.

"The Dutch police have informed me that a new member of our investigation team was involved in an auto/bicycle accident that damaged not only the bicycle but almost injured several pedestrians, while also destroying private property." He looked at Jana significantly. "And then that person fled the scene without trying to assist anyone who might have been injured."

There was a "tsk, tsk" of disapproval from Grosjean. Jana forced herself to say nothing, waiting for the scene to play itself out.

"Even though we have international immunity," Mazur went on, "this is not the appropriate message to give the public, and it is not going to be tolerated. If anyone is involved in possible criminal conduct, the circumstances will be investigated by the Dutch as well as Europol personnel. The Dutch police will then write a complete report directed toward establishing culpability, and forward the report to us for possible Europol sanctions to be applied to the officer who is the subject of the investigation." He looked very meaningfully at Jana. "Those sanctions may include the possibility of dismissal from Europol and transport on the next plane back to that officer's home country, where his or her own department will likely take additional action."

With that last blast, Mazur stood, stared fixedly at Jana for a moment, and stalked out of the conference room.

Grosjean rose and walked out after Mazur, closing the door behind him.

"Toady!" Paolo snorted in disgust, turning to Jana in explanation. "Grosjean the boot-licker. Asshole."

They all looked at Jana to see what she would say.

"I informed the Dutch police about the incident Mazur reported," Jana quietly responded. "They will get in touch with me in the next few days."

Laszlo fiercely rubbed his head as if trying to get circulation pumping through his thinning hair. "He's done this to us before when we have even a minor, anemic run-in with a grocery clerk. The son-of-a-bitch is afraid that the slightest incident might result in Europol's upper management faulting him."

Walsh sat with his arms folded, a disgruntled look on his face. "The whole organization is like that. The higher up the functionary, the more he quakes at the hint of a reproof."

"Watch," Ilica talked excitedly, bobbing his head, his heavily accented English getting worse. "In a while Mazur, he will call you to his office and he apologize. Not for being wrong, but to give the 'second chance.' Then, he give you a task to perform, something small, to show he still has faith in you. Naturally, he expect you to be grateful."

"We've all been most 'grateful' at one time or another," Paola grimaced.

"The organization is shit," Laszlo growled. "There is no real work."

Jana reacted to his statement. "What do you mean, *no work?*"

"The countries who are signatories to Europol don't send us cases," Laszlo explained. "Or they send shit cases no one but God can solve."

"The bloody European national police departments don't want us to be involved in their cases." Walsh groused. "They want to handle it themselves. No one wants to give their investigations over to us. It's all about national honor being upheld. If a case has international implications, that country's police would rather get directly involved with the other countries' police. On the other hand, the powers-that-be in our organization, those lofty individuals who run Europol, are economical with the truth. They tell lots of big fibs."

Jana thought about his characterization of the management at Europol as liars. "They give out misinformation? How?"

"Statistics," snorted Walsh.

"And claims of credit for cases we barely connect with," Paola affirmed, ruefully shaking her head. "The way they describe the cases we do get, it's as if we always have remarkable successes. There is never a bad result. If a case turns sour, they string it out under the guise of continuing the investigation, eventually burying it in the back of some report. On the other hand, they blabber about the depths of our involvement when we are only called on for something simple, like checking the file of some second-rate crook involved with the case, or tracing a foreign license plate."

"Remember my case on canned goods?" Walsh asked. "I was assigned a query on mislabeled cans of sardines. The Norwegians said they were being sold in Greece under false pretenses since the sardines were really caught and canned by Japanese rover ships, then shipped to Greece falsely advertised as being from Norway. A forty-thousand-euro shipment, very small by international standards, was involved. The Norwegians spent a year, the Greeks a year, with a total cost to the two countries of about 500,000 euros."

"More money than that was spent," Paola corrected Walsh.

"Probably," Walsh agreed. "We ran some shipping records for them. Nothing much. It took a couple of hours of my time. When the arrests were made, our head office wrote it up for our public records as if we had solved the whole thing."

Laszlo snorted. "If we touch it, no matter how teeny-tiny, we're the agency that saved the world."

"In reality," Paola added, "most of our jobs are make-work. We fill our own reports with crap to make us look good while we're really sitting on our hands."

"Getting fat-assed," Walsh appended.

"Speak for yourself," Ilica prodded Walsh. "I'm still Mr. Muscle."

He brought his arms up, flexing his biceps to show them all how fit he was. There was a chorus of boos, which Ilica enjoyed.

They began to file out of the room. Paola lingered for a moment, a sly smile on her face.

"Don't worry about Mazur. Like Ilica said, he's going to make nice."

They were right. There was a note on Jana's desk asking her to see Mazur. Paola winked at her as Jana went to his office.

Mazur rose from behind his desk, handing her a cup of coffee that he had already poured. It was as if he'd forgotten his disapproval of her.

"I'm so pleased that we have someone like you, a person who understands the command requirements that every supervisor must fulfill," Mazur declared.

"What would those requirements be, Assistant Director?" Jana watched him twitch, as if he had been jabbed in the ribs.

"The prime directive is to make this place run smoothly." He paused for a moment, as if rehearsing Europol directives in his mind. "I felt that you needed to know what the parameters of conduct were for working here. However, sometimes I am too abrupt in exercising my prerogatives as a supervisor. So if I was, if I spoke perhaps too harshly, I was simply voicing my perceptions."

"Perceptions are important," Jana agreed, wondering if she could keep up her pose of compliance for very much longer.

"Good. We agree. Some good news, now. Perhaps I should keep this to myself, but I won't. When I talked to the Dutch police, they personally indicated to me that they did not think they would have a case against you when they completed their assessment of the facts."

Then why, Jana wondered, had Mazur spoken as he had in the conference room? He was a frightened martinet, she concluded, covering his posterior in case things might yet turn sour. Another thought intruded. "Was the Dutch officer who contacted you an investigator named Jan Leiden?"

Mazur looked surprised, and a little anxious. "You know the man?"

"We met, briefly, over a cup of coffee."

"Oh." Mazur looked more anxious. "A friend?" It would not do for her to establish a back-channel source of information with the Dutch police; she might then possibly undercut him.

"We've just met."

"Hmmm." He fiddled with a pencil, then forced a smile.

"I've contacted the Slovak police with respect to the mix-up about your inappropriate job skills for the position they sent you to fill at Europol. I've received no answer as yet." He rubbed his hands together in a bad simulation of enthusiasm. "Now, I can't have you just sitting around not doing anything until I get some ruling on your status. So I have a little assignment for you in the meantime. You're an expert in homicide investigations. Our people receive continuing training through CEPOL, the European police college headquartered in England. However, since you're here, I'd like you to prepare and conduct an in-house training session for the people in our unit on how to investigate a homicide case. Merely a cross-training exercise, you understand, until we have further word."

Jana agreed, to make peace. The assistant director went back to his work. Jana walked out of Mazur's office with the realization that the man was a complete imbecile. Even worse, she began to think that this was the most absurd posting she'd ever been given.

When she got back to her office, Jana began to feel depressed, which set in motion a descent into a well of self-pity. Ultimately, she became angry with herself. Peter would not want her to respond in this way. If there were no chances of being assigned a real case here, maybe she would have time to investigate the cases that were still pending in Slovakia: the killing of Denis Macek, the phone blast that had killed Peter. And, also, the disappearance of Kroslak from The Hague. Fury replaced depression. Yes, she would find a way to work on those cases. There were difficulties, the long distance and a lack of access to witnesses and reports, but she would find a way. Peter would appreciate what she was going to do. Perhaps, even more importantly, she would.

Others, investigators who were not in her section, began popping in to chat with members of the team over morning coffee. There was Mayer from Austria, a stocky man who smelled of cigar smoke, then Ryan, another Irishman, who apparently shared a mutual antipathy with Walsh, the two of them bristling every time they neared each other, and Gunnar, a Norwegian whose hair and skin were so bleached out that he was almost an albino. They came and went, introducing themselves to Jana, or not, several of them mouthing "See you at 1700 hours" before they left.

Jana asked Paola what the "1700 hours" was about.

"Initiation party for the newbie. It's also an opportunity for everyone to get a little squiffed."

Jana winced. She knew who the "newbie" was.

Paola had a wicked look on her face. Whatever was on the horizon, Paola was going to enjoy it.

Chapter 11

The party began at 1700 hours. Everyone gathered at an even larger conference room one floor below. It was a typical cops-only event: vulgar, loud, tinged with anger. Swearing, cursing, and complaining comprised a large portion of the conversation. A large hand-printed sign on one wall said "Welcome Slovakia."

The conference table had been pushed to one side, the chairs stacked in the corners. A large punch bowl, filled with a purple-red liquid that looked like it would burn out one's insides, had been placed in the middle of the table with paper cups surrounding it. Another bowl containing ice cubes sat next to it. Three large thermos jugs stood on the other side of the punch bowl. Paola cautioned Jana not to drink the punch, describing its fiery contents as brewed by a genuine "Lithuanian witch." Instead, Paola referred her to the "purist's" choice, the contents of the thermos jugs: red contained scotch, blue vodka, and yellow gin. Jana poured herself a small amount of scotch on the rocks, then went through the usual mingling-with-the-guests process. All of them, not only the ones who had met her earlier, knew her name. This was, indeed, a small world she had come into.

They were an odd mixture. An Englishman named Peete was eternally embarrassed about something, and looked at the floor when anyone talked to him; a dark-skinned man who was clearly from the Middle East spoke

English with a very French accent and was more French in his mannerisms than anyone Jana had ever met; a Slovenian who looked more German than Zimmer, the Prussian, who stood against one of the walls, distancing himself from everyone. Jana tucked away all their names and faces in appropriate compartments of her brain. Most of her new compatriots were cheerful, talkative, and generally outgoing. It looked like it would be pleasant to work with them.

Everyone was now chattering away, the noise level fueled by the freely flowing alcohol. Jana eventually wandered over to Paola and Walsh, who were engaged in an intense conversation. The subject was Assistant Director Mazur, about whom Paola was ranting.

"The son-of-a-bitch doesn't know police work, he's ready to say 'no' at every opportunity, and he stalls or slows every investigation that I've ever been involved in."

"He's a little *shite*, and all little *shites* aren't even worth cleaning your ass with. So, take another sip of your gin and forget Mr. Craphead. Am I right, Jana; or am I right?" He flashed her a big smile.

"You're right, Aidan."

To show her agreement, she took a small sip of her drink. Heeding her example, and to illustrate how seriously he took his own advice, Walsh downed the last of his drink, then moved over to the gin thermos and poured himself another cupful.

"I've not seen Mazur at the party." Jana looked around the room. "Does that mean he disapproves of newbie parties, or just me?"

Walsh had returned. "He knows no one likes him, so he's afraid to come to the shindig. One of our laddies might get too drunk and tell him what he thinks in front of everyone, which would be splendid by me. Unnecessary for me to point out, I suppose, but that would mean lots of laughter at his Highness the Turd's discomfort."

"You'll notice that Grosjean is also absent," Paola added. She smirked, a wicked look in her eyes. "I sent him an anonymous letter today."

"Who?" asked Walsh.

"Grosjean. I wrote 'Stop Eating Shit'."

Walsh laughed uproariously. "I love it." When he quieted down, he leaned toward Paola, lowering his voice. "He'll know you sent it."

"He'll *think* I've sent it. That's a big difference."

There was a sudden fanfare of music from the speakers lodged in opposite corners of the room. The music stopped; a loud, falsely solemn voice declared, "Silence, and let us all pay reverent homage to the dear departed."

A number of men, including Gabi Laszlo and Gyorgi Ilica, slowly entered the room, solemnly carrying a coffin. They set the coffin on the table and reverently backed away, their heads bowed. A cardboard plaque was affixed to the coffin with Kroslak's name printed on it, RIP in gold letters under it.

Jana stared at the cardboard sign, realizing that the "Initiation for the Newbie" had begun. Law-enforcement officers develop a macabre sense of humor. It is one of the ways they stay sane. She was now to be the butt of that humor.

The voice blared over the speaker again. "Jana Matinova, replacement for our dearly beloved colleague who is no longer with us, will now come forward." As Jana hesitated, Walsh prodded her.

"Go up to the bloody thing."

Jana stepped up to the coffin. Everyone in the room looked at her expectantly, trying for mock solemnity.

The loudspeaker piped up again. "You will now unlock the coffin, Jana Matinova."

Jana opened the little chain-bolt that sealed the lid.

"Open the coffin, Jana Matinova."

Jana knew that whatever was coming would happen now. She opened the coffin.

As soon as the lid fell back, music suitable for a bump-and-grind striptease blared out of the speaker and Ryan, the Irishman she had met earlier in the day, jumped up from inside the coffin, grinding away to the music. He was dressed in nothing but a bikini bottom, with false breasts, a long wig, and garish makeup all over his body, a hermaphrodite gargoyle displaying his wares for the world to see. Most noticeable of all was a huge plastic phallus, jutting out from his briefs, waving in the air in rhythm to his gyrations.

He got closer and closer to Jana, brandishing the phallus until it was almost in her face. Jana knew she was expected to add her own touch to the revelry, perhaps scream, show feminine embarrassment, or fall over in a mock faint. None of those choices was acceptable to her, but she had to do something. Jana casually reached up, grasped the phallus, tore it off its tapes, then offhandedly tossed it into the crowd behind her as a bride would throw her bouquet. Ryan uttered a mock scream, clutching his groin, pretending that his own member had been torn away.

The people in the room cheered and laughed. A number jumped on the conference table to gyrate, people applauded, screaming for those on the table to "take it off;" others danced around the room, with nothing held back in this sacred moment. Jana moved a few feet from the table.

Walsh whispered in her ear. "I don't think I'd like you to get angry at me, Matinova."

"If I do it fast, it won't hurt a bit."

"Like hell it wouldn't."

"At least they didn't want *you* to take your clothes off." Paola had to raise her voice to be heard above the din. "To be accepted, you still have to take all this crap from the men."

"Well, did you?"

"Did I do what?"

"Take them off?"

"I stopped when I got down to my panties and brassiere."

"She looked pretty good in them," Walsh added.

"I know," Paola agreed. "I surprised myself by enjoying it."

"I could tell."

Paola punched him, and he rolled with the punch, gesturing toward the now phallus-less man standing on the table.

"This would have been a great party, except for that fat-ass Ryan up there."

Ryan was still gyrating away. Someone had tossed the plastic penis back up to him and he was whipping it over his head.

"For god's sake, will you stop with your crap about that guy," Paola snarled.

"Only when he's dead."

Paola shrugged. "What is it with the Irish and their feuds?"

Jana did not know the Irish well enough to answer the question. She glanced at the coffin. It still had Kroslak's name on it, the RIP sign now tilted at an angle symbolizing the off-kilter nature of the whole affair, silently asking "Whatever happened to Kroslak?"

Chapter 12

Jana's arrival had just been a pretext for everyone to have fun, so after a reasonable interval she slipped away from the party. By then, nobody missed her.

She needed to complete her work on the homicide investigation cross-training exercise she had been assigned to conduct for her sectionmates, and although she'd worked on it intermittently all day, she needed to put the finishing touches to her preparation before meeting the professor for dinner. She went back to her hotel room. But the investigation of the two killings in Bratislava and the question of what was happening within her own division in Slovakia kept intruding. She ultimately gave in and made a phone call to Slovakia: to Seges, her warrant officer.

When she got him on the phone, there was something decidedly different about the man's attitude. Seges was not only no longer deferential to her as his commander, he was decidedly truculent, with an edge to his answers that projected outright antipathy.

The first words out of his mouth when he realized it was Jana Matinova calling were, "What is it . . . Matinova?"

"I'm still a commander, Seges."

"Yes, Commander," he reluctantly said.

"Have there been any messages for me?"

"Nothing. No one has called."

There was a long silence.

"You wanted something?" Seges asked.

"Any word on the two cases?"

"Which ones?"

"The shooting at the hotel; the phone bombing in the prosecutor's office."

"It's my understanding that we are not supposed to discuss them."

"Are you saying that you don't discuss the cases among each other? That you haven't heard anything on the office water-cooler telegraph?"

"Just rumors."

"What rumors?"

"Rumors go in one of my ears and out of the other."

Seges was the biggest rumormonger in the Slovak police department. He had simply decided not to give her any information.

"I want you to check on someone for me."

"I'm not sure I can do that, Commander."

"Why not?"

"I'm not authorized."

There was always one way to get Seges to do something: threaten him.

"Seges, I will be back in Slovakia, maybe not tomorrow or the next day, but soon. I will recall your good humor, and your bad humor. I will remember your cooperation, or your lack of cooperation. Even more, I can still pull a personnel file and make notes in it. Do you understand the position you have now put yourself in, or shall I explain further?" There was another long silence. "Now, there is something I want you to do forthwith. And then, when you have the information, you're to call me back immediately. I expect this to be done in no more than a half hour. Understood?"

"I'll get to it right away, Commander," Seges said humbly.

"One more thing: who is going to replace me as chief of the division?"

"Unknown, Commander. There is not even a rumor about it."

That was strange. They had to fill her old position as quickly as possible. It was too important a vacancy to ignore.

"There must be someone doing the job at the moment, even temporarily."

"Colonel Trokan has taken personal command of the division. Everyone is reporting directly to him."

Why had Trokan put himself in that position, along with his other duties? What in hell was going on in Bratislava? Things sounded crazy back there.

Jana hung up on Seges after giving him another warning that the clock was ticking. He called back with the answers she wanted in twenty minutes, adding that he would be more than pleased to get her anything else she wanted. The information that Seges gave her was not surprising. In fact, she had expected it. The professor had no criminal record. Even though she was reasonably sure, she'd had to check. The stakes were too high for her not to.

Jana went back to her work, trying to prepare the lecture she was to give for her Europol section. Nothing she thought of was what she wanted. She tossed page after page of her work, crumpling up sheets of work-problem hypotheticals she'd outlined for the crew of SC 4 to consider. No matter what she came up with, after a few minutes she would dump it in the wastebasket as fit only for first-year students at the police academy. Jana didn't realize how late it had become until the phone rang. It was the professor, calling from the hotel lobby. She had worked past the time set for their dinner. Jana apologized, threw on a fresh blouse and pair of slacks, wasted a few moments fixing her makeup, and then took the stairs leading down to the lobby. Late, but as the professor said, taking her off the hook, only "fashionably" tardy.

They took the tram. The professor had brought tickets for them both, carefully clocking them in the time-stamp mechanism on the tram. He handed her one, then took on the role of tour guide as they passed through and out of the center of the city. First, he apologized. "I have decided that we are not going to the Scheveningen area. The bloody beach scene is too crowded. It's *commercial*," he muttered, making a disparagingly rude noise with his mouth. "People invariably become disgusting at beach areas. So, I thought, since I have decreed that you are, for tonight, true royalty in the city where the Queen of the Netherlands has her home, you shall be treated like royalty. Hence we are going to the Tampat Senang. Don't ask me what the name means, but there they know how to defer to royal visitors." He glanced out the window of the tram, lighting up as he pointed out a museum they were passing. "Old Dutch Masters are housed there. One of my favorites, Vermeer, has a painting which is not to be believed. This is a city of very fine museums, you know."

"I've heard," she said. "You like the arts?"

"I like the pure arts. Painting, yes. With a good painting we can perceive with our eyes twice as well as we ordinarily might be able to. Once through the surface of the painting; and then second through the eyes of the artist and our perceptions of why and how and what the artist himself has seen. But only with the good artists. Old Vermeers and new Van Dongens. And others," he smiled. "You must take advantage of being here."

He took out a blue handkerchief, which then became a red handkerchief, attached to a green handkerchief, then a yellow one attached to a purple one, then a polka-dotted one, then one striped in red, then another in fuchsia, going on and on until he blew his nose with an exaggerated flourish, then rolled them all into a ball and made them vanish.

Jana smiled, applauding his performance.

"Thank you; thank you." He bowed. "Now you see my problem. I have never quite been able to retire from bringing wonders to the world. My talent just pops up when I least expect it." He pulled a small orchid out from behind his ear. "This is for you. May I . . . ?" He pinned the orchid to her blouse. "A lady's eveningwear is never complete without a corsage."

"I thank the gentleman." Jana made her own small bow.

"I promise not to do any more magic for the evening. Everything shall be for 'real.' Besides, reality is always better than fantasy."

"Only sometimes. Magic has its place, Professor."

The tram passed over a canal, the professor gesturing at it to make his point. "Reality is also beautiful. You see the water, the greenery, trees, and lovely old homes that are cared for. They make a city feel cozy and comfortable. Liveable. Magic is already here."

"I'm glad you think so." Jana decided it was time for her to confront the professor with what she had learned from Seges. "I've also made magic. My crystal ball has conjured up interesting information. Your full name is Denis Macek. Your nephew was the young man who was shot to death at the Carleton Savoy hotel."

The professor winced but didn't seem surprised.

"I was going to tell you at dinner," he said, not by way

of apology, merely as a fact. "Denis was a good boy. Being around him was a pleasure." He quickly wiped away a tear that had formed in the corner of his eye. "I loved him. He was very curious, my nephew. We could spend lovely evenings together asking questions about life, and coming up with more questions. Great fun." He let his sadness show for a second, then suppressed it. "How did you link the two of us?"

"It was not hard. You performed magic; your nephew had a magic trick on his person. How many Slovaks take the same plane as I did to Amsterdam, then go on to The Hague as well? A possibility, but not a probability. I checked the plane's passenger list. Lo and behold, you have the same name as your nephew. I had my warrant officer check your background. So, simple."

"You notice, we don't need sleight of hand to find answers." He waved his hand in the air as if to conjure up a spirit. "That's how we differed, he and I. He was very practical. I, on the other hand, am not." He paused, reflecting, his lips moving slightly as if he were talking to himself. "I think he was going to bring me some of the food he was going to obtain at the hotel. He always did. Some pastry or other. Pensioners can't afford to eat pastry, and he knew I loved it."

"I'm sorry, Professor. I'm sure he loved you."

"I think so." He thought for a moment. "I was a performer at one time. I put on magic shows. I was billed as the Clown Professor of Magic." He smiled at the recollection. "That's where the 'Professor' comes from. I came out costumed as a professor, makeup, glasses, long string tie, lab coat mixing a chemical experiment that would blow up with a cloud of smoke and a big bang, and fall to the floor. I was never really very good at magic. So I capitalized on my deficit by making it into a comic clown act. I was Harlequin, Pierrot, a Merry Andrew. No, more than that! I was a Wise Fool.

"I deliberately made mistakes. People laughed and laughed. I was a comedian. I made my existence a joke. That was my fortunate—and unfortunate—calling. I made a good living, but spent my life mocking myself. A difficult task." He lapsed into silence, staring ahead of them, unseeing. Looking down, he whispered, "That explains the difference between a clown magician and a simple magician." He looked up. "A clown starts his act slipping on a banana peel, or something equally foolish. It tells the audience to expect more clowning than magic." He smiled at a thought. "Except for my nephew. I was never a joke to him. He thought of me as a skilled magician. A performing artist. Odd.

"My nephew didn't like seeing me as a clown. I was his uncle, so he thought it was not respectful. So for him I had to do good tricks. I practiced hard before every performance if I knew he was coming. He loved seeing me on the stage. For him, I became the larger-than-life Professor of Magic."

Jana nodded. "Professor, you are larger than life."

She reached into her pocket and pulled out the trick coin that she had picked up from the floor of the hotel restaurant where his nephew had been killed. "I think this was your nephew's."

He took the coin, turning it over and over in his hands, working the coin's mechanism to bend it, then bend it once more, then open it up again so it was an unmarked coin.

"I gave it to him when he was much younger," he said, his voice barely audible. "He wanted to do the inexplicable. This was his very first piece of equipment. He mastered other tricks. It didn't matter. The first one that you awe people with is always your favorite. So he kept this with him all the time. He didn't practice magic any more, except that once in a while he would pull this coin out and amaze someone." He continued to finger the coin. "Was this with him when he died?"

"At his feet. There was also a table napkin nearby. Did it mean anything?"

"The coin and the napkin are both part of the setup for a performance. You have the napkin in your left hand, you cover the coin with the napkin, and the trick is set up for *the turn*, where the magician makes the ordinary act extraordinary. My nephew was doing the trick. It did not meet with the appreciation that my nephew thought it would."

The Clown Professor of Magic kissed the coin.

"I must keep the coin," Jana informed him. "It may be evidence. If it's not, I'll get it back to you."

He shrugged, fighting to check his emotions. "He has no use for it any more. It's yours."

Jana put the coin away. "I think I told you I wanted to do magic when I was a child."

"Did you ever try it?"

"Once. Only, I tried to do real magic. I was not successful."

"Like my nephew."

"Perhaps." She thought for a moment. "I'd like to know how you found out I was coming to The Hague and why you wanted to talk to me."

"You're supposed to be a very good detective. I would like to see how your mind works. Can *you* tell how I knew you were coming here?"

"I've heard that magicians are not supposed to give

away their secrets, Professor. If they do, they meet a bad end. It's a cardinal transgression."

The professor looked sad.

"Since you tried to become a magician, it's quite acceptable for one magician to share secrets with another magician," he said.

"I'm not a magician, Professor."

"We can pretend."

Jana smiled at the thought of pretending to be a magician; then decided to humor the old man and his request.

"You remembered my name because of the publicity surrounding other crimes I've investigated. Then you read it in the newspapers because of my initial investigation of your nephew's death. You waited, perhaps a few days, calling my office only to find out that I was on leave. You kept calling, discovering that I had been taken off the case and that it had been assigned to another officer in the corruption division. You were referred to Investigator Elias.

"When you contacted Elias, he told you he could not give out any information. That's what the corruption division does; they politely tell you nothing. Your only hope for information was me, so you went back to my division. My new assignment is not secret, so they told you that I had been assigned to a new position here. They probably even told you when I was to start. The more serious question is how you knew what flight I was on and where I was to sit, so you would have the opportunity to talk to me." Jana mulled it over. "Government agencies all use the same travel service to book flights. There are not that many travel agencies in Slovakia. You knew which one the government used. When you were a traveling performer, I'll bet you used the same agency. You asked the agent to check with the airline for the flight I was listed on, then had him book a seat near me."

The professor confirmed her judgment by nodding a number of times as she talked. "So, you live up to your reputation."

Jana was embarrassed. "I wasn't solving a very difficult problem."

"That may be so. However, now you have to solve the very grave problem involving my nephew's murder." He hesitated, then continued. "I want to help you solve it. It's the least I can do for my nephew."

"I cannot use your help right now. I've been taken off the case."

He stood. "I hope you are still having dinner with me, even though you now know who I am." He rang for the tram's next stop. "The food here is too good to miss."

The professor was right. The Tampat Senang was unique. The inside of the restaurant was decorated like an old colonial rubber-plantation mansion, in the tradition of the Dutch imperial reign in Indonesia. The waiters, in native costume, catered to them with deferential service that was almost uncomfortable. The garden area where they were seated provided a graceful backdrop for the marvelous cumin-scented food they were served. It was all ethereally lovely.

The professor seemed to recover from his disappointment at Jana's refusal of his offer of help. The two of them talked freely about the changes that had been taking place in Slovakia, how the communist era was truly ended, about the new generation looking to the West and the EU. Small talk was used to fill up time, to avoiding the subject the professor wanted to talk about. They did not discuss that until dessert was served, in diminutive glazed bowls, scoops of both violet and tamarind fruit sorbets, their tastes gently soothing after the strong spices of the prior dishes. Then two small cups of strong espresso coffee to sip were brought.

"Would you like to hear about my nephew?" the professor started.

"I've told you that I'm no longer on the case."

"I don't believe that."

"What don't you believe about it?"

"That you would sit by and let the case be interred."

"It's being investigated."

"Not by the person who *should* be looking into it."

"That's what happens in the real world."

"But I want to tell you about my nephew."

"If you wish."

"He was investigating something."

"A crime?"

"It was a matter out of his area of expertise, but I think so."

"Did he tell you about it?"

"Not much. He was writing a dissertation for his doctorate. Like all students, he spent huge amounts of time on the computer. He collated reams of information. He went back into historical archives and pulled out files by the hundreds. Somewhere in that process, he found something that both disturbed and animated him. He became more and more agitated, more keyed up, saying that he had never run across anything like this before."

"You inquired as to what had made him so agitated?"

"I asked him," the professor confirmed. "All he would say was that he wanted to corroborate the information, and when he was sure he would tell me. Before he could do so, he was killed."

"You think he was killed because of what he'd found in his research?"

"Why else would anyone want to kill a starving student? His father died early on; I was his surrogate father. I knew him. He was not involved in any kind of criminality. I knew that boy. He was. . . ." The professor faltered, forced to fight the sorrow that was welling up inside him.

Jana reached out to hold his hand, squeezing it to give him whatever comfort the touch of another human can give.

"I know what you've experienced. We've both lost someone dear to us recently."

The professor looked at her, trying to make amends for showing his feelings. "I have probably depressed you by talking about my nephew."

"No, Professor."

"Is the information useful?"

"Very useful."

"I can help you more."

"Perhaps. We'll have to see how."

"You're going to investigate, then?"

She thought about telling the professor that she had already determined she would continue her investigation in earnest, and decided against it. "I hope you understand that as a police officer, I have to follow departmental orders. I've received those orders and I'm officially unable to directly participate in any investigation of the student Denis Macek's death. Of course, if, as you think, he had found out about some other crime, there is nothing in my orders that would stop me from investigating that crime."

The professor stared at her for a long moment before he understood what she was saying.

"Thank you."

"There's nothing to thank me for yet, Professor."

Jana obtained the professor's contact information. He assured her that if and when she needed any additional information about his nephew, he would be available. Before they took separate trams back to their respective hotels, the professor handed her another tram ticket.

"It wouldn't do to have a police officer riding the public transportation system without a proper ticket."

Jana kissed him on the cheek and boarded her tram. He had all his handkerchiefs out again, waving them all in a multi-colored banner, as her tram left him at the stop.

She felt sad at leaving him there, alone.

But the evening of conversation with the professor had solidified something in Jana's mind.

The killing of the professor's nephew was clearly a professional killing; the killing of Peter was also a murder committed by a professional. They were not "ordinary" killings. The methods used were very different. But, as she had already concluded, what were the odds that two such professional assassinations would take place within such a short time of each other in a small city like Bratislava unless they were connected?

She had to find that connection.

Chapter 13

The bath was as hot as Jana could tolerate, and she slipped into the water by degrees. She wanted to absorb the heat, still her mind, and let the water therapy take its course. Jana let everything drift apart for a while and then come back together as she relaxed.

The first thing that popped into her mind was the magic coin they'd found with the murdered student, and then the first time, when she was a little girl of eleven, that she'd tried to do magic. She even thought she had succeeded. Jana had walked into her house and told her father she thought she was magical. Her brother was in the same room, and he immediately started to scoff at her. Her father hushed him and shooed him out of the room so he could talk to the family *magician* by himself. Her father, a judge who listened as patiently to his children as he did the evidence he heard in court, asked her why she had come to that conclusion. Jana told him she'd been on her way home from school when she'd wished that Anna, a friend of hers who had been sick and stayed away from class that day, could be there. And, suddenly Anna was there. After a moment of consternation, with Jana excitedly informing her friend that they'd just performed magic, Anna had laughed and told Jana that she had been hiding behind a tree and just happened to pop out at the moment she'd been "wished" for. Nevertheless, Jana was still sure that it was her own magic that had summoned her friend.

Her father had nodded but suggested that one demonstration of her supernatural ability was not enough proof for him. Therefore, he would withhold his decision to allow his daughter to bring further evidence before his court. Of course, the court hearing would be in their living room and their father's favorite chair would substitute for the judge's dais. He set the *case* for the next day. Before Jana went to her room, her father suggested that he, too, might be a magician. The traits necessary to work spells and conjure apparitions might have been inherited by her from him. Considering how people in court always treated him as if he could work magic, he confessed that he had long suspected that he also might be a sorcerer.

The next day Jana tried to do magic. She had read fairy tales and used the conjuring spells and incantations in them to invoke a rain cloud or create fire from rocks, without success. The one she worked hardest at, transporting herself from one place to another without walking or riding her bicycle, failed no matter how hard she tried. When the time set for the hearing arrived, despite the fact that Jana now doubted her ability to perform magic, her father called the court in session, with both her mother and brother in attendance.

Her brother was called to give testimony. He testified that he had never done magic. Then came Jana's turn.

Jana's father put her under oath to tell the truth, and she never lied to her father, so she was forced to confess that she'd tried to do magic over the past day, and all of her spells had failed miserably. So, Jana guessed, she was not gifted, and that she had not conjured up her friend. It didn't matter, her father said. Because he'd discovered that members of the family were still gifted. It had been revealed to them that both he and her mother could do magic.

Jana stared at the two of them, her mouth agape. "You can both do magic, Father?"

He nodded, his demeanor very serious, announcing that he would demonstrate this by showing how Jana's mother could read the thoughts of inanimate objects.

Her father laid out three dishes in a row on a table, then asked her mother to leave the room. He pranced around, waving his arms and mumbling, casting a great spell over the plates so the plates would speak to their mother even though she was out of the room. Then he had Jana silently indicate a dish which their mother would then be called upon to identify. When he called Jana's mother into the room, she immediately picked the plate that Jana had selected. Her mother left the room again, and this time her father turned to Jana's brother and had him silently point out a plate for his mother to identify. Her mother was called back into the room and once more selected the correct plate.

She did this over and over again. Both Jana and her brother were agog at her uncanny ability. With that, their father said the court was adjourned, took off his robes, and demonstrated a simple word code he used to communicate with Jana's mother. Her father would call his wife into the room using slightly different words each time. The difference in words identified the correct plate. Then the judge had Jana and her brother perform the trick. It was very simple to play, once it had been explained.

All magicians are tricksters, he told them. All tricksters lie, but lie in a way that makes you believe them. They rely on the innocence and trustfulness of people. People want to believe. And every good magician makes his act a big show, an event, performing ordinary acts in an extraordinary way so the targets of his illusion are captivated. Her father had learned, in court, that great criminals had also learned the same tricks. It was all smoke and mirrors. So it was wise to be cautious.

Her father, the judge, had given them a life lesson: be skeptical. If it is too good to be true, it will be false. If great claims are made, disbelieve them. Use your senses and your mind. Above all, think.

Jana never forgot this lesson. It had paid off for her when she became a police officer: the *trick* had become the criminal act, the criminal, a *fakir* who was trying to fool the public. She owed it to her father to try to find out how the trick had been carried out.

Jana abruptly realized that the water in the bath had gone cold.

Her eyes popped open. She had napped. She quickly soaped herself, then rinsed off, climbing out of the tub. The killing of the student in Slovakia had been a trick; the killing of Peter a trick; the disappearance of Kroslak part of a trick. She had to maintain her disbelief, ignore the "smoke and mirrors," and see through the illusion.

Chapter 14

J ana was aroused by her wake-up call. This time she had slept through the newspapers being slid under the door. She tossed them onto the bed, then went through her wash, dry, dress, and makeup routine before she picked up the papers to read. Again, there was a Slovak *Sme* and an *International Herald Tribune*. A low-level government official, who asked not to be identified, suggested the possibility of nationalization of the oil field in Slovakia. Four had died in a gas explosion. A Slovak singer had filed a lawsuit alleging that a Slovak recording company which had released her records was cheating her on royalties. And the head of the Green Party was accusing the minister of economics of being corrupt, which was an oblique attack on the prime minister.

The *Herald Tribune* was not much different, only focusing on the international stage. A billionaire investment banker had been killed. The Georgians were accusing the Russians of firing a missile into their country. Oil and gas prices around the world were going up. All in all, the rest of it was the usual.

Jana tossed the papers into the trash container in the bathroom, took a last look in the mirror, and had started for the door when the phone rang. It was Colonel Trokan.

"Good morning, Janka."

"A little soon to be calling me about my next transfer. Where will it be this time? Uzbekistan, perhaps? Mongolia?"

"Janka, you hurt me by talking like that. You know I only have your best interests at heart. Look at the posh position I've sent you to. Everybody else in this country would give up any number of fingers and toes to be in Holland."

"Not me. I like my fingers and toes."

"I'm also outside of our beloved country. I'm calling you from Vienna."

"What are you doing in Vienna?"

"Ostensibly, I have taken a few days off by pretending to be on a vacation to placate my wife."

"Have you placated her, Colonel?"

"She screams at me in a slightly mellower tone."

"Why did you call me, Colonel?"

"I didn't want to telephone from Slovakia, either from my office, my cell, my home, or anywhere else. So, I came here on a 'vacation,' perhaps to take me a little out of someone's 'gunsights' and to be where I'm able to talk freely."

Jana hesitated, unsure for the moment if Trokan was still being humorous. Then she decided he was being very, very serious. She immediately thought of what had happened to Peter.

"Does it have anything to do with Peter's death?"

"The phones, the way Peter was killed, the disappearance of Kroslak . . . and the fact that there has been at least one informant who says that I'm now targeted for assassination. He's unreliable, and he says it's a street rumor, but I was concerned about calling or e-mailing you from anywhere in Slovakia. I'm making the assumption that any means of communication is suspect. I'm calling from a public phone in a hotel that I'm not registered at."

"Who else has been targeted?"

Jana knew one of the people even before Trokan told her.

"You. And Captain Bohumil, who was the head of the Anti-Corruption Division."

"You used the past tense."

"He asked me to relieve him of duty."

"They went after him?"

"His brother-in-law was driven off a cliff in the Tatras. They did an autopsy on the body. There were two bullets in his crushed skull. Bohumil's wife went off her head; Bohumil's ulcers then acted up, so he went on sick leave. The Hungarians are cooperating, so we were able to put the Bohumils and their kids in protective custody in a small villa near Budapest. I've taken direct charge of the Anti-Corruption Unit as well as yours."

"You're wearing a lot of hats."

"I like hats. I have a whole collection of hats. You know that."

"They made a try at me. The day before yesterday."

There was a long silence on Trokan's end of the conversation. Then he swore. "How?"

"They tried to run me down with a car."

"You're sure it was deliberate?"

"Absolutely."

"Damn them! We publicly registered you in another room at a cheap hotel in The Hague, and then let the word out here that's where you were staying." He told her the name of the other hotel. "Police officers don't room at places like the one you're actually in. I figured that might buy you some time. Now that they know where you're living, you have to move."

"Whoever they are will know it as soon as I check out and then check in somewhere else."

"Do you need one of our people to watch your back? Maybe I can send someone."

"That always looks absurd to the public: cops guarding cops. If we can't take care of ourselves, who's going to take care of them? So my answer is 'No, thank you'."

"What do you want me to do here?" Trokan waited for an answer.

After a moment of reflection, Jana plunged ahead. "With the killing of Bohumil's brother-in-law, at least we're now sure that whatever this is about is not connected directly to me, but to the anti-corruption investigation, and Peter's death. What did Bohumil tell you about investigating Peter's death? What do Peter's files show?"

After taking a moment to organize his thoughts; the Colonel plunged ahead.

"Peter Saris picked up the case he was working on from another investigation. He stumbled onto the evidence inadvertently. We don't know which case he pulled it from or what it was. He simply told Bohumil that it was a big one. He was apparently uneasy about saying anything until he had developed a complete picture. He wanted to be sure he was right. We now know that he was on the mark. He had reason to be afraid." There was a heavy sigh over the phone. "We looked for the file. No file was found."

"Taken?"

"Probably. Which has us all scared. It may be another police officer, or maybe *officers*. This is bad business, police officers afraid of other police officers. Even the minister of the interior is pissing in his pants. We're the government. *We're* supposed to scare *them*. The criminals are supposed to run from us! It's not working the way it's supposed to."

"So it would appear."

He sighed even more loudly. "I think we have bad trouble, Janka."

"That's the picture I'm getting."

"Also the reason I couldn't brief you in Slovakia. I didn't know where or how to do it safely. We're taking a chance now by doing it on the telephone."

"If they're listening, we haven't told them anything they don't know."

"Maybe."

"How is Elias doing?"

"Getting nowhere."

Jana thought of telling Trokan about the report she'd found in her closet at home, deciding against it. If they were tapping this conversation, or her room was bugged, they would come after the report and try even harder to get her. Better to be silent.

"You know what you need to accomplish, Janka?" Trokan's voice was stressed.

"I know what to do, Colonel."

"Luck to us all."

"Luck to us all, Colonel."

She hung up.

Chapter 15

J ana skipped breakfast at the hotel and went to the office. Outside the Europol building, a knot of people was gathered. There was a fire truck on the street; firemen were going in and out. The first thing Jana thought of was another bomb, just like the one that had killed Peter. Paola was in the group that had gathered. Jana went over to her as Paola answered the unasked question on Jana's face.

"A fire in the Records Section. The computer system is down all through the building. It's even hit the backup."

"How bad?" Jana asked, the conversation she'd just had with Trokan now very much on her mind. More records destroyed, she told herself. They were making sure Kroslak had left nothing behind.

"Who knows? The technicians will look at it; we'll look at it. Hopefully, the damage is limited." She gave a very Italian shrug indicating that it was beyond her control. "You have breakfast yet?"

"I could use toast or a roll."

They walked to a coffee shop that Paola selected and sat at a small table in the rear.

"I come here because the place is clean." She gave another shrug. "I think all Dutch places are clean. Which is too bad. I'd rather have it dirty if they would scrape up a little tasty food. That's the thing I miss most about Italy."

"I had good food last night."

"Indonesian," said Paola, very sure what the answer would be.

"Yes," Jana smiled.

They ordered pastry and coffees.

Paola focused more intently on Jana. "I understand you're going to teach us all about homicide investigations, Mazur's latest idea to keep us busy and prove he's a good manager. The man will never be a good supervisor. I understand he was a lousy cop as well."

"Give him credit." It was Jana's turn to shrug. "He has me thinking about the teaching session. It might turn out to be a good thing."

The coffee and pastries were served. The coffee was excellent, the pastries laden with enough sugar to rot their teeth.

"Are you going to look for Kroslak?" Paola asked.

Jana thought about the question and whether she should conceal her intentions. It would be stupid to mislead Paola, Jana decided. Anyone with half a mind would know that Jana would attempt to find the Slovak officer who had vanished.

"I'm not sure where to start."

"Maybe with his boyfriends?"

The statement startled Jana. "He was gay?"

"I met him on the street with a boy-toy once. He was very affectionate with the young man. The boy was slender, not too tall, not an ounce of fat. Dark hair, very dark eyes enhanced with mascara, hair black and pulled to one side, hanging over an eye partly to cover a scar that ran through his eyebrow. Very sexy. If the lad had liked women, I might have made a play for him myself. I admired Kroslak's good taste." She smiled at the memory of the moment, then brought herself back to Jana's question. "Kroslak never went out with women. He said enough for me to know he went to Amsterdam for his entertainment; so, after seeing him with his young man, I assumed he was gay."

Jana was surprised by Paola's disclosure. The issue had never come up with reference to Kroslak in Slovakia. The Slovaks still didn't know how to deal with overt homosexuality. Gays kept their sexual preferences hidden. It was just as well that Kroslak kept his sex life in the closet. If other police officers had discovered he was gay, they might have made his life miserable.

This opened up an entirely new area of investigation. It might explain the reason he did not use his listed apartment. He would have felt he could not bring any of his lovers to that address. If he did, and the people at Europol found out about it, his secret might have been exposed to the Slovak police. He would have been afraid to risk it.

"If he went to Amsterdam, where would he have gone? Is there a gay scene? Gay clubs?" After one small bite Jana put the pastry aside. She hadn't liked that much sugar since she'd been a little girl. The solid grains made her feel like she was chewing sand. "He would have talked to at least some of his partners in Amsterdam. Maybe he lived with someone?"

"Maybe. You can buy whatever you want in Amsterdam, depending on what club you go to. The Dutch don't care. They figure they have bigger problems than paying attention to how you get your sexual thrills."

"Did you get the name of the boy he was with when you met them?"

Paola thought for a moment. "Willem Albert. Whether those were his first and family names, or just first and middle name, I can't say. You want help in finding young Willem Albert?"

"I don't know Amsterdam. So, yeah."

Paola nodded, a warm smile on her face. They shook hands on it.

"I might suggest that we bring another body along."

"Who?"

"Aidan. He's got the bulk. If we need a persuader, he fits the physical profile of an arm-breaker."

"You trust him?"

"He's been here the longest of any of us. He would probably love the action. As to anything else about him, I don't have answers. So, your case, your call."

Jana thought about bringing Aidan Walsh into the process. Walsh could provide a modicum of protection. He was big enough. And she was in danger. Except, she told herself, *they* would assume that she would make an attempt to locate the Slovak officer. And, if Kroslak hadn't been captured and was hiding out, they might want Jana to find him for them. They might let her alone . . . up to that point. That would be the time to look for danger. Meanwhile, she hadn't much to lose using Walsh.

"I think bringing in Walsh might be a good idea," Jana informed Paola.

Paola used her cell phone. This triggered Jana's recollection of an item that had been nagging at her. There had been a Europol cell phone listed for Kroslak on the reports she had been given by Trokan. They had not found this cell phone in his personal property after he disappeared. He had also left Slovakia with his own cell phone, which had roving capabilities; he could call all over Europe. That phone had also not been accounted for. Both might still be active. If they were, they might be tracked to the users.

"Do we have tracking capability on cell phones at Europol?"

"Sure. Our system isn't bad. We can also go to the cell-phone providers, or the Germans and the British. Or the Americans. They all want to show how good they are." Paola began talking to Aidan, explaining what she and Jana had decided to do. Paola nodded, looking at Jana, making a thumbs-up gesture. Aidan had come aboard.

Jana gave Paola a victory fist. She was beginning to get excited. It was a start.

By the time they had finished their coffee, the Europol building was open again. As a simple check, to see if the fire had been a deliberate attempt to destroy information, Jana started up her computer and looked for Kroslak in the central database. He was not there. All references to Kroslak, even his personnel files, had been deleted. As far as their mainframe was concerned, the investigator who had come to Europol from Slovakia was a nonperson who had never existed.

Jana signed off, staring at her screen. She was beginning to get an idea just how big, efficient, and lethal the people who had killed Peter and the student were. Jana didn't think she'd ever encountered a group like this before. It was frightening. She shook off her fear. It distorted every-thing. It was time for her to start looking for them, and fear would not help her think efficiently.

Jana used her computer to type up the test problem she would use to "teach" the other investigators. It was a hypothetical, a fictitious series of events that would present a group of murders in several countries somehow connected together by a massive conspiracy. The students would be required to pool their various talents and the investigative resources of Europol to solve the crimes. Jana's argument to Mazur would be that this form of on-the-job training rather than classroom instruction was the best way to learn.

Jana used other countries and other names for the people involved, disguising the fact that the basis of the problem was the murders in Bratislava and the subsequent events that had occurred. The exercise would give Jana the room to operate, to do the things that were necessary to get the answers she needed here in The Hague, and any place else she needed to go, without arousing Mazur's suspicions.

She took the exercise to Mazur, who was too busy writing up his perceptions of the illegal immigration conference he had keynoted to pay much attention when she put the test problem she'd developed in front of him. She had also typed up an authorization giving her, and the other investigators, permission to pursue the project. Jana didn't have to use any of the arguments she had prepared to convince him that this was the way to go with her assignment. He simply skim-read what she had prepared, signed it without thinking, then casually dismissed Jana.

Jana, Paola, and Aidan Walsh went to work.

Europol had set up a cell-phone multi-tracking program through the multiplicity of European servers in their treaty countries. All of the server companies had been forced to subscribe to the system since the war on terror had been initiated. It cut across Europe, encompassing every country up to the Russian border. The first thing Jana did was to have the service run traces on both of Kroslak's cell phones. The answers came in very quickly. One of the numbers, the Europol phone he had been issued, had not been used since Kroslak had disappeared. It had probably been discarded or destroyed by Kroslak, or by whoever had made him disappear. The roving cell phone that Kroslak had brought from Slovakia showed that three calls had been made on the first day of his disappearance. Two of them correlated to clubs in Amsterdam. The other was to a number that Jana vaguely recognized.

She dialed it.

The man who answered the phone was Jan Leiden, the Dutch police officer who had followed her on the day she had gone to Kroslak's house. Jana hung up without identifying herself.

Leiden had to know that he'd received a call from Kroslak after he had disappeared. Jana corrected herself. No, someone other than Kroslak using Kroslak's phone might have called him. Only Leiden would know if it was Kroslak who had actually spoken to him. There was also another possibility: if Leiden had received a call from someone, not knowing it had come from Kroslak's cell phone, Leiden still might remember who had called him at the time listed. If he did, that information might be invaluable in assessing what had happened to Kroslak. Of course, it was all dependent on Leiden not being a part of this criminal conspiracy.

Before they began searching the clubs in Amsterdam, Jana had to talk to Leiden.

Chapter 16

L eiden insisted on meeting her on the south side of the Hofvijver, the lakelet in the city center of The Hague near the Binnenhof, the country's old parliament building. Jana walked to the site, then sat on a bench looking across the pond at the building, half-expecting women wearing the white caps and wooden shoes that she had seen in travel posters to come clicking along the walkway, carrying their milk pails. Instead, she saw civil servants walking by with the look of self-importance that characterizes the breed all over the world, the tourists with their children running over to the water to splash each other, and a particularly obnoxious derelict who insisted on peeing on the flowers near her. Jana moved to the next bench, then watched as Leiden came pedaling up, looking much the same as he had the other day.

He braked to a stop, pulling the back-carrier straps off his briefcase, and sauntered over to her. He opened the briefcase and pulled papers out of it before he spoke.

"I hope you are enjoying our sweet but very dull city."

"Not so dull a city."

"Yes, for you. I know what happened." He looked her over. "No scrapes or bruises."

"I was very lucky."

"Maybe you should bet on the lottery." He riffled

through his papers, changing their order. "I prefer to meet in the open air rather than in my office. I use every opportunity to get out." He indicated the little lake. "Nicer to be here by the water, even if it's so small and placid." After a moment he handed her the papers he'd brought. "I thought you might like these. It's a summary of what we have done to date to locate your countryman, Kroslak."

Jana took the report without looking at it.

"Aren't you going to review the marvelous effort we've put forth? Comment on our great investigative skills?" Leiden asked.

"Is there anything of immediate interest that I should study?"

"Nothing that I can think of."

"I'll check it later, then."

They sat in silence, looking at the water and the building on the other side.

"Lots of history in that place."

"I'm sure of it," Jana agreed.

"You asked me if I kept a phone diary."

"Lots of cops do. Some police forces require phone registries."

"Sorry, we have no registry of calls."

"Would you remember a call you received last Thursday at 1400 hours?"

"Only if there was a reason to remember it."

"Is your answer 'no'?"

"I had a reason to remember it."

The answer took Jana by surprise, Leiden looking at her with a sly grin. He seemed to enjoy the effect his reply had on her. Jana didn't like being played with.

"Who called you, then?"

"A man who identified himself as Kroslak."

Jana held up the papers she had just been given by Leiden. "Is that phone conversation written up in here?"

"No."

"Why did you omit it?"

"He asked me not to put it in the report."

"So you informed no one?"

"I honored his request."

Jana tried to digest what Leiden was telling her. He'd been in touch with Kroslak but let them all believe that the Slovak detective was still missing. There had to be a reason for a policeman to take that risk. Both Slovakia and Europol would call for Leiden's head if they discovered the omission. If his supervisors found out, they would suspend him, if not dismiss him outright.

"He told you something that you considered so important that you suppressed the fact that you'd received the call?"

"Yes."

"Why, then, are you taking the chance of telling me?"

"I need someone outside my own police department to help me. I checked on you. Your reputation as an investigator is superb. You've always done what's right, not what's politic. You've not been afraid to take chances to get the correct result. You're also new to this arena, which is a plus. You're not corruptible, as far as I can tell. So, I put myself in your hands, Commander Matinova."

She thought about what he'd said. It was clear that if she were to step forward and inform on him for suppressing information, he would be in trouble. It was also apparent that he wanted her to keep Kroslak's call secret. She might be at risk if she joined him. However, she liked the idea of Leiden taking the chance on her.

"I think you made the right decision, Investigator Leiden."

Leiden relaxed, leaning back on the bench, stretching his legs out to get comfortable. Jana joined him in stretching. They looked like a pair of close acquaintances quietly taking the afternoon sun, basking in its warmth.

"Are you sure it was Kroslak?"

"Reasonably sure. His speech was very fluent. There was no sign of rehearsal, no sign of preparation before calling me. He gave me stuff that there would be no reason to tell me about unless he truly was Kroslak."

"Have you talked to him since?"

"No. That's the reason I need you to share the problem. We were supposed to make a second contact. It never happened."

"What did he tell you?"

"That he'd discovered an international crime. It was so large that it involved national governments and international corporations and, of course, international criminals. Huge amounts of money were involved. There already had been killings involved, a number of them. He didn't tell me how many individuals he suspected had been killed, but I got the impression there were more than just a few. He said that he thought the people responsible had discovered that he had proof that would send them to prison. This was the reason he had chosen to disappear. I thought he'd gone slightly south of insane. Then he said something to make me change my mind."

"What?"

"He told me he was prepared to take his chances, but his 'partner,' meaning his current life partner, was now in danger. He told me of the killing of the prosecutor in Slovakia. I hadn't known about that. Kroslak said he'd been working with the man. That convinced me, at least for the moment, not to write him off as a madman. Kroslak wanted both his partner and himself to be given protection. He also said there was one other person involved who would probably need protection. He said he had yet to contact the person, and when he did, and received the person's consent to receive protection, he would call me back for the arrangements that would have to be made."

"There were no other phone calls?"

"Nothing."

"Why didn't you make another effort to find him?"

"If I tried to get the resources from my department to go after Kroslak, then I'd have to tell them about the call. I'd stir up more interest with the bad guys, create a more pressing motive for them to get Kroslak. That's when I started thinking about you. Are you the person Kroslak was talking about consulting?"

"I don't know anything about Kroslak's activity in Holland. Kroslak had to be talking about someone else." She thought about what had happened to Peter. Then about Trokan's phone call, and his telling her that both of them were in danger. Someone had to know what was going on. "You have no information about Kroslak's partner?"

"None."

"Kroslak gave you no information as to where he was?"

"He said he was in Amsterdam."

"That would appear, then, to be the place I should begin to look."

"Where are you going to start?"

"I can't say."

Jana stood; Leiden joined her.

"You must have some idea what you're going to do. Or you don't want to tell me?"

"I'm taking Kroslak's plea for secrecy one step further. There's no reason to tell you anything at this moment. I'd be telling one more person, who might tell one more person, which might be one person too many."

She began walking away.

"I'm not sure I deserve this," he called after her.

Jana didn't respond.

"Keep me informed," he called after her again.

"Only if Mr. Kroslak doesn't object."

Jana's voice was loud and firm enough to leave no room for doubt: if Kroslak was alive, Jana was going to find him, and ask him.

Chapter 17

Jana had spent the rest of the day going over the reports that Leiden had given her in a fruitless attempt to track Kroslak. Nothing pointed to what Kroslak had been working on or where he could possibly have gone. Jana had a quick supper, then went over the reports once again just to assure herself that she hadn't overlooked some small item that might be significant. One question kept coming up: who was Kroslak working with for whom he'd asked Leiden about protection?

Jana tried to watch some television in her hotel room, but Peter's face, recollection of the times that they'd spent together in each other's arms, prevented her from focusing on the screen. She decided to go to bed. Surprisingly, she fell asleep almost immediately.

The desk clerk telephoned, waking Jana from a sound sleep, to warn her that smoke alarms had been activated in the hotel and a number of guests had reported heavy smoke in the halls. As a precaution, the management was evacuating the guests. Jana promised she would use the stairs and not the elevators, then swung out of bed. She was just putting on her shoes when the stray thought of "smoke and mirrors" popped into her head. Set up the mirrors correctly and the audience can't see that the illusion is unreal. Use the smoke and the audience believes in the magical moment.

Jana tucked her gun into the back of her waistband under her jacket. She began to unlock the door to her room; then stopped. If she walked out through the door, would there be someone waiting to kill her? She decided to call the desk to verify that a general alarm had been issued by the hotel staff. The line was busy. Jana counted off a full minute before the phone was answered. The voice reaffirmed the evacuation. Jana hung up, again going to the door. Once more, she thought of the magic arts: do the obvious; help the audience think linearly, so its belief in an expected reality aids you in achieving your purpose. The public doesn't see the trick because of its preconceptions.

Jana checked the windows. There was no ledge, no fire escape, nothing that would get her down to the street level. She thought of tying the bed sheets to the radiator, but there was nothing there to anchor the sheets to, no guarantee the sheets wouldn't tear if she did find a way to secure them.

Jana finally decided that she was being paranoid. The smoke was real enough. When she looked out the windows, she saw at least one suite where windows seemed to be leaking smoke. If the fire was real, then it was already below her, which was not a comforting thought. Her path to safety could already be blocked. Jana unlocked the door, pulled out her gun, chambered a shell, and then opened the door, at the same time stepping into the bathroom which was immediately adjacent to the door. Smoke began to billow into her room. Jana instantly went down on her knees to take advantage of the clear air near the floor. It saved her life.

Bullets from the hall began to stitch through the wall, punching a series of irregular holes through the lathe and plaster, zinging over her head. Then a second automatic weapon opened up, shredding the door. Jana went down on her belly, edging back farther into the bathroom, then pulled the shower curtain half off its rod, propping it up so it presented a barrier that would not stop a bullet in the least but which would, at least, partially hide her. She needed just a moment of hesitation in the actions of the men who had come to kill her, a moment in which to perform her own trick.

What remained of the door to the room was kicked off its hinges. A man darted from the hall into the room; a second man, directly behind him, turned toward the bathroom, firing the assault rifle he was carrying, spraying bullets at chest level. Jana fired four slugs into the man, smashing him back against the wall. She angled her line of fire at the wall, targeting the area she could not see but where she estimated the first man would be standing. Jana emptied the gun, realizing that she had no more cartridges. If she had missed, there was nothing left to defend herself with.

The room was absolutely silent. Smoke, still drifting inside, partially obscured everything. Jana edged to the bathroom door and then popped out into the vestibule leading into the rest of the suite, her gun held in front of her at the ready as if she could still fire it. More smoke and mirrors, she thought. There was no way to fool the man in the room if he was alive; he would open fire immediately.

He was sitting on the floor with his back against the dresser, bleeding from his mouth, unable to move, ineffectually trying to reach the assault rifle on the floor two feet away. He saw Jana's feet, his head tilted back slightly to look at her, his body shuddered, and he slumped over. One of her shots had hit him in the left center of his chest. She had managed to kill both men.

Jana sat on the edge of the bed, surveying the two bodies, the damage to the room, the blood pooling around both men. She coughed at the smoke, wiping her mouth with her forearm, still not quite sure that she had survived.

A hotel employee chose that moment to check to make sure all the guests had been safely evacuated. He stuck his head in the door, gasped at seeing the man in the doorway first, then let out a "*Godverdomme*" in Dutch when he saw the second man, mumbled an incoherent short babble of words when he saw Jana, then darted out of the room screaming for help and ran down the corridor. His screams galvanized Jana into action.

She grabbed her bag, pulling clothes out of the closet, prodding the dead man out of the way with her foot as she emptied the drawers, piling everything into a suitcase haphazardly, hesitating only long enough to take her reserve bullet clip from the night table and slap it into her gun, which she tucked into her waistband at the small of her back. She picked up the bag and suitcase and sprinted out of the suite and into the hall, heading for the stairs. She passed two of the smoke bombs which had been used by the intruders. Jana had been right: there was no fire. It was all "smoke and mirrors."

She took the elevator to the first floor. There was no reason to avoid the elevators. No fire, no danger. Then she took the stairs down to the lobby, in case the two dead men had backup on the main floor watching the elevators, then walked to the rear and into the massive shopping center behind the hotel. A huge crowd of both guests and passersby had gathered at the entrance to the mall to gawk at the firemen who were now pouring into the hotel. Nobody glanced at Jana as she pushed her way through.

She had to find another place to stay. Whoever was

after her would eventually find her again, but she had to buy herself some time. They were determined, that was clear. And to an organization, as she now thought of them, that determined and with enough resources to find her, she presented a very large target. Two minutes later, Jana was headed to the only place she could think of where she wouldn't have to register: the apartment that Kroslak had leased but never occupied.

When she got there, in case she'd been tracked, she took a tour of the entire building, familiarizing herself with the layout. The roof led to other roofs, which might provide an escape route; unfortunately, it was also a method of gaining entry to the building from adjoining structures without attracting notice, a strong negative. The only other portion of the building that she was concerned about was the basement. It was very small. But there was a locked door apparently leading to the building next door. At one time they had shared an understructure which now included a partitioned basement. It, too, was a possible avenue of escape if she needed it.

Having found out what she could, Jana went back up to her new apartment. The maid had done an amazing job of creating order out of the chaos that Jana had left. She silently thanked the young woman, then crawled into bed.

Chapter 18

In the morning, when she got up, aching from the stress and discomfort of the night's battles, Jana puttered around the apartment putting her clothes away. She was not hungry, but she needed to keep up her stamina, which meant putting food in her stomach. Jana walked to the café where she had first met the Dutch police officer and sat at the same table as before, ordering a black coffee and toast, thinking about her predicament as she sipped the strong coffee. Jana was in a bind, no longer sure she was safe anywhere.

Why had the "enemy," as she now thought of them, made her a priority? Most likely it was because they knew she was hunting Kroslak, which probably meant that Kroslak was still alive and that it was important for them to prevent her from reaching him. And Jana could not stop thinking about the murders in Bratislava. Peter's death, of course . . . and the college student's murder. In her mind, they had merged.

There was nothing that connected the two, really, except the professional aspect of the killings. Jana forced herself to focus on Peter's killing, to break it away from the Carleton Savoy hotel murder in the hope that the intense focus on the one would heighten some aspect of it, some salient factor, which she could then compare with Denis's murder.

There was one other item she had not given much thought to, the papers that she had found in the closet of her house where Peter had kept his things. Jana had them with her. She waited until she had finished her breakfast toast, then pulled them out of her shoulder bag. They were still encased in their clear plastic covers. Jana fanned the pages out on the table top. They were numbered one through four, and she began her examination in that order. On the first page, after what appeared to be an introductory section, there were graphs, each one with multiple plotted lines. The graphs had numbered indicators on the left and bottom. Jana eliminated years and weights in deciphering the mathematical markings. They were measurements or indicators of some other type. The language used was Western in origin, but not one of the major languages Jana was familiar with. She checked the word endings. There was enough Latin in their construction for Jana to eliminate everything except Portuguese and Romanian.

Not close enough to Spanish to be Portuguese. If you eliminate all the rest of the possibilities, no matter how improbable, you generally have your answer. The language was most likely Romanian. Jana immediately thought of Gyorgi Ilica, the Romanian cop in her section at Europol. She'd take a chance and ask him to translate.

All the pages were similar, with nothing she could decipher, until the last page, which was more curious than the others. The text ended about a third of the way down the page. There was a stamp with a signature and date: March 1, 1944. It had been written during the middle of World War II. Immediately below, but toward the left-hand margin, was another scrawled signature and date: March 17, 1944. The signature, which looked like it might be

"Haider" or something close, had all the spiky earmarks of German script. The note, in German, which was more legible, was translatable by Jana. It simply read: "I agree. No further action recommended."

At least as curious was a notation at the bottom of the page. This one was in Russian, also signed and dated. Jana had learned Russian as a child in communist Slovakia, so it was easy to translate. It read: "Further tests indicative of prior results. No further action recommended," and it was signed and dated July 8, 1975. Romania was still a Soviet Socialist Republic then and behind the Iron Curtain that contained Eastern Europe. Jana put the papers back in her shoulder bag.

Someone had left a Dutch newspaper on one of the adjoining tables. Jana picked it up and read portions of the front page. There was a large photograph of two bodies being rolled out on stretchers from her hotel. Headline news. Jana could not see any reference to her name in any part of the article. They had to be looking for her, but they were keeping her name out of the paper. Why?

Jana used a public phone to call Slovakia. Trokan was back in his office, so she would have to be guarded in her conversation because of the possibility of a tap. However, she and Trokan were so familiar with each other that they could communicate almost in monosyllables without giving critical information to whoever might be eavesdropping.

Trokan immediately answered his phone.

"Colonel Trokan," she said.

"Janka, how have you been?"

"Not so good."

"I called the hotel."

"So you know."

"Yes."

"From the Dutch or Europol?"

"I talked to the Dutch."

"Someone we know?"

"Yes."

"What do you think?"

"I have nothing to give you. The cop was polite. He seemed to recognize that I had nothing to give him other than what he already knew. He didn't even ask if I had heard from you. However, I volunteered that I had not. He was professional. I had some confidence and trust in him when I hung up."

"Anything new in Slovakia?"

"Things are hectic here. There is a more-than-strong rumor, which has been reinforced by our minister, that the prime minister is going to nationalize the oil field. The other parties are taking positions, the nationalists on his side, the Europe or America worshipers taking the other side, and everybody in between making noises of one sort or another. We've been put on full alert in case there are disturbances, so everyone is working overtime out in the field looking for the first sign of trouble. I haven't a man to spare."

"I was thinking of taking a vacation."

"It's not the time for a vacation. Besides, I think you've used up the days you're entitled to."

Jana hadn't used any days off. He was telling her that he was not pulling her back to Slovakia. Nor did he have any other specific plans for her, other than the orders she'd already been given. Which also meant that Trokan would not be sending her any assistance. She was to carry on with her assignment, to stay out in the wilderness until whoever was hunting her made themselves known. Then she was to act. He was not giving her any other options.

Jana didn't like the "no option" approach. It left her hanging in the wind, vulnerable. Jana tried to press him to change his mind.

"I could have sworn I had days left."

"Nothing, Jana. I checked. The records are very clear."

Trokan had thought of pulling her in. He had asked the minister, but the minister had vetoed it. Trokan was saddled with this decision, and so was Jana.

"I have sightseeing I wanted to do, so I think I'll take a day or two of sick leave and just wander around. Europol won't miss me." Whoever they were would be looking for her there. "Perhaps I'll go to some other part of Holland and do some sightseeing."

"Enjoy yourself."

"I always like new experiences."

"All good investigators do. I'm going to Vienna tomorrow."

"A pretty place."

"We've both been there before."

Trokan would be staying at the same hotel he generally did when he went to Vienna. She could call him there tomorrow.

"Give my regards to your wife."

"I'll tell her you said so. Fact is, you can call her yourself if you want to."

Trokan's wife hated Jana. He was simply confirming it was all right to call in case she had missed his signal.

"Thank you, Colonel."

"Good-bye, Janka."

They terminated the call.

Jana found a reproduction shop and had three copies of the Romanian papers run off. They were bad copies but still legible. Jana put the reproductions in plastic sheets she bought from the same shop, put those sheets into separate plastic bags that were sealable, then went back to her new apartment. She took the originals out of her shoulder bag, checked the bag for airtightness by running water into the plastic that would contain them, then set the original, still in its container, into the tested bag, placing the bag into the cistern of the toilet.

The apartment had assuredly already been searched by the enemy. If they tried to search the apartment again, they might not think to look for papers in a toilet. For the moment, it was the best hiding place Jana could come up with. It was time now to get to work on her investigation.

Her first stop was to talk to Paola.

Her second would be Amsterdam.

Chapter 19

J ana called Paola on her cell, making the call brief so that anyone who attempted a tap would not come up with much. Paola suggested that she and Aidan Walsh meet her at Le Café Hathor, a neighborhood joint with good beer and tapas on Maliestraat, a narrow side street. They could sit on the terrace overlooking a small canal and nobody would give a damn who they were or who was looking for them.

They arrived at the same time, sat, and ordered beer and a plate of tapas ostensibly to sate Aidan's large appetite. The beer arrived quickly.

"You made a big boom," said Aidan. "My guess is that hotel will think twice about welcoming you back."

"*I* didn't lay down the smoke bombs."

"You did the shooting."

Jana shrugged. "I didn't do all the shooting. They shot at me first."

"Your shooting instructors have to be bragging," Paola suggested. "I got a look at the photos the Dutch gendarmes developed. Your room was shot to pieces. The bad boys tried hard."

"Who is after you, and why?" Aidan asked. He emptied his glass, holding it up for the waitress to bring another. She studiously ignored him. "The Dutch are great at making the beer, but they crap out on the service side."

He pushed himself erect. "I'm forced to go after my own lager." He walked toward the bar.

"He eats a lot, drinks a lot." Paola took another sip of her own beer. "But he's a good man. His question was on point: who sent two goons to kill you?"

"I hope that you're saying that the Dutch police have concluded that the two men I shot were trying to kill me, and not the other way round?"

"The Dutch want you to go through the numbers for them." She eyed Jana. "So, are you going to traipse in to them and explain what it's all about?"

"No."

Paola was taken aback.

"Why not? You'll walk away clean."

"If I walk away at all. I think whoever is out to kill me is determined to do the job. And I think they will if I go to the Dutch police. I don't trust cell phones; I don't trust safe houses. Even more serious, I don't know the police who will be dealing with me."

Paola looked even more surprised.

"You think that our Dutch cousins are in on this?"

Aidan shouldered his way back to the table carrying his beer in one hand and a plate of tapas in the other. "The miracle man has succeeded." He sat, pushing the tapas toward Paola. "Have you determined what in bloody hell the Slovak lady has got herself, and maybe us, involved with?" He took one of the tapas, biting into it. "They have good tapas here, which is strange 'cause they're not Spanish." He talked while he was chewing, peering over his beer at Jana. "Okay, so people are after you. We increase our chances of getting those people before they get you if we know why they're after you. If we know that, then maybe we know them. And if we know them, we kick the crap out of them, or maybe take a cue from you, Commander Matinova, and blow the hell out of them before they do the same to you. Good plan, eh?"

"Not so good," Paola responded, looking slightly glum. "She doesn't have the vaguest idea who is after her, or why."

"I think it has to do with Kroslak's disappearance," Jana told them.

"Have they killed him?" Aidan asked through a mouthful of tapas.

"I don't think so."

"But you're not sure?" Aidan suggested.

Paola hit him on the arm. "She's telling us we have to find out."

"Okay, we find out," Aidan agreed. He started on another tapa.

Jana handed them copies of the problem that she had worked out for her seminar on homicide investigation. She also pulled out the duplicates of the material she had recovered from Peter's closet.

"You have other things to do," Jana suggested. "Do we trust Gyorgi Ilica, our Romanian?"

Walsh and Rossi exchanged glances.

"He's a good guy," Walsh said.

"He knows what it's about," Paola added.

Jana slid one set of the duplicates across the table to them. "I'm reasonably certain these are in Romanian. I need a translation as quickly as possible."

"No problem," Walsh said.

Paola fingered the copy of the problem that Jana had given her. "What do we do with this?"

"Use your instincts. The thing that jumps out at me, first, is identifying the shooter of the student. Go through the files. Look for professional shooters, killings where someone did the job with a close circle of shots. Then, look for technicians who fit telephones with explosives."

"There are a few of those around," Walsh affirmed. "The Israelis have some of them. The old KGB did. Probably the current Russian FSA. A few Lebanese I know of. Even a few IRA people. We'll get a list and see who their last employers were and try for a geographic fix."

Jana mulled it over. "One more approach: see if there's an assassin in the files who's current, an individual out there that has both characteristics we're looking for: a good shooter as well as an explosives expert."

"And the witnesses?" Paola asked.

"The insurance guy, Fico." Aidan said, finishing off the last of the tapas. "See who he works for, see what his statements to your department's people were. And who's this investigator, Elias? The name doesn't sound Slovak to me."

"We're a hodgepodge of names. The Slovaks have been run over and conquered so many times by other countries that we've been a breeding ground for everyone else in Europe. The names have lingered on."

"The Roman legions and their sex drive rolled over you guys too?"

"If it wasn't them, it was the Turks, or the Hapsburgs, or Nazis."

Aidan playfully nudged Paola. "Very passionate, the Romans. Except for this one."

"Piss off, Walsh."

Jana looked pointedly at both of them. "Elias has all the witness statements under lock and key. They'll have done tests on the explosive used in the telephone attack. There will be ballistics reports on the weapon used in the student killing. We'll have to run them through Europol without it being picked up internally. How?"

Walsh looked very pleased with himself; the solution rolled off his tongue. "We open up a case file so we have a case reference number, then make a request to the Slovaks citing that case number. By treaty, they're obliged to cooperate, so they send us the information."

"It can't be on the master case list or they'll pick it up in the front office," Paola cautioned. "We don't want them to know what we're doing."

"Use current case numbers which are already assigned and approved," Jana suggested.

"Nice idea. We spread the requests around so no case gets noted with multiple requests," Aidan recommended, then laughed at himself. "I've just realized how devious I am. I could have been a great thief."

"You just stole all the tapas," Paola pointed out.

"You weren't hungry anyway." He finished off his beer, wiping his mouth with a napkin, then waved it at Jana. "What's on your agenda while we're playing with this stuff?"

"I look for Kroslak."

"You'll need a place to start."

"I have an idea."

"Where?" Paola asked.

"I'd rather not say."

Paola and Aidan both looked at her with surprise.

"I'm putting myself in Kroslak's head. Just disappearing. Let everyone look for me like they looked for him. If they can find me, I'm not thinking enough like Kroslak. From this moment on, I'm a fugitive looking for another fugitive." She got up, laying money on the table. "My treat."

"How do we get you the information we come up with?"

"You don't. You just get the information. I'll call, or send for it in a way that's safe."

"Good luck, lady," Aidan murmured.

"Amen," Paola added.

The two of them stared after Jana as she walked out of the café.

She didn't look back.

Chapter 20

J ana called the professor at his hotel. Following her directions, he rented a car, then drove the vehicle to Grote Markt Square, avoiding the cyclists, circling the square several times while she watched to make sure he'd not been followed. After satisfying herself that he had not inadvertently brought an unwanted tail with him, Jana signaled him to pick her up. The professor then followed her directive to drive northeast.

"Thank you for calling me," he said.

"I needed help, so *I* should thank *you*."

"Why are we going to in this direction?"

"When we get to a tram station, you get out and take it back to The Hague. I'll drive the car on from there."

"I've been brought up to protect women. So I'm staying."

"I'm a police commander, Professor."

"That does not make you any less a woman. I make no distinction for your being a police officer."

"Thank you, but I'm not concerned about myself. I'm concerned for you, Professor. There are some very bad people moving around out there. And they do ugly things to human beings they don't like. They've already decided they don't like me. I don't want them to dislike you."

"The risk doesn't bother me."

"That's because you don't know enough about the risk to be concerned. I do."

"I read about what happened at your hotel. That involved you, didn't it?"

"I'm not about to discuss it, Professor."

"Why not?"

"Because the more you know, the more you're at risk."

"You're going to drive to Amsterdam, aren't you?"

"Again, no comment."

"You asked me to get a car because you're afraid of the train or bus stations. Or airports. There is no reason in the world for you to want to go north unless you're going to Amsterdam. So please listen to me. This is not a negotiable issue. Realize that I'm a stubborn man, and I'm going to drive this car. It's my car. I rented it. I have the keys to the car, and unless you beat me up, I won't let you have them. So, we both go to Amsterdam."

Jana sat in uncomfortable silence, not quite knowing what to do.

"Of course," the professor continued, "you can abandon me in Amsterdam; but before you do, think of the possible help I can offer."

"There's no help you can give me."

"You didn't think so until you needed me for the car, right? And that will happen in Amsterdam, once we get there. Surprises happen; things change; assistance is needed. Think about my offer . . . and don't be as obstinate as I am. I know that whatever happened at the hotel, two men are dead. I'm an adult. I'm informed enough to decide what chances to take. So, Amsterdam!"

They drove toward Amsterdam.

Jana tried several times to talk the professor out of his determination to come with her. But, as he'd pointed out, if she needed to Jana could lose him in Amsterdam. Meanwhile, there was no choice.

As they neared Amsterdam, Jana had begun to think of herself as a fugitive. She played with that in her mind. Odd, to be a fugitive. She was now constantly checking behind their car, looking for threatening vehicles gaining on them, watching the speedometer and making sure they didn't commit any traffic violations which would result in their being stopped, wondering how she was going to get the money to keep herself going, thinking about what means she could use to conceal herself, and who she could turn to for assistance. Jana eventually concluded she didn't want to go to a hotel and be a walk-in without a reservation, which might make the desk clerk scrutinize her more closely.

Before they got to Amsterdam, Jana selected the American Hotel in Amsterdam from a phone book at a gas-station pay phone. She picked it because the name conjured up cleanliness, plainness, solid bourgeois patrons, no particular frills. Not a place that would draw attention to itself, a place which the police would not be particularly interested in.

She was surprised when she and the professor arrived there.

It was anything but American. Built in an odd-looking Art Nouveau style, a fancy patterned brickwork building with stained glass amid neo-Gothic arches greeted them. Opportunely, there was one additional reason Jana had picked the hotel which made it acceptable despite its appearance. The American was located in the hub of the nightlife area, a place where Jana thought she might begin looking for the boy-toy who might lead them to Kroslak.

Jana and the professor checked into two rooms under the professor's name. The desk clerk gave the apparent May–December relationship a briefly raised eyebrow. Each went to a room to freshen up; then they met downstairs in the hotel's Café USA and ordered hamburgers, to go along with the spirit of the hotel. Relieved at being out of The Hague and the immediate danger that the area presented, Jana's appetite flared. She ate everything on her plate, including the garnish.

The professor wiped his mouth; sat back, satisfied; then looked at Jana expectantly. "What's our next move?"

"*My* next move," she corrected.

"I hope we are not going to fight that battle again," he said. "You will see, I'm a very helpful person."

"I don't need the car any more, Professor."

"How many times have you been to Amsterdam, Commander Matinova?"

Her answer, when it came out, emerged grudgingly. "Once."

"I have been here six times, the second time for a two-week period and the fourth time for ten days. I have begun to know the city quite well. With your lack of familiarity, you can't wander around the city without looking at a map. How can you pay attention to what you, as a detective, must pay attention to when you are constantly checking the street signs to make sure you haven't made a wrong turn?" He looked at her appraisingly, watching her digest his argument. "I told you you would need me. And I promise to not get in your way."

Jana recognized defeat, smiling despite her misgivings. "You're a persuasive man. Can you also promise me that you'll stay out of harm's way?"

"No. But I can tell you I won't go looking for it . . . unless it has to do with my nephew."

"That's not much of a promise, Professor."

"We promise only what we can deliver. So. . . ." He pushed his plate away. "What's our first step?"

"I need to find a man who is, or was, an investigator with the Slovak police. He has information that will assist the investigation."

"What is he doing in Amsterdam if he's a Slovak?"

"Running, like I am."

"He's in hiding?"

"If he's still alive."

"How do we find him if he doesn't want to be found?"

"We look for a friend of his." She described the young man who Paola had seen with Kroslak.

"You think he's in Amsterdam?"

"My educated guess is that Kroslak met him here, and then took refuge in this city. It's harder to find someone in a big city. If he stayed in The Netherlands to hide, and I think he had to, he couldn't go to a city where a Slovak would stick out like a worm in an apple. But Amsterdam is cosmopolitan. No one would give him a second thought here."

The professor nodded. "I understand." He reflected on what she'd said. "The boy is the key to finding the man?"

"I think so. The young man visited Kroslak at The Hague, which means he and Kroslak were close. I think Kroslak may have been staying with him in Amsterdam when he was supposed to be living in The Hague. Now, wherever that place is, it's the only safe haven he has."

"Do you know where to start?"

"The gay bars and nightclubs. We look for the man with the little scar just above his eye. We throw his name out to the regulars. Then, we hope one of them knows handsome Willem Albert and points us in the right direction."

"I have another small idea. It might make our search easier."

"Tell me."

"There are, maybe, one or two places in the city that are information centers for gay men and women."

"Registration places?"

"Informal registration. You want to find a lost lover, you ask. Maybe they have the information, maybe not. It's iffy, but worth a try."

"Bookstores? Phone services? Escort services?"

"They have a few of those."

"You know where these places are?"

The professor suddenly looked uncomfortable. "I've not been there before. I've read about them," he explained hastily. "I just know they exist."

"An Amsterdam guidebook is in order."

They paid their bill, then walked to the hotel gift shop. There were a number of Amsterdam guides sitting in wire racks at the entrance. Jana rifled through them, picked the one with Amsterdam street maps and a full section on the Red Light district and environs. It also included the COC, as the gay and lesbian social center of Amsterdam. It was located on Rozenstratt, an easy stroll from their hotel.

As they walked, the professor became more and more nervous. Jana had to pull him back to safety as he stepped into the street in front of an oncoming vehicle.

"Professor, we are not entering the jaws of hell. I thought you were a brave man."

"I've led a quiet life. Well, not so quiet. But not danger-ous. There is a difference between stage danger and real danger."

"You can go back to the hotel."

"No."

"I warn you, I have something planned. You may not like it."

"What?"

"Even though they have information, the people who staff these places may not want to give it to us. They protect their people. We have to use a ruse."

"What ruse?"

"Smoke and mirrors."

Jana spotted what she had been looking for on the street. "The place I was looking for." She pulled the professor into a store advertising *"Produit de Beauté"* on its window, a cosmetics store catering primarily to male gays. "We need to make you more presentable."

The only clerk in the salon, a man who had a very faint blush applied to his cheeks, was only too glad to help them, taking enormous enjoyment at what he was asked to do. By the time they walked out, the professor had mascara on his eyelashes, a very thin eyeliner on the base of his upper lids, a faint lip gloss, and the merest dab of rouge on his cheeks. The professor held himself very stiffly, taking hesitant steps as if he wanted to bolt and run.

"Why have you done this to me?"

"Pretend that you're in your clown makeup."

"I chose my clown face. I put it on. It also appealed to a different audience. I knew what I was getting into."

"You spent your professional life as a performer. Think of this as just another performance. You actually look good: healthy and younger. So relax," she ordered.

"How can I relax wearing this . . . ?" He hesitated, unable to find the right words. "Why is this necessary? I admit to being a jester, but this is absurd."

"Professor, think of your magic tricks. You're the left hand; I'm the right hand. I want them to look at you while I'm doing the work. You're the illusion, I'm the reality. All you have to do is relax and, if possible, be a little sad."

"I'm feeling very uneasy."

"I want you depressed, not uneasy."

He tried to change the expression on his face.

"Good. Keep it up. And stop cringing. The people in this city are used to gay men."

They reached the COC. It was a combination of offices, social center, gay nightclub, and café. Everyone inside was gay, except for a pair of tourists who had entered by mistake and were rapidly retreating.

"You're sure I have to do this?" The professor's voice had taken on a plaintive tone.

"A small reminder: you wanted to come. You're needed for the plan. Try not to shake so much, and keep walking."

They entered the social center area. A number of men and women sat talking. Jana propelled the professor over to an armchair.

"Stay here." She checked his makeup. "Almost perfect, although he could have gone easier on the eyeshadow."

The professor started to get up. Jana pushed him back down into the chair. "I'm teasing. Remember, it's for your nephew."

Jana stepped over to a desk area staffed by a man and a woman.

She introduced herself as the niece of the man sitting in the chair. Both staffers looked over to him.

"My uncle has a problem," Jana confided.

"I know. He's getting old," whispered the man. "It comes to all of us, you know."

"How can we help?" asked the woman.

"I'm looking for his lover."

They both eyed the professor again.

"His lover deserted him?" suggested the woman.

"That happens when you age sometimes," the man whispered.

"His lover didn't leave a forwarding address, a phone number, anything. My uncle thought the relationship was for life. The young man apparently didn't. And my uncle needs closure. He sits and broods; he doesn't eat. I'm trying to help him. That's why I came here. You advertise that if a gay needs help in Amsterdam, this is the place."

The staffers nodded in unison. People are people. Like helps like. Problems need to be solved. For the next twenty minutes, the two moved heaven and earth to help. They called the Gay and Lesbian Switchboard, a number of the boy-toy bars and clubs, and several gay and lesbian bookstores. Surprisingly, they found the information at MVS Radio, the gay and lesbian radio station. The young man had worked for them as a sound engineer until last week, when he'd suddenly called in and quit.

When they left, the woman staffer insisted on giving Jana her home phone number. Jana did not want the woman to take it as a rejection if she refused her offer. She said she might call in the next day or so. The male staffer gave Jana a kiss on the cheek for being so caring, and she and the professor walked out. The professor immediately insisted on going to the nearest straight restaurant, where he used the restroom to wash all the makeup off.

He was not happy with Jana. His *persona* had been tampered with. On some basic level he felt desecrated. The professor hadn't enjoyed being the misdirection for her trick.

Chapter 21

They went into the area called the Jordaan, just to the west of the city center, a strait lattice-work of narrow streets and canals, following the original *polder*, strips of farmland separated by canals, with houses in a hodgepodge of styles ranging from the seventeenth century to the present. In the old days it had been a refugee enclave filled with people speaking different languages.

The address they were looking for turned out to be a structure with bottleneck gables and slightly faded red shutters. The house, like a number of the others in the area, had been divided into apartments. Two of the three mail slots bore other names. The third slot had no name. Jana tried its buzzer. There was no answer, so she tried the other two. Within seconds they were admitted.

As they walked up the broad rococo staircase to the second floor, the tenants who had buzzed them in with typical Dutch credulity, in a nation with a very low crime rate, stuck their heads out of their doors to see who their guests were. The professor and Jana, smiling, waved at them in reassurance. Jana mouthed a *hallo* to greet them and a *dank u* to thank them for their politeness, two of the three or four Dutch words Jana had picked up since she'd arrived. Aside from their slightly bewildered looks, no one tried to stop them.

The second floor, smaller than the ground floor, had just one apartment. Jana walked over to it, the professor lagging a few steps behind her. She signaled him to step to one side of the door. Jana then slipped to the other and placed her ear to the door. There was the sound of movement from inside. Jana knocked, immediately pulling back beyond the doorjamb as a precaution. Almost instantaneously there was a loud crash as if some large object had been thrown against the door. This was followed by several more thumps. The door shook each time it was hit. Then there was a moment of silence, followed by a voice howling from inside.

"Get away from my door. I have a weapon. I'll kill you if you try to get in. Leave me alone. Go away."

"Willem Albert, my name is Jana Matinova. I'm a police officer. I'm here to help you and Mr. Kroslak. Please talk to me."

There was another crash against the door.

"Get away. I told you, I'm armed. I'll use my weapon."

Jana relaxed slightly. Willem Albert did not have a weapon. Anyone with a weapon does not pound on his door with furniture to scare you away.

"That doesn't help anyone, Willem Albert. Your furniture is going to be all smashed if you keep this up. Just open the door."

There was another crash.

"I've just called the police."

Jana was sure he had not called the police.

"I *am* the police, Willem Albert. From Slovakia. Like Mr. Kroslak."

There was a long silence, followed by the sound of a lock being tinkered with. A young man who Jana supposed was Willem Albert peeked through a crack in the door.

"I told you to go away. Leave my apartment." He looked Jana over. "You don't look like the police."

Jana reached inside her shoulder bag and pulled out her credentials.

"I can't read them."

"They're in Slovak."

"Go away."

He shut the door. Jana heard him fasten the latch again. She was tired of trying to coax him to let her in. She stepped back two feet, then kicked the door in.

The professor was shocked.

"Force has its place, Professor."

Jana pulled her gun from the small of her back, then quickly stepped inside. As soon as she entered, Willem Albert began to throw things at her, crockery, a vase, anything and everything he could get his hands on, screaming epithets at Jana in Dutch. Jana dodged the objects, ultimately getting angry, pointing her gun and cocking the hammer with a loud metallic *snap*.

"Time to stop being so inhospitable, Willem Albert."

He stopped. The young man's fear was so palpable that it came at Jana in perceptible waves. She had to calm him down; otherwise, she'd never be able to get any information.

"I'm putting my gun away." She uncocked it, then tucked it into her waistband at the small of her back again, holding her hands out to show him that they were empty. An old scuffed wooden chair was lying on its side on the floor. Jana righted it, then sat on it, keeping her hands in sight, crossing her legs and leaning back, hoping that he wasn't now going to rush her while she was in such a vulnerable posture.

"You see? No gun. No threat."

The young man stared at her. She used the opportunity to look him over. There was no doubt that it was the same Willem Albert who had been described to her by Paola as Kroslak's handsome significant other. He had the scar through one of his eyebrows.

"My name is Jana Matinova. I'm a commander in the Slovak police," she said again.

The professor chose that moment to come in. He took the situation in, paused, then quickly sat on the floor, trying to appear unobtrusive.

"My friend doesn't look like he's going to attack anyone, does he, Willem Albert? He's much too nice a man." She sank deeper into the chair. "Neither of us is trying to be menacing. We're all friends here, just trying to help each other." She waited for a reaction from Willem Albert.

After a moment's hesitation, his body posture began to moderate, the stress on his face easing. Jana allowed herself to relax.

"What do you want with me?" Willem Albert finally got out.

"We're looking for Martin Kroslak, your partner."

"So were the others, a few days ago."

"What others?"

"Two men. They beat me up. They cracked one of my ribs." Tears began to appear in his eyes. "Look what they did to my face."

Even through the pancake makeup that Willem Albert had applied to his face, Jana could see bruising. He quickly opened his shirt, eager to show his other injuries. His upper body was purple.

"You see? One of them had a blackjack. The other man would ask the questions and when I gave an answer they didn't like, the one with the blackjack would step in and slam me with it." Willem Albert began to weep, and sank to the floor.

Jana slowly got up, walked over to the young man, sat next to him, and put her arm around his shoulders. All three of them were now sitting on the floor.

"It must have been terrible," she murmured. "They were thugs."

The two downstairs neighbors took that moment to stick their heads in, both of them worried about the noisy events going on in their upstairs neighbor's apartment.

"We heard the crashing. Are you okay, Willem Albert?"

Willem Albert looked over to them.

"I'm fine," he sniffled.

"You're sure?" They eyed the broken door and the damage to the room. "We're here to help."

Willem Albert waved an all-inclusive arm at the professor and Jana.

"My friends are helping me."

"We're just downstairs if you need us."

"Thank you," Willem Albert wiped his eyes. "I'll be fine."

"You'll have to call someone to repair the door. Would you like us to do it?"

"Thanks, I'll do it myself, later."

"Be well, Willem."

They backed out. Jana waited for them to get out of earshot, then took Willem Albert by the elbow to help him stand.

"Thank you," he whispered. "I'm glad you're not one of the gangsters."

"They gave you a bad beating."

"Yes, they did."

She led him over to a corner love seat. The professor stayed seated on the floor, looking at a show he didn't quite fully grasp.

"Why do you want my friend?" Willem Albert asked.

"Mr. Kroslak has very important information for us."

"They wanted it also."

"The two men who beat you?"

"They kept asking for papers he had. I told them he didn't talk about his business with me. That's when they started beating me up."

"Did you tell them where Kroslak was?"

"I told them I'd filed a missing person report with the police. I didn't know."

Jana noticed he had used the past tense.

"Has he been in touch with you since?"

There was a long reluctant silence. Willem Albert was still not sure he should tell her anything.

There is a rule in police questioning: one confidence breeds another.

"The ones who beat you tried to kill me. If they catch up with Mr. Kroslak before I do, they'll certainly kill him. You don't want that to happen."

"No."

"When did he call you?"

"Yesterday."

Jana felt a surge of relief. As of yesterday, Martin Kroslak was still alive. She still had a chance of getting to him before the killers.

"Those gangsters killed two friends of mine in Slovakia. One of them was my lover," Jana revealed.

Willem Albert let out an audible gasp.

"The other person they murdered was an innocent student." She indicated the professor. "The professor's nephew. So you see we have every reason to want to find those men and bring them to justice before they commit any other brutal acts. So, if you want to save your lover, you have to tell me what he said."

Willem Albert finally nodded.

"He said he loved me."

"I'm glad. What else did he say?"

"That he'd have to be away for a while. That he needed to leave Amsterdam. I told him about being beaten up. He told me that he was sorry. That it was his fault for not realizing they would know about me. He was going to Prague. There was a possible witness to see about a case he was working on. If he . . ." Willem Albert's voice quavered. ". . . If he survived, he would come back to get me."

"He truly needs you."

"And I need him."

"Did he tell you where he was going in Prague?"

"Only that he'd be looking for a record."

"A music record, a city record, a birth record?"

"Just a record."

"That was it?"

"Yes.

She had come close, but not close enough.

"Did Kroslak have any friends he might have talked to?"

"We kept to ourselves."

"Kroslak lived with you when he was in Holland?"

"Yes."

"His clothes, his other possessions. Where are they?"

"They took everything. They brought boxes with them. Every last item of his went in the boxes. They took all the papers in the apartment, including all of mine."

"Nothing of his was left?"

"It's all gone. Every scrap."

Jana thought of coming home and finding that all of Peter's clothes had been taken from his closet in Slovakia.

"The two men who beat you, what did they look like?"

"Both big, one taller than the other. One had dark hair. Both, maybe, in their thirties. I was too frightened to think about what they looked like. And they were beating me."

The tears began again. Jana waited until they slowed down.

"I want you to e-mail me if you come up with any more information." She looked over to the professor, at the same time pulling the Mont Blanc pen and some paper out of her handbag. "It would be better to use your account instead of mine, Professor."

The professor got to his knees, struggling to rise as he grunted out his e-mail address. Jana tried to write, forgetting that the pen had no ink, shaking it several times. Willem Albert looked intently at the pen.

"You recognize the pen, Willem Albert?"

"It was *his* fountain pen."

"It was in Kroslak's desk at Europol."

"It doesn't work."

"No ink." She shook the pen again to demonstrate that it was dry.

"It never worked. He took the insides out."

Jana examined the pen, unscrewing the top. Willem Albert stared at it with anticipation, as if hoping it contained a note, a message from his lover. The top came off, exposing an empty ink chamber. Jana saw the disappointment written on Willem Albert's face.

"Nothing there," he mouthed. Tears appeared in his eyes, Willem Albert ineffectually trying to wipe them away with his knuckles. "He would scribble little notes for me and leave the pen so I could find what he'd written inside. We passed it back and forth. When it was from me he'd open it when he got back to The Hague." He made a face. "Now it's empty again."

"When people go away, they leave empty spaces."

"Big spaces."

"Hard to fill them."

"Yes.

Jana and the professor departed a short time later. She left the pen with Willem Albert.

Chapter 22

Jana and the professor headed toward the professor's rental car.

"I have to go back to The Hague, Professor."

"Why?"

"I left some papers there. Colleagues of mine are participating in the investigation with me. I have to know what they've discovered."

"Telephone them," he suggested. "More practical than us driving there."

"I'm not sure the telephone is a safe way to communicate right now. You don't have to go, Professor."

"I'm going if you're going," he said matter-of-factly. "We'll check out of the hotel."

They passed two men in a parked car, both with their heads buried in newspapers. Jana recognized Jan Leiden, the Dutch police officer, in the passenger seat. She leaned into the window.

"Investigator Leiden, nice to see you."

"Are you sure its 'nice,' Commander Matinova?"

"Why wouldn't it be, Investigator Leiden?"

"The last time I heard from you, it was in connection with two men who were shot to death in your hotel room. Did you shoot them?"

"They certainly tried to shoot me, Leiden. Are you going to arrest me for their deaths?"

"No. File a report with the police, Commander. If you need a little more time, a day, you may have it."

"That's good of you. What do you expect me to say in the report?"

"That two well-known Czech gangsters with long records of violence, using smoke bombs as a ruse, tried to kill you with assault rifles. You, being Slovak, a neighbor of the Czech Republic, knew who they were, naturally, and also know why they tried to kill you."

"They didn't wait to inform me before they tried to shoot me."

"I was hoping you could fill in the gaps."

"I'm trying to fill them in myself."

"When you write your version of the events, forward it to me."

"You'll be the first to get it. Thank you."

"I believe in helping a fellow officer."

"No, you're just hoping a fellow officer will lead you to whoever sent the men to kill me, here, in your country."

"That's also true."

"How did you know I'd come here?"

"His boyfriend filed a missing person report on Kroslak. I assumed you would be trying to find Kroslak, which meant stopping off at the address in the report. We waited for you."

"Kroslak's lover was beaten up a few days ago."

"By different people than the ones from your hotel room?"

"I think so. Two teams. Both teams probably had the same employer, just slightly different agendas."

"One team after you, the other after Kroslak."

"It looks like that."

"How many of them are there?" There was an edge

of disbelief to his voice. "Whatever the answer, there are more than I like." His voice took on an accusatory tone. "And you brought them all to my country."

"How do you know that they weren't here already?"

". . . Maybe," he acknowledged reluctantly.

"Thank you, Investigator Leiden."

She stepped away from his vehicle. He leaned out of his window.

"Be cautious, Commander. I don't like cleaning up blood."

"Neither do I, particularly if it's mine."

She and the professor walked to their car.

"He didn't ask about me," the professor complained.

"That's not a good sign."

"Why?"

"Because it means he already knows all about you."

"How would he know?"

"He's been in touch with Slovakia."

"Is that bad?"

"It depends on who he talked to, and how much information he gave them about us, your car, what we've been doing, where we may be going, and everything else he's collected on us."

"I see."

They got into the professor's car.

"Now they know about the vehicle we're driving. When we get to the hotel, we have to leave the car in a parking area and find another way to get back to The Hague. We have to do it without the knowledge of Leiden or the people who are after me."

"What other way?"

"I'm thinking."

They drove back to the hotel. On the way, Jana removed

her gun from the small of her back, placing it at the bottom of her shoulder bag. With the items she rummaged through to make room was a piece of note paper. It had the name, address, and telephone number of Adele, the woman who had aided her at the gay help center. She had been eager to see Jana again. There was a chance she might help.

They parked two blocks from their hotel and then walked the rest of the way, Jana prodding the professor, before they had even entered the lobby, to forget about his belongings and continue on out the back door.

"My clothes are in my room. I will need them," he insisted.

"They won't have had time to put anyone at the back of the hotel if they're following us. If we walk straight out, we lose them. If we don't, we probably lose that opportunity to get rid of them."

"What do I do for fresh clothes? I need clean underwear."

"We buy clean underwear when we get back to The Hague."

"And my shirts?"

"We buy more."

They kept walking through the hotel and went out the rear exit. After they had gone a few blocks, they found a small phone store where Jana purchased the cheapest cell phone they had. A calling card was included in the price.

"You can use my cell instead of spending so much money," the professor offered.

"They now know about you. That means they also know about your cell phone and can listen in. This new phone will be good for today and maybe tomorrow. Then we have to toss it and pick up another."

Jana dialed the COC woman's number. Adele answered very quickly.

"It's Jana calling. I hope you remember me, the woman who came in with her uncle for help in finding his lover."

The professor bristled. He was still smarting over the masquerade at the COC and its threat to his masculinity. Jana ignored him for the moment.

"I need additional help. I was wondering if I could see you."

Adele invited Jana to meet her at her home, perhaps in an hour. Jana took down her directions.

When Jana hung up, she began to fault herself for taking advantage of the woman's attraction. On the other hand, she couldn't think of anything else to do. She needed a way back to The Hague, a way that was not immediately traceable. She had to act quickly and ignore the niceties.

Adele opened the door to her apartment with a welcoming smile on her face, which faded when she saw the professor. She ushered her guests in, offering her cheek to Jana for a kiss. Adele poured wine for the three of them, and then seated herself next to Jana, peering at her over the rim of her glass, hoping for an affectionate response.

Jana decided to tell her the truth right away. First she apologized, told Adele she was a police officer, showed Adele her credentials, and related the information she'd obtained from Willem Albert, including a description of the beating he had been given. Then came the hard part: she skimmed quickly over the two murders in Slovakia, but told Adele about the deaths of the men who had tried to kill her. By the time she was through, Adele had moved as far away from Jana on the couch as she could.

The professor saved the day. He sat on the floor of Adele's apartment, facing the women.

"I'm asking for help, too. Please listen to me for a moment?"

Adele grudgingly nodded.

"I'm sorry about fooling you at the center. We thought it was necessary. By helping us, you truly helped Willem Albert, and his lover, and you brought us closer to our goal. That goal is not only to survive, but to find some very bad men who've done terrible things. I'm just a . . ." he hesitated, "a clown. But I am also a bit of a father. I helped raise my brother's child, who was murdered. He was my only living relative. I don't want to believe that my nephew died for no reason. There is one other thing: they are also after Commander Matinova. We have no one else to ask. If we stay in Amsterdam, we will both probably be killed. If we can get to The Hague, we have a slim chance. I ask that you give us that chance by helping us."

The professor spoke with absolute simplicity. There was not an ounce of performance about what he said, no false note. No clowning. It was impossible to turn him down.

Adele made them a late snack, then called a friend in The Hague, preparing to spend the night with her when she got there. She called another friend and borrowed a car. In less than an hour, she was driving them to The Hague.

She kissed the professor on the cheek when she dropped them off at Kroslak's apartment. She lightly kissed Jana on the mouth, then hugged her.

"We could have had fun," she said regretfully, then drove off.

Chapter 23

When they walked into Kroslak's apartment late that night, it was as if an industrial-sized mixer had whirled through the place. The professor was aghast at the wreckage; Jana angry. No matter what, the people who were after them seemed to be able to match her moves. Jana paused for a moment before walking into the bathroom to see if the originals of Peter's papers she'd recovered from her closet were still where she'd hidden them

The back of the cistern had been pulled out; the papers were gone. She felt angry and disappointed, and then tried to console herself. All was not lost. She still had copies, but originals have a convincing quality that copies lack, particularly if it comes to presenting evidence in a court of law. Her hope that the killers might not revisit Kroslak's apartment was wrong. Which portended they might revisit it again. Not a comforting prospect.

Jana walked back into the living room. The professor had taken his now usual position: on the floor, gloomily surveying the wreckage around him.

"This is getting to be a habit, Professor. How will your audience react if you sit down when you perform?"

"There's no furniture here to sit on," he grumped. "It's all been destroyed." He tossed the wooden arm of a casual chair that had formerly decorated the apartment into the largest pile in the center of the room. "The people who created this carnage do not seem to like you at all."

"Nor Kroslak; and by now, probably, not you. If you recall, I suggested you stay away from me." She kicked at a table leg on the floor. "There is one consolation: if they're this mad at us, then they think we're a substantial threat. Which means we're going about things in the right way. We're getting closer to them."

"And they're getting closer to us." He could see the frustration on her face. "Did you find what you came for?"

"They got it." She saw his face fall. "I have copies, Professor," she reassured him. "We can go forward." She pulled one of the copies from her shoulder bag. "You should look at this, Professor. You talked to your nephew. It might trigger something if you read this. It's not in Slovak, but maybe you have some idea of what it could be?" Jana handed the report to him.

Before he began reading, the professor crawled over to a ripped couch pillow.

"Comfort is paramount when the mind is called to action." He propped the pillow against a wall, bracing his back against it, then began to read. Almost at once he stiffened, holding the report out, as if to keep it as far away from him as possible.

"It can't hurt you, Professor," Jana joked.

He softly began reciting a phrase over and over again, a mantra he reeled off to protect himself. "That which does not kill us makes us stronger. That which does not kill us makes us stronger."

Jana listened for a moment, then knelt down next to the man. "Professor, what's happening? Can I help?"

The professor put the papers down, rubbing his hands

on his pants, his voice apprehensive. "Why is it that you want to forget and the rest of the world won't let you? You try to ignore things and hope you've left them in the wake of fading conversation or bad memories locked away. Then they suddenly dance around you, costumed, even louder than before."

"Something in these papers, Professor?"

He reluctantly picked up the report again.

"Are you all right?" She put her hand on his arm, trying to ease his fear. "I need you to be okay, Professor. If either of us is not okay, then both of us are in even worse trouble. So, are you okay?"

The mantra faded away. The professor took a deep breath, then another.

"I'm merely tolerable. That's all one can hope for on occasion. This is one of those occasions."

"The papers brought back some bad memory?"

"The past wormed its way back. Perhaps seeing the swastika on the page. Did I tell you I was terribly afraid of the Nazis when I was a child?" He began reading again. "I don't understand this language." The anguish in his voice had abated. "Words, and feelings, have to mean something." He didn't look up, continuing to study the report.

Jana watched him. The professor seemed to have recovered from whatever had bothered him, so Jana walked around the room, looking for anything the intruders had left. There were candy wrappers where the couch stood, and, going back into the bathroom, she found one that had been tossed in the bathtub. Whoever had raped the apartment hadn't gone hungry. She gingerly picked up the wrappers by their ends and found a piece of torn curtain to put them in, carefully folding the cloth over them so as not to smear potential fingerprints, then put them in her handbag. If there were prints, a chemical fuming process might bring them out.

Jana walked back into the devastation of the living room just as the professor looked up, finished with the report.

"I couldn't understand a word, except for the German."

"It was the same with me as well."

"The rest of it is a scientific report. I think it may be a geology report."

"Are you saying that because your nephew was studying geology?"

"I'm looking for a connection."

"So it's a guess?"

"There is the word *petro* here. It means rock or stone."

"What does *petro* mean in Romanian?"

"I don't know." He handed the papers back to her, disappointed with himself. "I'm old. Nothing comes easy anymore."

Jana tucked the papers into another section of her capacious shoulder bag.

"Thanks for trying."

"You're welcome." He tried to make himself more comfortable by plumping the pillow. All he succeeded in doing was disgorging more of the pillow's stuffing. "The only things that have been attached to me in the last few days have been feathers."

Jana began moving the pile of debris to the front door, blocking entry to the room.

"If they come back, this won't stop them for long, but it may be enough time for me to prepare a warm greeting before they get to us."

"If they read the papers about what happened to their comrades when they broke into your hotel room, I think they will hesitate." He turned on his side, adjusting the pillow so he could sleep more comfortably. "Do criminals read? This time, I hope so."

"Good night, Professor."

There was no reply. The old man was already sleeping.

Chapter 24

When you are presumably under surveillance or being monitored, particularly with electronic devices, it's difficult to arrange a meeting place. Although it was Saturday, Jana called Paola's cell phone, recording a message to respond from a public phone, and then went out for a breakfast pastry with the professor, giving him explicit instructions on what to do when they parted. She walked with the professor to the busiest part of the central district of The Hague, watched him go into a building; then she began to stroll about the streets until Paola called. They arranged to meet in a safe place, at the business of a friend of Paola's.

Thirty minutes later, after going through a variety of evasive moves to throw off anyone who might be following her, she arrived at the Crescent Supermart, a Dutch–Arab food store catering to the substantial Arab community in the area. Paola had alerted her Palestinian friend, the manager of the market, that Jana was coming. As soon as Jana entered the store the woman, who looked more European than Middle Eastern, except for the head scarf, walked up to Jana, and when Jana identified herself, escorted her through all the smells of the open spice sections, to the back of the store where a small office had been created. Paola and Aidan Walsh were already there, Walsh unsuccessfully trying to make himself small enough to fit comfortably into the cramped space. Paola thanked her friend, who nodded, then left.

"Greetings and salutations," Aidan offered, helping himself to a plate of dates that had been placed on the desk. "Any buzzards follow you here?"

"If there were, I think I left them fighting the hordes of Dutch cyclists I had to battle crossing the streets."

"Better than fighting us," Walsh muttered.

"These people seem able to find me wherever I run."

"Run faster," he advised.

"There has to be some place to run *to*. I haven't found it yet."

"Are you sure this is not part of your homicide training exercise? I won't like it if it is."

"I guarantee that this is no part of any training program I had in mind." She turned to Paola. "They got the originals of the report I brought from Slovakia."

"More shit hits the fan," Paola murmured. She took a breath. "The Romanian was away today. I'll get the copy to him when he comes in tomorrow."

"Is it safe?"

"My friend the Palestinian lady has it under safekeeping. Her husband works out of their house. He also has a few *bad* cousins who are going to assist him. So it should be okay, at least until tomorrow. I'll pick it up in the morning."

"Anything from Slovakia?"

"The reports on the witness interrogations and the rest of the investigation your compatriots have completed are due in tomorrow. There was an argument, but your Ministry of the Interior affirmed our treaty rights to copies of the reports." She wrote an imaginary check mark in the air. "One battle won."

"Did anyone find out what caused the computer wipe-out in the records-area fire?"

"Nothing. The crime was committed in Netherlands territory, so the Dutch indicated that they would investigate. They came over and talked briefly to our people. Had them sign some statements . . . and that's that! I think they've decided we should clean up our own mess."

"Piss on these local police forces." Walsh pushed the now-empty plate of dates away from him.

"I need some possible fingerprints run." Jana eased the cloth-enfolded candy wrappers from her shoulder bag, handing them to Paola. "Kroslak's old apartment was tossed again. The furniture-breakers ate while they were tearing up the place. The candy wrappers in here may give us prints. If we have prints, we might identify the wreckers."

Walsh looked dubious. "Professionals wear gloves when they search a room."

"Have you ever tried to tear off a candy wrapper when you were wearing gloves?"

He thought about it. "It would be clumsy."

"All we need is for the room-butchers to have forgotten for a minute where they were and why. Maybe one or both of them took off a glove when they fed their bellies. Presto, we may have a print."

Paola gingerly placed the packet containing the candy wrappers in her own purse. Jana sat back, thinking about what she was going to say, then began speaking almost as if she was having a conversation with herself.

"Think about this: where did the papers we hope Ilica can translate for us come from?"

"You got them from your closet. Your boyfriend had them," Walsh reminded her.

"I know where *I* got them; I know who put them there," Jana snapped. "Peter. . . ." She stopped, fighting back the sudden rise of her feelings about Peter's death. "Okay, we know a prosecutor had the papers. He told us, by hiding them, that they were important to whatever it was he was investigating. I think we can safely conclude that it's because of this report that they're after me. Then there's Kroslak on the run."

Walsh interrupted her. "You don't think he's dead?"

"I think he's alive and in Prague. He's looking for something. I think it has to do with the same events we're involved in. I couldn't say this before, but I think, now, that he's a good investigator. You don't keep at it as he is doing unless you believe in your job. It also takes a strong will to survive," she added.

"Like you," Paola pointed out.

Jana looked at her, wondering if Paola was joking. She decided she was not.

"Thank you for the compliment."

"I'm just stating the obvious."

Jana smiled her appreciation, then continued. "Kroslak's in Prague. That means I have to go to Prague and find him."

"Today? Tomorrow?"

"As soon as possible, after you quietly book a plane ticket for me." She looked at Walsh. Walsh took the cue, using his cell phone while Jana and Paola continued the conversation.

"Someone acted as a liaison between Kroslak and Peter. Kroslak and Peter would have felt that going back and forth between Holland and Slovakia would be too obvious. I think Peter knew he was being watched and that even the attorney general's office or police headquarters were no longer safe, so he hid the papers in my closet. Someone other than Kroslak transported the papers to Slovakia, and to Peter. The mail's not safe and electronic transport's no good. It's only a copy of the original, and he'd want the original to examine and verify, and, most of all, to be able to introduce the evidence in court."

"We need Kroslak to tell us who he used."

"Maybe not. Do you know the people who work in our computer area by sight? Our records people? People in the area where the computers were probably attacked?"

"Some of them."

Jana pulled out the photograph of the woman the landlady had given her and who she'd seen in Peter's apartment. She handed it to Paola. Paola looked it over, shrugged, then passed it to Aidan Walsh. He also failed to recognize the woman.

"I still believe that Peter and Kroslak used a courier. They also may have been mailed a copy which put them in the sights of the people who eventually killed Peter and the young man shot at the hotel. Then the killers went after Kroslak. But Peter had an original." She mulled over what she'd said. "Before I go to Prague, I want you to help me access the personnel records at Europol headquarters. I figure I'm safe, with you and Walsh and everyone else around."

Walsh hung up the phone. "You wing it home on Czech Airlines. Tomorrow at one."

"Good. Now, the office."

Chapter 25

At the Europol building Aidan Walsh split off from them, going to his office to get a computer printout confirmation of Jana's flight. Jana and Paola went to the Information Management and Technology Section. The first thing Jana asked for was a list of staff who had taken time off in the past month. There were twenty-seven of them. She shortened the list to women who had taken two or more days, which brought the number down to twelve.

If Kroslak had persuaded someone to transport his reports to Slovakia, he would want that person immediately accessible, someone whom he could just casually pass by without creating any unwanted attention. Three people worked off-site, so Jana deleted their names, which reduced the list to nine. Jana had Paola order their personnel files and went through them one by one, hoping there would be a distinctive characteristic, some item of information in the forms contained in the files, anything that would suggest that that person had been working with Kroslak. When Jana came across the photo, she almost missed it.

The woman was Czech. Her photograph attached to the file was eight months old. She was extremely fat, her hair done up in an elaborate coif that made her look even pudgier. Jana studied it for a long time just to be sure she was right, then passed the photo to Paola.

"You know this woman?"

"No."

"It's the woman in the photograph I showed you earlier."

Jana placed the photograph taken from Peter's apartment side by side with the file photo.

"Hard to tell with all the fat, but it's her," Paola eventually acknowledged. "Humph," she grunted. "The lady must have gone on one hell of a diet since that was taken."

"Maybe she looked in a mirror and couldn't stand what she saw," Jana hazarded. She checked on the woman's current assignment. She was listed as working in the Information Integrity Section. Jana took the woman's file with her as Paola led the way to IMT 7, the woman's work area. She was not at her desk. The woman's supervisor informed them that she had been called away by someone who told her there was a home emergency. Some sort of plumbing problem in her apartment, the supervisor thought.

Jana became uneasy. It did not feel right.

"Her apartment, as quickly as possible," Jana said.

The two of them dashed out of the building. Paola quickly drove them to the woman's apartment complex on the outskirts of the city. They went through the buildings, hurriedly searching, cursing the time that was wasted, eventually locating the right apartment on a corner of the first floor of one of the buildings, and knocked. There was no answer. Jana went to the next-door neighbor, inquiring if she was aware of any emergency repairs that had been done or needed to be done at her neighbor's place. The neighbor had heard of nothing. Jana knew she needed to get inside the apartment. Paola agreed.

Jana used her elbow to break the glass of a front window,

reached inside the frame to unlock it, eased her way through, and then opened the front door for Paola. Together they searched the woman's apartment.

They found her in a clothes closet. She had been garroted. The woman's tongue hung out, her face distorted from fighting both her attacker and her lack of air. Jana checked her pulse. Nothing. They laid her on the floor next to the closet.

Paola called the Dutch police, told them about the murder, and, at Jana's direction, asked them to get in touch with Investigator Jan Leiden. The Dutch crime-scene cops arrived very quickly, Leiden shortly after the first team's arrival. Leiden found the two women outside the front door to the apartment. He nodded curtly at Jana, not pausing as he went into the apartment, saying, "I assume you brought a killer virus with you when you came from Slovakia." He didn't wait for an answer. Five minutes later, another investigator came over to them to obtain their statements. Thirty minutes after that, Leiden appeared from inside the apartment. He was not happy.

"Why did you come here?"

"To talk to her," Paola answered him. "That's in the statement that the other officer took."

He looked directly at Jana.

"I want *you* to tell me why *you* came here. I want *you* to tell me what *you* wanted to talk to her about. Then I want *you* to tell me who killed the lady, and why."

"We came to ask her why her photograph was found in the possession of a prosecutor who was murdered in Slovakia."

"You have this photograph?"

Jana gave him the photo she'd had taken from Peter's landlady in Slovakia. Leiden looked it over.

"Why did the prosecutor have the photograph?"

Jana believed she now knew the answer to why the photograph was in Peter's possession.

"I think the Slovaks needed a liaison between the prosecutor in Bratislava and Kroslak. They went to their cousins to the north, the Czechs, because they knew a Czech officer was working in Europol. I believe that person was our murder victim. I also think the Czechs introduced her to the prosecutor in Slovakia through this photograph. They put the date on it for verification. It would say to the prosecutor, when she introduced herself, that she was who she claimed to be so he would work with her without fear of retribution by the killers. Thereafter, she delivered information acting as a courier. I believe that she delivered documents I have in my possession from Kroslak here to the prosecutor in Slovakia. And I think it's part of the reason the prosecutor was murdered and Kroslak went on the run."

Leiden still looked disgruntled.

"I think you both had better explain in my office, with a tape recorder going." He called over one of the uniformed officers guarding the scene. "Drive them to my office, and make sure they stay there. They're not under arrest, so there's no need to handcuff them. But if either of them tries to get away, you may shoot. A kneecap shot will do."

He walked back into the apartment.

"Nice man," Paola offered sarcastically.

"I'd have done the same."

The officer led them to a patrol vehicle. When they got into the car, Jana asked him to make a short detour and pick up an old man who was waiting for them at Jodenbreestraaton, the Rembrandt house museum. The cop was reluctant. It took Jana two blocks to persuade him, the man agreeing only after she told him that if he didn't pick up the little old man, the little old man would almost surely be killed. Then, of course, Investigator Leiden would blame the cop, and the newspapers would blame him and, eventually, the chief of police would blame him as well.

The professor, looking a little tired, was waiting at the front of the museum. He was very surprised when the patrol vehicle stopped and the officer ordered him inside. But when he got in, he was very glad to see Jana. "I like your new limousine," he said.

They were taken to the station, and then up to Leiden's office, a fair-sized workplace, redolent of long occupancy, with photographs on his desk and original artwork on the walls. It was a lot less grim than Slovak police headquarters. Jana focused on the professor, asking him to explain what he'd done during the day.

"I followed your instructions exactly." He eyed the paintings on the walls. "The man who owns this office has taste. Adventurous taste. He is not afraid of innovation. Not conservative at all."

"Is that good or bad for us?" Paola asked.

"People who think are always good," the professor decreed, looking pleased with himself.

"Professor, I asked what you did today," Jana reminded him.

"Exactly as you ordered." The professor beamed at her. "I kept on the move. Always looking, watching. I went from one busy place to another, never anywhere I would be alone. I even made up games in the big arcade behind your old hotel. I ducked behind counters, moved in one direction, then darted in another. It was exciting."

"You never saw anyone following you?"

"Only once." His face dropped slightly. "I kept trying to lose him, I'd think I had, and then there he was, back again. It was very discouraging." His expression became brighter. "Then I ran toward an escalator, looked back, and I saw him leaving from an exit on the other side of the floor. Boom, he was gone. I did well," he suggested. "Pretty good for an old man, no?" He looked to both of them for approval.

"What time did he break away from you?"

"*I* broke away from *him*," corrected the professor, annoyed.

"Professor, he only left you because he'd either completed his job or he'd been called off. You didn't lose him."

His face fell again.

"Well," he consoled himself. "I stayed alive."

"You did your job, Professor."

"Staying alive?"

"That, and keeping them occupied for a few hours. They weren't sure of your objective. Why would I leave you alone for half a day, possibly put you in jeopardy, unless I had sent you to complete some task? It was enough to distract them, until they found out what it was."

"I was a decoy? Just a wooden duck on a pond?"

"Everyone has limited resources, even the group that is coming after us. It was to thin them out, so I could do my job. And you did your work admirably, Professor."

He was placated.

"Professor, what time of the day did he leave you?"

"About eleven."

Jana turned to Paola.

"Just about when we went to IMT 7."

Paola nodded.

"You think he was called away to deal with the dead woman?"

"There's nothing to confirm that." Jana mulled it over.

"Yet they'd want to silence her before she could talk to us."
She shook her head, not happy with her reasoning. "How
did they become aware that we were on to her?"

"Damned if I know," Paola said.

Again, the hunters had been one step ahead of them.

"Professor, please describe the man you saw."

He reflected. "He was tall, thin, dirty-blond. He wore
a jacket and tie." Sheepishly, he said, "Not much to go
on. He was always too far away for me to see him clearly.
I've got old eyes, and my eyeglass prescription hasn't been
updated for years." He heaved a sigh. "I guess I didn't do
as well as I thought."

"You did fine, Professor. I have no regrets."

An hour later, Leiden arrived. He sat at his desk, still
angry that another body had popped up in his jurisdiction and that Jana was, in one way or the other, responsible. Leiden wanted to know everything that Jana knew,
from the very beginning of her investigation in Slovakia
until the moment he had seen her at the dead woman's
apartment. He pulled out a tape recorder from a drawer
and turned it on.

Jana went over her movements and surmises, giving
him a detailed explication of her investigation, omitting
nothing. Whenever he felt that he needed clarification, he
asked for it. Both of them raised possibilities for discus-
sion. It took them two hours. The last thing Jana did was
give him one of the remaining two copies of the report
written in Romanian that she'd brought from Slovakia.
He looked at it briefly without grasping the nature of its
contents, and dropped it into a drawer.

When her debriefing was over, Leiden had no more
idea than Jana about the whereabouts of the conspirators.
He agreed that they had to find Kroslak.

Paola went home. Before she left, she offered to put Jana and the professor up for the night, but Jana declined. It was time to spend a safe night in a safe place, and Leiden had offered them cots in the police officers' rest area. If they weren't safe there, there was no place in Amsterdam that they would be.

Jana walked Paola out to the stairs, reminding her that they should have gotten some reply to the queries they had made to other European police agencies with respect to the pattern of the two murders that had occurred in Slovakia. Paola informed her that there hadn't been the slightest nibble. Nothing. She promised to get on it as soon as she got back to work.

The cots did their job. At least Jana slept through the night. The next morning, they used the police showers and then shared the prisoners' breakfasts. At eleven o'clock, Leiden arranged for a police vehicle to take them to the airport, and at 1300 on Sunday they were on their way to Prague.

Jana was glad to get out of Holland.

It had not lived up to its peaceful reputation.

Chapter 26

They flew out of Schiphol on Czech Air to Prague's Ruzyně Airport. The professor, who'd had a restless night, fell asleep as soon as the wheels lifted off the runway. Jana had brought with her the fairly extensive Europol personnel file on Gizela Dinova, the woman who had been garroted.

Dinova lived in Prague before being sent by the Czech government to The Hague as part of their required contribution to Europol. Jana thumbed through her dossier, paying particular attention to certain subjects. The woman's area of expertise was information security, with a focus on international liaisons with other countries. She was on loan from the Czech Ministry of the Interior. Her personal information indicated that she had previously been married to a man named Vilem Tuma during part of her tenure in the Ministry of the Interior; he was to be notified in case of medical or other emergencies. Apparently, she had stayed friendly enough with her former husband to so designate him. Not the usual arrangement when a childless couple gets divorced, and there were no dependents listed in the file so Jana assumed they'd had none. His address was in Dejvice, outside the immediate center of the city of Prague, to the northwest.

One other item struck Jana as odd: Dinova was listed as speaking six languages, certainly an asset, but not what you would expect from a woman in what was essentially a routine technician's job. Jana would have expected her to have held a more prominent position.

The flight took an hour and a half. Jana reflected on Dinova's murder during the entire time. One thing kept disturbing Jana: a number of the facts in the file did not match the lifestyle of the woman that Jana had been imagining. One other fact, not in the file, kept intruding on Jana's thoughts: Gizela had been killed immediately after Jana discovered the connection between her, Peter, and Kroslak. That, in itself, was ominous. She pushed it out of her mind for the moment, promising to come back to it later. Gizela herself, and her activities, had to be Jana's focus for the moment.

Why put Dinova together with Kroslak and Peter? It had to involve their need to have a secure line of communication. It would have been easy to work with a Czech whose language was so similar to Slovak that members of the two neighboring nationalities could communicate with each other with ease. Jana became inpatient. She was still missing something.

Would either man put his life in the hands of an individual about whom he knew nothing? There had to be something about Dinova that both men would have agreed on as safe and reliable. Gizela being a Czech civil servant would not, by itself, do it for them. There had to be another factor. The contents of the file did not give Jana a clue until just before they landed.

There was a section on leisure pursuits. It listed Gizela's hobbies as sports such as tennis, volleyball, and skiing. The woman was an athlete. That didn't compute when Jana considered the picture of the woman in her personnel file. Gizela had been obese when she'd come to Europol.

Jana went to Dinova's birth date and did a rapid computation using Dinova's starting date of employment with the Ministry of the Interior. She had been thirty-seven when she'd taken that position. No prior jobs were listed. However, she must have worked before the age of thirty-seven. Posts at the ministry were highly sought after. They were very picky over whom they selected and would have demanded some type of prior job references that would qualify her for the assignment. Gizela's jobs, whatever they were, had deliberately been excluded from her file. Jana thought she knew what at least one of those jobs was: Dinova had been a police officer.

An athlete would consider police work a satisfying career, an often physically demanding profession in a milieu where teamwork was emphasized, but rugged individualism accepted.

Then Gizela Dinova had gone to fat.

Why?

Jana had seen it before, a police officer who was an athlete putting on weight at a desk job. The ministry, and then The Hague, had not been kind to her. It had almost happened to Jana when she'd been promoted from patrol work. She'd had to force herself to exercise regularly.

When the opportunity came by for Dinova to go to The Hague, she would have jumped at the chance to get back to where the action was. The Czech Ministry of the Interior oversaw the police, so they could reach into their pool of officers for an individual who had the qualifications needed, a certain type of person who could fit in at The Hague. They would see her ability to communicate in six languages, and assume she'd blend well into an all-European force . . . except, what was she doing in information security? If Dinova was a cop, but working at The

Hague in, what was, essentially, a technical position, she was working undercover. She was still a cop, acting as a cop, but none of the officials at Europol would be aware of this.

So she was a part of a criminal investigation that had come to involve Kroslak and Peter as her allies. As a cop, Gizela would have Kroslak's and Peter's trust. They were working together. And the Czech government and Colonel Trokan had to know about it.

Whatever crime they were investigating had Europol at its nexus. And, even worse, the criminals involved were at the very center of the police structure of Europe.

Who would look inside an organization like Europol for criminal activity?

It was the perfect cover.

They landed. Jana put the file away just as the professor woke up. They waited until all of the other passengers had disembarked before they left the plane. Jana was thankful that there was no one there to greet them.

Chapter 27

J ana had an instinct as to where to go next. She trusted
her decision. She had been right in the past; she was
correct now.

She couldn't rent a vehicle. She didn't want to be pin-
pointed, and car rental registrations and their associated
computer entries were a quick way for searchers to pick
up her tracks. So, even through she and the professor
were now carrying small hand luggage not quite filled with
underthings and toiletries provided free of charge by the
Dutch police, she decided to travel by tram. Jana obtained
a free city map from one of the hotels, located their destination, and asked the concierge at the hotel how to get
there by public transport. She and the professor arrived at
Vilem Tuma's address in Dejvice in thirty minutes.

Gizela Dinova's ex-husband lived in a small, tile roofed
house in a pleasant but nondescript area outside of
Prague's center. The house was undistinguished except
for an elaborate tracery of blue vines and leaves painted
around the edge of the white façade of the house. There
were a number of people standing around the front of
the dwelling, some dressed in mourning, somber-faced,
making quiet conversation. The front door of the house
was open.

"They're having a memorial service," the professor suggested. "Not a good moment for us to intrude."

"Professor, we haven't the time to pay attention to niceties right now. There's no alternative but to intrude. Besides, I don't think it's a real funeral."

"What is it, then?"

Without answering, Jana walked inside. Reluctantly, the professor followed. The place was well lit. A number of sedately dressed individuals were quietly talking, a few with drinks in their hands. Plates of food were scattered around the room, with many framed photographs of Gizela Dinova prominently displayed. There were also a number of uniformed police officers present, mingling as guests with the other mourners. Jana had been right. The woman had been a police officer. She looked around the room, hoping to identify Vilem Tuma. One of the guests, a woman, came over to a short, thin man who was beginning to go bald, and hugged him; then her husband extended a hand to the man, both of them whispering condolences. It had to be Tuma.

Jana waited until the three were finished talking. When they stepped away, Jana moved over to the man and murmured, "Mr. Tuma, my sympathy on the death of your ex-wife." She extended a hand, Tuma looking at her quizzically.

"I'm Commander Jana Matinova. I worked with your wife at The Hague."

He looked even more perplexed. "I'm afraid I have no recollection of your name. She didn't speak of you. Perhaps you were part of her secret life."

"That's what I wanted to talk to you about."

"She kept her life as a police officer to herself for the last year."

"Perhaps I can tell you something that you'd like to have clarified."

He reflected on the possibility. "She didn't want me to know. She specifically said that I had to distance myself from her. And she was right; look at what happened to her. They killed her."

"Did she give you any idea who 'they' were or what she was working on that might affect both your lives?"

"That was the point. She separated herself from me. It was her way of keeping me safe."

"From who? She had to have given you some indication."

Tuma's face took on the look of a frightened deer. He backed away from Jana, his expression reflecting his increasing apprehension. Jana watched him back away knowing that very soon they would have answers to some of their questions. Then she went to the professor, who had taken up a position in the center of the room, uneasily standing to the side of a group that he had nothing in common with, and with no clear picture of what Jana was planning.

"Why are we still here?" he muttered.

"Professor, there is going to be a commotion in a moment."

"What do you mean, a *commotion*?"

"People with guns are going to come out of every corner of the house."

There was the sound of a siren approaching.

"They're not going to do anything to you as long as you keep your hands in sight and don't fight."

"Why would I fight?"

"Just keep what I've just said in mind."

"You said they would have guns?"

The room suddenly erupted with "mourners" who created a constricting circle around Jana and the professor. A number of them had guns in their hands, all of them pointing at Jana or the professor, ready to use their weapons if they were given the slightest reason. One of the uniformed officers came up to them. His collar insignia was that of a full colonel in the Czech police.

"You are Jana Matinova?"

Jana nodded, knowing what was coming next.

"You and you accomplice are under arrest as complicit in the crime of murder."

Other officers moved in quickly to handcuff them.

"What have I done to deserve this?" the professor yelped.

"Professor, they're doing the right thing."

"Why is arresting me the right thing?"

"Because I said so, Professor."

"This is unbelievable."

"Believe it, Professor. Believe it."

The circle of police officers began walking them out the front door. A police van was just pulling up, its siren sound tailing off as it stopped. Men jumped out of the van at the ready, taking them both into custody. The professor's protestations to the men that he'd done nothing were ignored.

Chapter 28

The hoods blinding them were very uncomfortable. They had come as a surprise, their use far from usual when prisoners are taken into custody. The two sat in silence until they felt the vehicle come to a stop. Seconds later, they were taken out of the van and walked into a building, down a long corridor, then into a room. The echoes of their footsteps on the wood floor suggested a larger room than one would normally expect in an office building or home. Jana and the professor were placed in cushioned seats, their handcuffs taken off one wrist and fixed to their chairs. The footsteps of their police escorts receded, the door to the room closing with a reverberating finality. The subsequent silence became much more apparent and threatening than the sounds had been.

"Is there anyone here?" Jana finally asked.

She waited, then used her free hand to remove the black hood over her head. A man was seated at the other end of the huge conference table at which she and the professor now sat. He was an older man in civilian clothes, his white hair crew cut. He stared at her silently. Jana waited for him to break the quiet, then turned to the professor.

"Professor, take your hood off."

"Are you sure it's okay to remove it?" His voice quavered. "I don't want to offend anyone."

Jana glanced back at the man at the end of the table. He had not moved, merely waiting for her to take action.

"I assure you, Professor, you can pull it off."

The professor gingerly removed the black hood, his eyes narrowing when he saw the man seated at the other end of the table. The professor nodded at the man, who did not respond. The professor turned to Jana, whispering.

"Is he angry at us?"

Jana answered in her normal speaking voice.

"He'll tell us if he is."

"You knew we were going to be arrested at the house. How did you know?" he asked.

"There were too many people gathered together that quickly for a wake. It takes a few days to get that kind of an affair organized. The murder of Gizela Dinova only took place yesterday. She's still in the Hague morgue. The police were there to protect her ex-husband, just in case someone came after him because of what he might have learned from her. In other words, it was a sting to catch any stray murderers who happened to wander into the net. I think they were also there for the two of us in case we promenaded by."

"Why did we go in, then?" he hissed.

"I wanted them to arrest us."

"What for?"

"If I had asked the Czech police about Gizela Dinova's secret life at The Hague they would never have told me. Outsiders aren't welcome when it comes to giving away secrets. This way, the right people have found us, and maybe I can talk them into taking us into their confidence."

"It doesn't look like he wants to talk to us." The professor indicated the man in the crew cut. "Maybe he's a mute?"

"I don't think so."

The professor surveyed the room. It was quite large; the ornate ceiling had several baroque scenes painted on it, the sections of the painting separated by gold-leafed interstices which extended to the edge of the walls, giving the room a golden glow. There were a number of paintings around the room, all of them suggesting a seventeenth or eighteenth-century provenance. And the very long table they were seated at was topped with a mahogany surface that was so polished, it could have served any lady-in-waiting as a mirror.

"This doesn't look like a prison," the professor observed.

"We're not in prison, Professor. My guess is that we're sitting in a palace located somewhere around Prague, an out-of-the-way former noble's residence. Our friend at the end of the table felt he could talk to us here with comparative security. I don't think the gentleman wanted to take us to one of the usual haunts for prisoners." She looked down the table at the man. "I've always liked coming to Prague. There are always beautiful buildings to see. Of course," she shook the arm handcuffed to the chair, "when I visited before, it was under more agreeable circumstances."

"Who is he?" The professor's voice had strengthened.

"He's either from the Ministry of the Interior, or he's the head of the police. From the haircut, I think the police."

"Why are we here?"

"I told you: he thinks it's safe to talk to us here."

"Why not at the police station?"

"Because it's not safe for us there. Or private. Maybe it's also not safe for him." She looked at the man at the end of the table. "You're the general who is the head of the police?"

He nodded. "Jana Matinova?" His voice was a scratchy baritone. "I *thought* you might come to Prague."

"Now you can tell everyone how right you were."

"You've become a suspect in a number of killings: in the Netherlands, Slovakia, Ukraine, Luxembourg, Switzerland, Finland. . . ." His voice trailed off. "Actually, there are twenty-some-odd killings you might be associated with, and probably a number of others that we haven't been able to connect up yet, maybe a lot more."

"I don't think you believe I'm guilty of murder. If you did, you wouldn't have brought us here."

The professor shifted uneasily in his seat, glancing at Jana, whispering again. "The man at the end of the table is crazy."

"He's not crazy, Professor."

The man responded by tossing a handcuff key the length of the table. The key bounced once, leaving a small scratch on the table's pristine top, before it reached Jana. She used the key to unlock her handcuffs, then handed it over to the professor, who had to work at it a little but finally got his handcuffs unlocked.

"Can we go now?" the professor asked.

"He's not ready to let us go just yet."

"He doesn't really believe you're a murderer if he gave you the key. We should be able to walk out of the door."

"There are police officers standing outside the door to stop us if we leave without his permission."

"I see." He settled back into his seat. "He wants something from us before we can go?"

"Yes."

"Yes," the man at the end of the table echoed.

"I hope it's not money. I have very little money," the professor declared.

The man at the end of the table almost smiled. "I think, from what I've been told about your reputation, Matinova, that you are not likely to have committed murder. Please convince me that I'm right."

"I assume you've checked on my whereabouts during the course of *all* these killings, not just the ones in Slovakia and in Amsterdam?"

"Yes."

"I don't know the times or places of most of these murders. However, I'm reasonably sure that if you checked Slovak employment records, I was almost assuredly working in Slovakia at the times of most of the killings that occurred out of my country. I suppose you could object that I planned them from Slovakia and had someone else carry them out. Except there would have to be some kind of links, phone calls, e-mails, connections through intermediaries. I have to believe that you've also found none of these. You haven't unearthed any of them, because they're nonexistent."

"There are none that we can find."

"Which brings us to the two murders in Slovakia. The times, events, and facts that you know of surrounding those murders have to tell you that I did not commit them. I was investigating another crime. There will be reports verifying what I've suggested to you."

"Now suggest what I should look at to show that you had nothing to do with the Dinova and Kroslak killings."

"I was with other police officers when Dinova was killed. As to Kroslak, I don't think he's dead."

"Where is he?"

"Perhaps in Prague."

The man at the other end of the table studied her.

"If Kroslak is alive, why would he come here?"

"Don't you mean: if Kroslak is alive, why hasn't he contacted *you?*"

The man nodded.

"I assume Kroslak has been working on a joint investigation, which includes you in some capacity. During the course of that investigation, Kroslak and Dinova began to work together. Peter Saris, the prosecutor killed in Slovakia, was their designated contact." She analyzed her facts, going over the rest of her suppositions, fitting them in with what she had learned from the man at the end of the table.

"There have been a number of murders in various locations throughout Europe. They appear to be professional killings. From the nature of the killings, there are connecting links, perhaps through the victims themselves, the method of the killings, or events surrounding the deaths which indicate that whoever has committed these murders has some inside knowledge of investigative activities both before, during, and after their acts. That points to insider involvement. And from where Kroslak and Dinova were placed, at Europol, you think that someone in Europol is guilty. Who that person or persons are, I don't think you know, or we wouldn't be here sitting in a gilded room which used to belong to some long-dead member of the aristocracy."

The corners of the man's mouth twitched in the semblance of a smile.

"I had heard you could do extraordinary deductive work. Perhaps they're right." He nodded his appreciation. "Please go on."

"The prosecutor who was killed in Slovakia was the designated receiver of all information because you have leaks in your own department in Prague. Leaks that you haven't been able to trace. The investigation necessitated absolute confidentiality. The fewer people who knew about it, the better. So, you selected a Slovak prosecutor, someone trustworthy, but outside of Prague and even outside of your country. You're so concerned about leaks that you decided it was not safe for us to talk at your office, or even in the jail, so you selected a location that you hoped would be private. Here, in this room."

Jana reflected on what she had said, coming to one more conclusion.

"And you want me to do something for you that you don't want anyone else to know about. Otherwise you wouldn't have brought me here."

"Also true."

"I'm not used to having the police handcuff me." She flicked the handcuff which was still attached to the arm of her chair.

He nodded. "I understand. However, I would ask you to listen to me despite that."

Jana acquiesced with a slight nod. He went on.

"We have agreed, your government and mine, that we have to keep this information within as tight a group of people as possible. Law enforcement, in a number of countries, has developed into a data spigot that we can't turn off. We tried to alert Europol. They said they would investigate. Soon after that, the man charged with heading up the inquiry died from a heart attack while out in his boat. He had never had any health problems and had just had an uneventful medical examination. The next man appointed by Europol is now in South America. We think he fled to avoid being killed. Of course, he could have just decided to suddenly retire. Except he is now living exceptionally well in Brazil, living much better than one would have thought possible, given his prior salary as a civil servant. Our belief is he was both paid off and scared off, a wonderfully effective approach to silencing an individual."

"How did you become aware of this problem?"

"Rumors. We got the same rumor from several countries: large corporate frauds were being committed; contracts involving large corporations were laden with graft, major corruption existed in a number of governments involving government procurement fraud, with the culprits obtaining tens of millions in illicit funds. Every time there was the hint of an investigation, or an individual tried to bring the matter to public attention, he was silenced. Some were bought off. Most of the time, they were killed."

"Were the people who were involved in the frauds or corruption the actual killers?"

The man finally sat back in his chair, his ramrod posture easing slightly.

"People who commit the illegal frauds or acts of corruption in all these countries seem to be totally unrelated to each other. But the killings seem to be related, by technique if nothing else. We think that there is a group of people out there who become aware of ongoing investigations, for example, of government fraud. Those people then contact the criminals and offer to stop the investigations, if necessary, by murder."

Jana reflected on the geographic scope of the crimes, what it would take in the way of resources to carry them out, then escape without leaving traces of themselves.

"You indicated the killings have gone on all over Europe. I presume that would require a centralized group with ties to law enforcement and access to their files, and investigations. Considering everything that has gone on, that does suggest it is coming from Europol."

"Yes."

"A catastrophe," suggested Jana.

"Worse, if that's possible." The man sighed.

"And you can't identify the individuals involved?"

"That's what our people, yours and ours, were trying to do."

"I see. What do you want from me?"

He held up his hands, palms up, shrugging as if it were all very simple.

"Not a great deal: to keep on investigating. To make lots of noise while you're doing it. While you are looking for them, we'll try to catch them as they look for you."

"You want them to come after me?"

"They're doing that anyway, aren't they?"

"It would appear so."

"Consider this: how can we do anything unless we know who the players are? There has to be a desirable piece of bait dangling out there just waiting for them to reach for it. Once they reach for you, we'll know who they are. You have to *entice* them into the open for us."

"Dangle?"

"Dangle," he agreed.

"Dangle in the air, look helpless, and hope they miss their first shot at me."

"Yes."

The professor looked from Jana to the man at the end of the table.

"I'm not at all sure I want to do this."

Jana smiled at him.

"No one ever is, Professor."

Two police officers came into the room, each carrying a small box. The man at the end of the table nodded at the two officers, who set the boxes in front of Jana and the professor. "Your personal effects," said the man.

The professor shuddered.

"*Personal effects.* It sounds like we're about to go to a funeral."

The man at the end of the table made a face.

"I hope not," said the man. "Funerals are such sad events."

Chapter 29

The phone rang for a long while before Trokan answered it.

"I'm harried, overworked, and ready to shoot the prime minister," he explained when he finally answered it. "He has nationalized the new oil field and kicked the foreign oil company out. The opposition is using the opportunity to call for new elections. The students have taken to the streets to complain about the dictatorial methods of the prime minister and his party. So the entire police department is out following the strikers around the town to make sure that they only commit noise and littering violations."

"I'm in Prague."

"There is no trouble in Prague. Why are you in Prague? And how are all the little Czechs? Or is that unimportant?"

"I arrived yesterday. I'm doing what I'm supposed to be doing. How much I've accomplished is another question."

"I got a call from the Dutch police. They're still demanding that you file a report on the killings in Holland. Reports are more important to the bureaucrats than finding murderers. However, that still doesn't explain to me why you're in the Czech Republic."

"Kroslak was alive as of two days ago. He announced he was coming to Prague, so it seemed reasonable for me to come after him."

"A rational move, Janka."

"Did you have any other ideas for me?"

"No."

"How are the investigations of the two homicides in Slovakia coming?"

"Everything has been put on the back burner until the national situation is resolved. I expect it to quiet down enough by tomorrow so we can get back to business on the important things. Have you contacted our friend in Prague? A nice man, isn't he?"

"The general is a little gruff."

"Gruff is good in our kind of job."

"I'm sure that kind of approach would keep up the morale of the troops in Slovakia, Colonel. Wouldn't you agree? Perhaps a new approach to our officers is necessary?"

"Are you being sarcastic, Janka?"

"Never, Colonel."

"Good."

He hung up.

Jana put the phone down on its cradle. She'd had the faint hope that some type of help or advice might be coming from Trokan, but she was disappointed. Which meant that she would have to go forward with the plan that the Czechs had come up with: become an inviting target in an effort to draw out the people who were committing the murders. It was not pleasant to contemplate.

She and the professor had been put up by the Czechs in a hotel suite. The electronic gear they had been given was still on a table top. The elements looked like pieces of dead insect skeletons that had been painted different shades of black and gray. The professor came in from his bedroom looking rumpled in the terrycloth bathrobe the hotel had supplied, fiddling with the tracking device he'd been given.

"I've decided that magic is much better than the things these crazy inventors of arcane modern artifacts come up with."

Jana rose and took the very small oval device out of his hands, peeling off the plastic covering from its back to expose adhesive.

"I would suggest you put it under your arm. They always look for it on your back or in your underwear, but seldom under the arm." She folded back his bathrobe, pressed the tracking device into the space between the chest and arm; then pulled the bathrobe back into place. "It shouldn't be too uncomfortable there."

"It feels like I've got a tumor," the professor grumbled. "Why can't they just follow us?"

"That's what the bug is for, Professor. There are too many people in the central city. The crowd may swallow us up. This way they'll be able to track us electronically, as well as visually, without worrying that we'll become lost in the multitude."

She went over to the coffee table, picked up her tracking device, removed its plastic covering, and fixed it under her own arm. There was also a tiny black box, which she looked over as she checked her watch for the time.

"We're at the point at which I have to activate the alarm." She pressed an even tinier switch on the end of the device, then slipped it into a side pocket of her pants. Almost immediately, there was a ring on the telephone. Jana answered it just as quickly. "All okay," she answered the phone; then, "Every hour, as agreed." She hung up.

"What was that?"

"A reminder to press the button on the alarm every hour to tell them we're okay."

"We'll forget."

"Not with you to remind me."

"I always forget things like that," he warned. "Besides, you're responsible for our safety."

Jana gave him a jaundiced look.

"Have you felt safe since you've been traveling around with me?"

"No."

"So don't forget to remind me." Watching the professor's face drop, Jana tried to lessen his unease. "It's just a backup alarm. If I forget to push it, they swoop in to save us from ourselves. Or, maybe, they save us from our murderers."

"We hope."

"Optimism, my friend. It's the key to success—and survival."

The professor watched her as she checked her gun, then stowed it in her shoulder bag.

"As I watch what you're doing, I have this feeling that neither of us is very optimistic."

Jana hesitated, then changed her shoes to a lower heel.

"Just in case we have to do some running."

"The right costume is important. Think through your rehearsal. When I used to perform, I always thought it was safe only after we rehearsed until we hated it. Then I was ready for showtime." He snapped his fingers, brightening up. "Maybe that's a good sign. I already hate what we're doing."

"This is real life. We don't get the opportunity to rehearse."

"That's why I became a magician. Who wants real life? Look what's happening to us in the real world. Comedy is better than tragedy."

"I agree, Professor."

He was struck by a sudden thought. "Maybe this is all a fantasy and we're actually performing on a stage?"

"This is real, Professor." She finished her preparations. "Time to go."

He grimaced. "I always get nervous at curtain time."

Twenty minutes later, the two of them were walking down the street.

Their rooms were at the Leon, a modern hotel situated close to Old Town Square, a plain looking building on a quiet street. On the inside everything was ultra modern. However, once you walked fifty meters from the hotel in either direction you were in the middle of the hubbub of bars and restaurants and knick-knack stores that catered to the tourists that flooded Prague. Jana made no effort to be unobtrusive. Appearances were the key to the operation. They were supposed to look confident, as if they felt safe.

Showtime, as the professor had said.

Nonetheless, a rehearsal would have been nice.

Chapter 30

They walked for hours, stopping only to eat a quick meal at the rear of a large café. Jana found them a table where they could sit with their backs to a wall. She didn't want to be surprised, so she frequently glanced at the door, sweeping her eyes over the customers, looking through the plate-glass front window. The customers at the outside tables in the fresh air were enjoying themselves, everyone flirting with everyone else, the waiters serving copious amounts of Czech pilsner guaranteed to lift even the most morose spirits. The people at the tables were living in the moment, which was a state, a feeling that Jana had not experienced for herself since Peter had died. She envied them.

The professor finished mopping up the last of his *knedliky*, took a final sip from his glass of *mineralka*, and pronounced himself ready to go. "I want to visit some friends of mine I haven't seen for a while."

"Not good. You may be bringing trouble with you if you visit them."

"Stage people always have trouble. We expect it. If it doesn't happen today, it will tomorrow, so what the hell."

"Not this kind of trouble, Professor."

"In the theatre, everyone dies at one time or another. If it's not the audience throwing things at you, you're killed by the hero. The trick goes wrong and the manager fires you, and no one else will speak to you because they're afraid of getting fired too. This is a kind of murder. Everybody in Shakespeare's *Hamlet* dies, not to speak of *Lear* and *Macbeth*, or of Arthur Miller, or Godzilla. I once had a jealous husband come after me with a large carving knife. Fortunately, he tripped and cut himself on the arm, and the lady in question went back to him to comfort him . . . so that was a kind of death as well."

"Professor, we're talking about real-life dying. Like your nephew," she reminded him.

He nodded. "Of course." A brief, sad smile appeared. "I was just trying to cheer us up. Nobody really dies in the theatre; everyone dies in real life. That's why I liked the theatre."

"Why did you leave it?"

"I got old. No one wants to see old magicians or old clowns. They're too close to the truth. And I was a combination of both." They watched the other customers for a few minutes, then the professor suddenly stood. "I've decided where I want to go."

Jana put money down for the check, slowly standing, still checking out the room. Now that they were about to leave, she focused on the exterior of the café.

"Where to, Professor?"

"In the old days, the really old days, they used to go up to Hradcany and St. Vitus's Cathedral. You would either petition the king or some noble at the castle to sponsor you or pray to God at the cathedral for success if the nobles had spit on you. So we go to the Mala Strana on the hill. Besides, a lot of my friends have settled in the 'little quarter'."

"I was hoping you'd given up the idea of seeing them."

"I'm still thinking." There was a stubborn edge to his voice. "We'll let things play out, see how it goes, okay?"

She nodded, resigned. The professor was determined to see his friends.

When they left, Jana concentrated on trying to avoid the people crowding the inner streets of this part of the city. It would be too easy for an anonymous assailant to hide among the thousands of gawkers and to shoot her and the professor as they walked by. She steered them toward Smetanovo Nabrezi, the long avenue running along the murky Vitava River. The area they needed to get to was on the other side of the water. Meantime, they had to negotiate their way through the crowds of tourists that infested Prague like hordes of gnats. All of Europe, America, and Asia appeared to have come to see the historic capital of central Europe, but the avenue along the Vitava was one of the few places where the crowds thinned out slightly.

From time to time, Jana would casually glance back, trying to spot the guardians whom the police had promised would keep the two of them under protective observation, but except for a guess at some magazine-stand browser or river-embankment leaner, there was nothing to indicate that their protectors were nearby, which disturbed Jana.

Perhaps, Jana rationalized, since she and the professor had their monitors on, their guardians were hanging well back or tracking them from adjacent side streets to keep from being spotted. If Jana could identify their protectors, the murderers could as well, so she consoled herself that it was probably better that she couldn't spot their guardians.

They reached the Charles Bridge, the span across the Vitava connecting the New and Old Towns with the Mala Strana. As usual, the passage was jammed with pedestrians, buskers, vendors, and street artists making it almost impossible to push through the mass of bodies. They walked under the Stare Mesto bridge tower, slowly making headway past the statues of saints lining the bridge, Jana pressing ahead as quickly as she could, the professor following in her wake. Just as they reached the sculpture of St. Anthony of Padua, approximately in the middle of the bridge, Jana glanced back and saw Gyorgi Ilica, the Romanian investigator from Europol.

She grabbed the startled professor, pushed him past a mime who was dressed all in white and presenting himself as Jesus on the Cross, to the side of the bridge where they would have a wall at their backs.

"I was going as fast as I could," the professor protested.

"I saw someone I shouldn't have, Professor." She eased her gun out of her shoulder bag, holding the bag so it concealed the pistol. "If he's here, then there will be others as well." Jana pressed the alarm activation in her pocket.

"Who's *he*?" the professor got out.

"A man I worked with, a man who shouldn't be on this bridge."

She looked back, but she had lost Ilica in the crowd. Her eyes ranged over the bridge, in both directions. She focused on smaller sections, quartering the area, trying to concentrate on individuals in the hope of spotting Ilica or anyone else who had been at Europol. There was no one who looked even remotely familiar.

"Shouldn't you hit the alarm button?" the professor asked. "The police will come to help us."

"I have. But they won't be able to get through the crowd quickly enough. Come on. We'll run for it." She pushed the professor ahead of her, prodding him to go faster, alternately checking behind them, then scanning the area ahead, all the while hoping that they could reach the other side of the huge pedestrian bridge before they were attacked.

Almost miraculously, a space cleared in front of them, allowing them to pick up their pace to a rapid jog. The professor counted the saints aloud as they went past them, as if hoping that naming them would shorten the distance between the statues.

"Saint Luitgard . . . Saint Phillip . . . Saint Adalbert. . . ." He began to wheeze as he struggled to breathe.

"Stop talking," Jana growled. "You're using too much air."

"I'm depending upon the . . . saints . . . to hear me. Saint Vitus. . . ." Now he was beginning to stagger; Jana had to hold him up. "The Blessed Ivan . . . Christ and Saint Cosmas. . . ."

He almost went down. Jana pulled him erect. "We're almost there, Professor."

"Saint Wenceslas. . . ."

And they were suddenly through the arcade of the Mala Strana Bridge Tower and off the bridge, on the other bank of the Vitava.

Jana steered the professor to the side of the arcade, looking back.

"Shouldn't we go on?" the professor wheezed.

"We choose the battleground this time, Professor. They have to come through a very narrow space if they want to get to us. It reduces the odds. So we stay."

They waited for a good ten minutes. At long last, Jana signaled that it was time to go on and put her automatic back in her pocketbook.

"It appears that they decided against taking that final step to get to us."

"Are you sure you were right? You're positive it was one of them?"

"As positive as one can be under these circumstances. Ilica is easy to recognize, but there were a lot of faces in that crowd."

They hurried on, up to the castle.

Jana had the childish hope that the castle walls would protect them.

Chapter 31

As they climbed the long hill to reach the castle the houses seemed to get older and smaller. They had been built wall-to-wall; none of them afforded a safe place to hide. Oddly, now the professor didn't appear eager to arrive. He had retreated into himself and appreciably shortened his steps, lagging behind. Eventually, the truth came out.

"I want to go somewhere else first." He wanted to see his friends, or at least a particular one, a woman. "I want to see Marketa."

"Marketa?"

"Yes, Marketa."

"A lady, naturally. Men do stupid things over women," she warned him.

"I never claimed to be smart."

"She's a special *friend?*"

"She was my special friend."

"The love of your life?" Jana guessed.

"Yes."

"And she lived around here?"

"The last I heard."

"And when was that?"

"Ten years ago. When I stopped performing."

"Ten years is a long time, Professor."

"We were angry at each other. It was my fault. I wouldn't move here from Slovakia."

"It's hard to conduct a long-distance romance."

"It is."

Jana checked the immediate neighborhood. Aside from the people trudging up the hill, all of them comparatively innocent-looking, there had been no hint of trouble since the bridge.

"You know the danger we may bring with us if we go to her house, Professor?"

"She was a very brave woman. I think she would want to see me."

"Don't confuse your hopes with reality. She's probably found someone else."

"She *had* someone else."

Jana blinked at the statement.

"Another boyfriend?"

"It doesn't matter now."

"You're still intent on going?"

"I want to go."

"I can't persuade you not to?"

"No." He gave it a few seconds' consideration. "I would like you to come, too."

"I should think that the two of you would want to be alone together."

"It will be more awkward, at first, to be alone. If things work out, you can quietly excuse yourself later." He let her think about his invitation to join him. Then he said, "Please."

"I'm uncomfortable with this."

"We're partners in jeopardy, aren't we? Partners humor each other." He looked at her with pleading eyes; then, once more, said "Please."

Jana gave in.

They doubled back, actually a good strategy, Jana concluded. No one would expect them to turn so quickly. Then they veered onto Karmaletska, set back slightly on the hill. They were walking roughly parallel to the river, only this time on the west side.

Just in case, Jana kept a grip on the gun in her purse, ready for any eventuality, but no one looked at all suspicious. Unfortunately, she could not see any of their supposed police chaperones. She had pressed the alarm. They should have come running to their aid. They hadn't.

Perhaps they were following them from the air, perhaps using a helicopter at an angle and altitude high enough that it would not be easy to see even when she looked up? But then ground support would be so far back, it would take them half of forever to arrive if the two of them were attacked.

Jana scanned the sky. No helicopter, of course. She quickened their pace, the professor hard put to keep up even though they were no longer climbing.

"You seem to be in more of a hurry than I am," the professor observed. "Let's take our time so I'm not winded. I will need my wind for the meeting I'm contemplating."

"We're too exposed here."

She pressed on, the professor trotting to keep up with her.

"Is there a problem?" he asked. His head swiveled from side to side. "Are they after us? Are they back there?"

"I don't know, which is why I'm hurrying."

They turned onto Proposka, then twisted left on Malteske, heading down into a separate little declivity of old stucco and stone houses, a few little shops and restaurants, to an area generally inhabited by artists and writers who liked the bohemian life. They passed a graffiti-covered wall commemorating John Lennon's death, something totally out of place in Prague, particularly in this section. A segment of the graffiti depicted a bullet exiting a bleeding heart. Not a good omen, Jana thought, then chided herself. The stress was getting to her. Omens are for witch doctors, not investigators. Focus on reality, she told herself. That was the only way to get out of the mess they were in.

The professor tugged at her sleeve to pull her to a stop shortly after passing the wall. The yellow building housed an old restaurant with a smiling pig over the door, a sign underneath in fading candy-striped letters proclaiming *Veprove Zahrada*, the Pork Garden. The professor looked up at the sign, and hesitated.

"Just standing in front of the door isn't going to get you far, Professor."

"I'm planning."

"What are you planning?"

"What to say."

"If you still love her, you'll know what to say."

"It requires careful thought."

"Telling a woman that you love her is a good beginning."

"What if she says 'Go away, I don't love you any more'?"

"Then you go on to the next dream. Meanwhile, I think you have to explore this one." Jana opened the door, nudging him inside.

The restaurant was dimly lit. A number of long wooden communal tables took up the floor space. Several people at one of the tables were being served large glasses of dark beer. The guests nibbled pretzels from a large bowl in the center of the table before taking their first sips of the heavy beer. At the same time, they played a dice game, shouting every time a cup containing the dice was shaken and rolled. The waiter who had served the beer, a heavyset older man with a completely bald head that shone even in the dimness of the inn, waved them to a table.

"Beer?" he called as they sat down.

Jana signaled for two small beers.

The waiter walked back to the rear of the place, pouring the beers out of a pump spigot.

The professor gazed intently at the man.

"It's him."

"Who is him?"

"Marketa's husband."

The revelation that the professor's beloved was married shook Jana.

"You didn't tell me she was married, Professor." She eyed him disapprovingly. "We didn't come in here to confront a husband. If you had informed me of that, I would have handcuffed you and dragged you back to the hotel."

"It was okay. He knew about us. He had another lady who he was seeing. It was okay with both of them. That was the way it was. She was my assistant in the magic act. Every magician has to have an assistant. What happened between us came naturally."

"Professor, she's no longer your assistant."

"That's why she left me," he sighed. "She liked being on the stage. When I retired and asked her to marry me, she walked out."

"So she no longer loved you."

"Of *course* she loved me. It was just her way of trying to make me stay in the business. I got angry and left Prague. I thought she'd follow me."

"You're fooling yourself, Professor."

"I *know* she loved me. Men can tell about these things."

"Professor, it's supposed to be the women who can tell, not the men."

"You forget, one of the items I did in my act was to read minds."

"Professor, it was a trick."

"With me and her, it was real."

The bald waiter who was Marketa's husband came over to the table and set the two beers in front of them.

"Hello, Konrad." The professor nodded at the waiter. "How have you been?"

The waiter nodded back without any sign of recognition.

"I'm the Professor, Konrad. The magician who Marketa worked with."

The waiter looked at him more closely, the light of recognition finally appearing.

"How have you been, Professor?" he asked, without really caring.

"Fine, Konrad. And how is Marketa?"

"I haven't seen her in a while. She always liked the bright lights. This life was not good enough for her. You know that."

An older woman, slightly younger than Konrad, came out of the back carrying a small bowel of pretzels that she set in front of them. Then, without saying a word, she walked over to the table where the men were throwing dice.

"I see Jolana is still with you."

"We get along."

"Do you know where I can get in touch with Marketa?"

"Sure." He reached into his pocket, then pulled out a small wallet and extracted a card. "She went into business for herself. This is her club." He laid the card down in front of the professor. "If you see her, tell her that her husband says hello." He walked to the dice-thrower's table, sat down next to Jolana, and kissed her on the cheek.

"They make a nice couple," Jana commented.

The professor picked up the card. "K5," he read. "That's all it says, with an address in Stare Mesto." He admired the card. "Very classy."

"Gold embossing," Jana pointed out.

"Good-quality paper."

"You still want to see her, Professor?"

"She's my one true love," said the professor.

"You said that before."

"I meant it before; I mean it now."

"You're crazy," said Jana. "And I'm crazier for going with you."

They finished their beer, left money on the table for the drinks, and left.

Chapter 32

The club was in one of the taller buildings in the Stare Mesto area. It advertised "K5" in ornate neon lettering a half-story high. When they stepped out of the taxi and looked up at the sign, the professor thought they had come to the wrong address.

"Obviously this is not it." He turned back to the taxi driver, showing him the card Konrad had given them. The driver pointed at the card, then the neon sign, then drove off talking to himself about the idiotic clients he had to service. The professor yelled a few ineffectual words after the departing taxi, then turned back to Jana.

"We will have to talk to someone else who can tell us where the club is."

"Professor, I think this is it."

"Too expensive; too garish. She always had taste, even in the costumes she wore on stage. Never too much skin. Merely suggestive."

"It's a different era now, Professor. Glitz is good."

The professor was rooted to the spot, staring up at the sign. Jana took him by the arm and marched him toward the lobby door. There was an elevator next to the door which was surrounded by red neon. A liveried doorman hurried over to punch the call button. The elevator door opened, and Jana pulled the professor inside.

"We follow the directions, Professor."

The doors closed and the elevator began to ascend. The professor looked at the panel.

"There are three floors to the club," the professor murmured, a tone of awe in his voice. "I don't believe this is hers. Maybe she's just a hostess?"

The floors on the panel were labeled with small gold plates that read CLUB/BAR/RESTAURANT, THEME ROOMS, and RELAXATION AREA. Jana wondered what went on in the relaxation area.

The elevator doors opened, and they walked into the club. It was stylishly appointed, with an ultra-modern décor that managed to maintain a touch of elegance. Even at six o'clock in the early evening, it was nearly full. But the clientele was not yet boisterous, the soft hum of music being piped in not yet overcome by the ambient noise. Unlike the sign on the outside of the building, all was softly lit, the rosy glow of indirect lighting suffusing much of the room. It made everyone look better.

They were met by a very attractive young woman wearing a strapless gown who led them onto the floor. "I can see the way you're looking around that you haven't been here before. Welcome to the K5. There is a cover charge that you must pay when you're seated, which will be deducted from your tab at the end of your stay. Eat and drink enough and you pay no cover. This is the best club in Prague. Three floors, fifteen individually themed rooms in which you can enjoy yourself, with over forty girls working tonight. If you have any questions, just ask any of the ladies, who have been selected by the management for their intelligence and beauty."

She led them to a central table with a notebook computer in its center. "The fifty-euro cover fee is payable now." She tore a slip from a small pad, setting it on the table. "Just show it to the waitress and it will be progressively deducted from your food and drink bill." She patiently waited while a slightly bewildered professor dug into his wallet and came out with a fifty-euro bill.

"The computer on the table?" Jana asked.

"You'll find it's simple to operate. It tells you which girls are working tonight, what their interests and statistics are, and allows you to make a decision about which of them you want to spend your pleasure time with."

"Pleasure time?" gulped the professor.

"Everything here is pleasure time," the hostess said. "The computer also tells you what other activities are available in the club. Any other questions?"

"We're here to talk to Marketa. Is she around?"

The hostess hesitated. "We have several Marketas. Which one do you want?"

"She was in show business. I don't know what name she's going by now. A very pretty woman," the professor suggested.

"All of our women are pretty." The hostess was impatient. "Check the computer."

"I don't think she's on the list," Jana asserted. "I think she owns the club."

"Yes, maybe she owns the club." The professor's voice came out in a reluctant squeak.

"Perhaps just a piece of it."

"You want to see the owner?" the hostess asked.

"If she's Marketa," Jana asserted, "we want to see her. Please tell her that the professor is here, and that he still loves her."

"That's not fair!" the professor yelped.

"You want her to *come*, don't you?" Jana looked back up at the hostess. "Go ahead, tell Marketa."

The hostess nodded, then walked away.

"I think you've done me a disfavor," the professor scowled at Jana. "I am not a lovesick buffoon."

"Lovesick, yes; a buffoon, no. If there was any doubt that the woman would come out to see you, there is no doubt now. She won't be able to resist hearing the declaration of love from your own lips."

"I'm embarrassed. The whole world will think I'm a dolt."

"This is a nightclub, not the whole world." She scanned the club, looking for threats. There were none that she could see. "Being direct is a virtue."

"Not in this case."

"If it truly is 'your' Marketa, I will wager my share of the cover charge that not only will she be here, but in the first minute she's at the table she'll tell you how lovely it was to hear that you still loved her."

The professor was silent.

"Do you accept the bet, Professor?"

"I never bet against myself."

"Why not?"

"Because I may win."

He surveyed the club, the girls lounging at the bar, the computer at the table.

"It's a glorified brothel."

The professor stared across the floor. Jana followed his eyes. A woman in her fifties, dressed in a designer business suit, a diamond necklace at her throat, a matching diamond pin on her lapel, and a diamond bracelet on her wrist, was making her way through the tables toward them.

"Is that her, Professor?"

"Yes," he gulped out. "It's Marketa." He took a deep breath. "She looks very different."

"It's not reasonable to expect the same woman you knew. Change the picture of her on that shrine in your mind, Professor."

"It's still her."

When she got to their table, without any other prelude, Marketa pulled the professor's head around and kissed him on the lips.

"The message you sent me was truly lovely, my sweet." She pulled back just enough to look closely at his face. "It is so good to finally see you after all these years." She kissed him again, this time on the cheek, affectionately rubbing her hand up and down his arm. "You haven't changed a bit."

"Well, you have!" he blurted out.

Marketa's eyes narrowed.

"How have I changed?"

"The diamonds; you are covered all over with diamonds."

She tossed her head. "You would never buy me any, so I had to find the money to buy them for myself." She looked over at Jana. "No need to tell you how expensive they are. So, once a woman gets them, she's entitled to flaunt them, right?"

"Right," Jana agreed.

"I am Marketa," Marketa announced somewhat imperiously to Jana. "And you are . . . ?"

"Jana Matinova."

"A pleasure to meet you, Ms. Matinova." She stroked the professor's arm again. "Has he told you that we used to be in a magic act together?" She went on without waiting for an answer. "My darling professor finally got tired of sawing me in half and decided to leave the stage. Of course, I was too young to retire."

"Of course," agreed Jana.

"He wanted me to go to Slovakia. Can you believe that? Leave Prague and go to the Slovak Republic? That was not a change for the better."

"You weren't so young any more," the professor interjected.

"Young and still beautiful enough." Irritated, Marketa moved away from the professor. "I simply had to find another man who was willing to put up with me."

"And you did," suggested Jana.

"He gave me a little. I had savings. I knew the business of entertainment. Eventually, I had these. . . ." She indicated her diamonds. "Then I had this." She swept her arm around the room.

She moved back closer to the professor, kissing him on the cheek again.

"Unfortunately, the kind of magic we had only lasts for a while."

A very handsome young man, deeply tanned, dressed in tailored leisure clothes, his silk shirt collar flared at his neck, came over to the table, crouching down in front of Marketa.

"Marketa, I'm going shopping. Would you like to come?"

"Not right now, Jiri. Do you have enough money?"

"I thought I could take some from your purse."

"Always, darling. It's in the office."

He kissed her on the mouth, both of them lingering over the kiss.

"I'll be back soon," he called back over his shoulder as he sauntered away.

The professor looked thunderstruck.

"I can't help myself," Marketa confided to Jana. "I like them young." She looked at the professor, sighing. "You used to be like that, darling. And so was I. Being young is lovely, having a young one is only slightly less so." She patted the professor's arm. "I'm so glad you stopped by to see your former flame, old sweetheart." She pinched him on the cheek. "Still cute."

Jana noticed a man walk over to a nearby table. He seemed to be determined to look in any direction but Jana's. And he was too watchful. He was ready for what was to happen, knowing it was going to happen. Jana felt a chill in her stomach.

She looked at the entrance of the club. Two other men were talking to the hostess.

Jana felt an even colder chill. One of them was Ryan, the Irishman from the Europol party who had tried to embarrass her by dangling his false member in her face; the other was Ilica, the Romanian. She had not been wrong when she thought she'd seen him on the Charles Bridge.

"Professor, they're here."

He stiffened, looking around the room. Marketa, no stranger to problems in a club like K5, caught Jana's tone as well.

"Do we have trouble?"

"There are three men in the club who want to kill us."

Marketa quickly ran her eyes over the clientele in the club.

"The two at the entrance?"

"And the one at that table." Jana indicated the table with her eyes.

"If you can get through the back, near the restrooms, there is another elevator. It's a private route down to the parking lot. There's a black BMW sedan parked immediately next to the elevator doors. I keep the keys in the ignition. You never know when you'll need to make a fast exit from the stage."

"Thank you, Marketa."

"Yes, thank you, Marketa," the professor echoed.

Jana pulled her gun out of her purse, clicking the safety off.

"No shooting in the club." Marketa hissed. She kissed the professor one last time. "Come back when you have more time to talk, darling."

Jana slid out of her seat and walked quickly over to the man seated at the nearby table. He saw her coming, but a fraction of a second too late. Jana placed the barrel of her pistol at his neck before he could do anything.

"Up!" she said, pulling him erect, stepping behind him. The two men at the entrance now had guns in their hands and were walking toward her. Jana stood behind the hostage she had taken, pulled the hammer of the pistol back, and rested the gun on the man's shoulder, aiming at the two men who were advancing on her. The sight of her gun stopped them for the moment.

The professor yelled a few last words at Marketa: "Your husband says hello." Then he darted behind Jana, the two of them backing toward the hall containing the private elevator.

Someone saw the gun in Jana's hand and screamed. Others screamed, causing mass confusion, giving the two of them the cover they needed as people darted between them and the two advancing gunmen.

They reached the corridor, passing the restroom doors. A woman emerged from the ladies' room; a small noise came out of her mouth when she saw the gun. She retreated. A second later, they reached the elevator. As soon as its door opened, Jana hit the thug she was holding behind the ear. The man crumpled. Jana's next move was to fire two shots down the corridor, into the floor so she wouldn't hit any of the nightclubbers with a stray bullet. It created a hesitation in their pursuers that she and the professor needed. Once inside the elevator, the professor pushed the PARKING button, the doors closed, and the car started down.

Jana put her gun back in her shoulder bag. The professor frowned at her.

"Marketa asked that you not fire the gun in the club," he scolded Jana. "Didn't you hear her?"

"My hearing is very good."

"Then why did you shoot?"

"Would you rather we were dead, Professor?"

"No."

Within minutes, they were driving Marketa's BMW sedan out of the garage.

Almost as an afterthought, the professor asked, "Why didn't you activate the alarm the police gave us?"

Jana glanced at him.

"I did. Three times."

The professor's mouth fell open. "They didn't come to our rescue."

"No, they didn't, Professor."

"They didn't *want* to come to our rescue."

"Unfortunately, you may be correct, Professor."

They drove on in silence, contemplating their situation. It was not good.

Chapter 33

Jana drove to a residential side street on the outskirts of Prague. There were lots of trees, the secure feel of families around them, and a quiet that suggested safety. She pulled under an overhanging willow tree that made them less obtrusive, satisfied she had done what she could for the night. They slept in the car.

Jana awakened before the professor, got out, and did stretching exercises for a good ten minutes trying to get the cramps out. During the course of her exercises, the professor climbed out of the car, heeded a call of nature by going into a bushy area a few meters from the car to relieve himself, then stiffly walked back to the car. He eyed Jana with a skeptical look as she finished her workout.

"Stretches would do you good, Professor," Jana suggested.

"I'd rather rust."

Jana could feel the beginning of a light rain. The sky was clouded over, with even darker clouds coming. It looked like they were going to get a heavy downpour. Jana climbed back into the car. With an audible groan of pain, the professor got in.

"The last time I had to sleep in a car, the lady I was with was more obliging."

"You were younger."

"More *virile* might be a better word. After seeing the

young man that Marketa is now so enamored of, I realize that I lack a certain sexual aura."

"It happens."

"Maybe I should have stayed in Prague? Show business is attractive to a certain type of woman."

"Marketa would have moved on, anyway."

"You think so?"

"She has that look."

"Perhaps you're right."

"She still loves you a little, Professor. She wouldn't have given us the car if she didn't."

He smiled, then winced. "Even my jaw muscles hurt." He very carefully shifted his position.

"Marketa will report the car stolen soon," Jana suggested. "She'll want to make sure she gets it back. Or at least the insurance money."

He sighed. "She always loved money." He thought about it for a moment. "She won't report it for another twenty-four hours. She will want to give us time to get away. It's an old show-business custom. If an act skipped on the rent, nobody else would give any indication to the landlord until they were sure the act had made a clean escape. Remember, they used to put us in debtor's prison if we owed money."

"Did they ever put you in jail, Professor?"

"No. I was the one who always fled first."

Jana opened her shoulder bag and pulled out her last copy of the Romanian report, examining the signatures at the bottom of the page.

"The Nazi's name was Haider."

She handed him the report.

"It appears to be." He checked the Russian name. "This one I can't make out."

He handed the report back to her.

"The Russian communist bureaucracy was convoluted and kept miserable records. Checking Cyrillic on the Internet will also be a task, so we'll stay with the German for the moment."

"The *Internet*?"

"The Nazis kept good records. Lots of them have been posted." She put the report away. "I think we may be able to identify this man and find out what his job was. That may key us into the report and tell us where Kroslak was heading when he came to Prague."

She put the car in gear, and within five minutes they were parked outside of a small café that advertised Internet access with a big "@" in the window. They had to wait for a half-hour before it opened.

Once inside, the professor looked nonplussed. "I don't know how to use one of these," he confessed.

"I thought you were a magician," Jana chided him. "It's a magic box."

Jana went on the 'net.

She searched for Czechoslovakia, the old union between the Czech Republic and Slovakia, then went back to the Second World War period, searching a variety of headings that included the Nazi Protectorates of Bohemia and Moravia and the puppet Slovak Republic that was created by the Nazis immediately before the start of the war. Her primary interest was the officials who had been appointed by the Nazis to oversee the governing of the puppet states. It took several hours, until, by a lucky accident, she found Haider listed in the body of a report on German wartime need for war materials from the occupied countries.

"Bruno Haider," she pointed out to the professor. He was Administer-Adviser of State Material Reserves for the Protectorates of Bohemia and Moravia. There was an asterisk after his name, the reference at the bottom of the page indicating that he was also Special Adviser in Resource Management to Josef Tiso, the President of Slovakia under the Nazis.

"What does it matter, now that we know who he is?" a growingly impatient professor asked. "My stomach needs food."

"This is a café. Order a pastry," suggested Jana. "They're better here than they are in Holland."

"What are you looking for now?" he asked.

"Someone has the Nazi wartime records. The questions are: who, and where?" She continued with the search. "Haider was involved with material reserves, which might mean anything from tanks and planes to salt and pepper."

After spending another half-hour on futile searches, Jana decided that during the war, Haider, as an overseer to the Czechs and Slovaks, would have had nothing to do with tanks or guns. The Czechs had none, and the only Slovaks who had been conscripted for the German side were on the Eastern Front fighting the Soviets. The Nazis would not have been concerned with food supplies for the Czechs and Slovaks. As far as they were concerned, all the Slavs could die and the world would be a better place for National Socialism. Haider's jurisdiction had to be items vital to the Nazi war effort—iron ore, coal—anything that would benefit their war machine and which they could plunder from a subservient nation.

Kroslak had told his lover Willem Albert that he was coming to Prague to find a *record*. He could not have meant anything but an official record, considering the report that he had left behind him, a record that was so important that a series of murders had probably occurred because it had been found. Who would be the successor, the heir and keeper of all the Nazi records abandoned in the Czech Republic?

Jana finally zeroed in on the present-day Czech Department of Industry and Trade, and then the Ministry for Regional Development. Under the subheading of Administration of State Material Resources she saw an additional subheading, Records Management and Archives. It was as close as she could come.

They drove back nearly to the center of Prague, found a parking place to leave the car, then walked into the Stare Mesto area, stopping to have a quick hot chocolate to keep Jana's stomach from growling. When the rain became a heavy downpour, they purchased a large man's umbrella and shared it while walking to Staromesteke Namestie, the center of the area, and entered Number 16, an ornate Gothic structure like most of the buildings in this sector of Prague. The signs in the building directed them to the basement and a warren of offices. They finally found a small sign that announced RECORDS AND ARCHIVES. It led them to the rear of the basement.

There appeared to be no one tending the archives. The professor loudly called for a clerk. An extremely short woman came from deep in the shelves of records that filled the cavernous back area.

"*Prominte*," she excused herself. Her voice was high, almost like the chirping of a bird. "We have a buzzer on the door to announce visitors, but the system has a short." She climbed up on a special ladder-stool. "You're here to see a record?"

"It may be in the archives," suggested Jana. She handed the little lady the report that had been signed by Bruno Haider. "We're looking for the original and any communications that might have originated from or to Mr. Haider around the period of the date near his signature."

The woman scanned the report and looked up, slightly bewildered. "This isn't in Czech. I can't read it."

"Neither can we. So we'd like a name search for him. Hopefully, some of the documents may be catalogued under his name. Perhaps under State Material Reserves for the Protectorates of Bohemia and Moravia, or perhaps under Special Adviser in Research Management to Slovakia. Both would be under the Nazi occupation."

"Some years back, we put everything for that period of time on microfiche." She looked a little doubtful. "You want *all* of the microfiche for that period?"

"Just the ones that might be associated with Haider or the Adviser for State Material Reserves or Special Adviser for Slovakia."

"Odd you should ask about this. In the three years I've been here, we've had two requests for these items: one by a man about two months ago, and another by a woman just yesterday."

"Yesterday?"

"Yes."

"Can you describe the woman who inquired yesterday?"

"Taller than I am, but most people are. Let's say petite. A little too much makeup. Dark skin."

A picture of Paola appeared in Jana's mind.

"Was she blonde?" Jana asked.

"Blonde," the clerk nodded. "You know her?"

"Perhaps. Did she speak with an Italian accent?"

"We spoke in English. I can't distinguish one accent from another in English, except for people in American movies who are supposed to come from their South. *Soouuthh*," she drawled, trying to imitate the accent.

"One of them?" the professor whispered.

"Yes," Jana reluctantly agreed. "Did she go through all the records on microfiche?" she asked the clerk.

"She didn't have to," the clerk responded.

"Why?"

"She asked me for the microfiche that the man who was here two months ago had viewed."

"Do you know the man's name?"

The woman checked a sign-in log. "His name was Kroslak."

"Did the blonde-haired woman leave a name?"

The woman again checked the log. "Donna Bourg. She had Austrian credentials."

"False," said Jana.

"False?" parroted the little woman.

"The fiche you pulled, that's all she looked at?"

"Yes."

"Did she copy anything?"

"She did. But not this report. She copied everything on the fiche using our reproduction machine." The woman edged off her stool, then copied a list of numbers from a large ledger, went to a row of wall cabinets in which the microfiche were stored, and pulled out several box containers. She came back to Jana and the professor with a stricken look on her face.

"These microfiche are missing," she announced.

"You're sure?"

"I'm sure."

"Did you put them back yesterday?"

"I put everything back." Her hand went to her mouth as if trying to stifle what she was about to say. "I'm going to be held responsible for their loss." Tears appeared in her eyes.

"I'm sure it was not your fault," the professor tried to reassure her.

"Did you make any other copies of the material that was reproduced?" Jana asked, hoping against hope that there might be even a partial record of what had been taken.

The woman thought about it, then nodded.

"I automatically make one copy to ensure the machine is functioning properly. The reproduction machine makes a record of all copies, so I have to keep the proof copy and save it with the other proofs. We charge for all copies, and the administration wants to make sure we're not cheating, so I have to account for all copies with either money charged for the copies, or the proofs."

She ran to a pile of papers next to the reproduction machine, then pulled out a sheet, hurrying back to them. She thrust the single sheet of paper at Jana.

"Here it is."

There was a small sign on the wall indicating the amount charged for the reproductions of a single sheet of paper. Jana dug out some change, laying it on the table.

"For this copy."

The woman examined the coins, then scooped up the change. "Thank you. But what am I going to tell my supervisors about the lost records?"

"Report the person who stole them to the administration. They'll tell the police," suggested the professor.

"A pencil and paper, please," Jana asked the woman.

The clerk slid a small sheet of notepaper and a pen over to Jana. Jana wrote Paola's name, the full name of Europol, the address, and the telephone number on the piece of paper, then slid the pen and paper back to the clerk. "That's the thief."

The woman read the word "Europol."

"Why would she steal?" the woman asked. "Isn't she a police officer?"

"Ask her," the professor volunteered.

"A good idea," Jana agreed.

Jana stepped away from the counter, standing directly under a ceiling light to read the copy the clerk had given her. It was in German, so it took Jana a few minutes to understand what was written. It was the beginning of a query letter to a list of German personnel asking for an assessment of the natural resources that were available in their countries. The list included virtually everything the German war machine needed. The Nazis were searching the occupied countries for booty, ready to seize their natural resources to keep German industry going.

Jana checked the date on the document. It was two months earlier than the other "Romanian" report that had been signed by Haider. Jana was sure that the document that Peter had hidden away was at least one of the responses to the original order that they'd just uncovered.

Jana explained what she had translated. The professor was perplexed.

"What does it all mean? Why are people still hunting for these documents, so many years later? Why kill for these pieces of paper?"

Jana still had no answers to these questions.

Chapter 34

J ana and the professor entered the lobby of a five-star hotel two blocks away from the records center. She wrote down the number of one of the hotel's public telephones, then from another of the phones in the hotel called the general who had set up the sting operation that had gone so badly the day before. When he got on the line, she told him to call her back as quickly as possible, using a telephone other than his own office land line or his cell phone to avoid any possible taps. She gave him the other number she had copied down, then hung up.

Within five minutes, he was on the second phone, using the interior minister's personal phone. Just to make sure to avoid any "quick" taps being made on that line, Jana told him they could only talk for five minutes.

"What happened yesterday to the guardians you said would watch over us?"

"Defective equipment."

"I don't believe that," Jana informed him.

"Neither do I," he responded. "The tracking equipment failed after it had been checked out. It had to have been tampered with."

"You know all the people who had access to it?"

"Yes."

"It had to be one of them."

"I concur."

"Do you have photos of the people involved?"

"I can get them."

"Bring them when we meet." She related what had happened the night before. "We were attacked by three men." She gave him the names of the two Europol cops who had participated in the attack. "There was a third man with them. I haven't seen him before. I think he may have been one of your men."

"The way things have gone, that's possible." He muttered a quiet curse. "No, judging from everything, it's quite probable."

"I struck your man on the head. Did any of your men come in with a wound? Perhaps one of your officers was in pain, acting as if he had a hangover?"

There was a moment of silence. "One of my men called in sick. He had access to the equipment. I'll bring his photo."

Jana told him about what had occurred at the archives unit, giving him Paola's name.

There was another quiet curse from the chief. Jana looked on the bright side of events. "The sting wasn't a complete failure. We now have three of them identified, with a possible fourth if the photo fits."

Jana could hear the frustration in the general's voice. "I'm not so sure. By the time anyone gets around to questioning them, they'll all have plausible reasons for what they were doing. They'll claim it was part of an investigation. Or that they were after *you* as a suspect. We don't have enough on them yet." He paused, this time taking an audible breath. "I have more bad news."

"What?"

"Kroslak. He's dead."

It took Jana a while to recover from this blow. Martin

Kroslak had been a good man. She had hoped that he would make it out of this alive. Jana fleetingly wondered how Kroslak's young lover in Amsterdam was going to take the news. Not well. She felt sorry for both men.

Now their task was going to be even harder. Even worse, she was not sure she and the professor themselves were going to make it out alive.

"How did he die?"

"Ligature strangulation."

Jana thought of Gizela Dinova, the ligature around her neck, her eyes almost popping from their sockets.

"Your agent Dinova was killed like that. I think one of them from The Hague did this as well."

"Kroslak had been dead for only a short time."

"Was he killed yesterday, when the professor and I were out walking?"

"Probably."

"Perhaps that's why they dropped us and didn't pick us up again until the evening at the club. His death was more important than ours. So they took him first."

"Be very careful, Commander. I have to believe that you are now the first item of business on their murder list."

"That depends on who else they have on their list. Have you looked in a mirror lately?"

"Not very funny," the general said.

"It wasn't meant to be funny."

There was silence on the other end of the phone.

"I want to view the body. Call the coroner's office and tell them that we're coming. I also want access to any of his personal effects that were recovered."

There was a grunt of acquiescence.

"I also want you to call Colonel Trokan in Slovakia."

"After what's happened, I'm not sure he'll take my call."

"Tell him to go to Vienna and register at 'our' hotel. He'll know where it is. I want him there tomorrow. Tell him it's a matter of my life if he is not there. I'll contact him."

There was another grunt of agreement.

"I want to thank you for all hospitality we've received in Prague. It was a pleasure."

The phone stayed silent.

"That was a joke," she informed him, hanging up.

Jana sat at the phone, trying to come to grips with what she'd learned. The professor took in her body posture and the expression on her face.

"He told you something very bad, didn't he?" the professor asked.

"Kroslak, the man we were looking for, is dead."

The professor considered what she'd said. "Does that mean we can go home now?"

"Not quite yet. We have a stop to make at the morgue. Then a brief meeting at a street corner, and then *dovidenia* to Prague."

"I would have hoped you would think of a nicer place to go than the morgue."

"Mr. Kroslak would appreciate the attention we are going to give him."

"Do I have to look at his body?"

"No."

The professor attempted to cheer himself up as they left the hotel, humming an off-key tune, trying to take the bad news in his stride, pretending just like so many professionals do when they encountered this sort of setback. Jana thought about her own feelings. It was never easy,

Even more worrisome, sometimes things got even worse.

Chapter 35

Prague's morgue, just like any morgue in a big city, was cold and dreary and very ugly. No perfume that had ever been made could take away the odors in the air or the anguish that had seeped into the walls. Jana and the professor tried to ignore the quick pang of depression they felt as the attendant took them through the halls to the back where the dead were kept. He selected the tray that had the number corresponding to the name Kroslak on his list, then slid the metal gurney out on its rollers and lifted the plastic sheet away so Jana could view the body. The professor hung back, refusing to look at the dead man.

Jana remembered the last photo she'd seen of Kroslak, taken during promotional evaluations in Slovakia. Hard to compare a picture from a few years back with the body in the drawer, but the high forehead and prominent ears were there, and a mole in the very center of his chin gave her enough to convince her that it was him. "Yes, it's Kroslak," she said, more to herself than to the attendant.

The ligature had been removed, leaving a huge red welt. She quickly checked his face, then the rest of his body. His face was badly bruised, nose broken, large contusions on his body. Several of his ribs must have been broken, probably as the result of kicks. Kroslak had sustained a vicious beating before he'd been garroted. The people who had attacked him with such ferocity might have been trying to force information from him; but from the widespread bruising and the other injuries, Kroslak had been savaged simply to inflict injuries on him. The people who had murdered Kroslak had wanted to hurt him, to avenge themselves on an individual who had been close to them and who had then placed them in jeopardy.

Jana took a last look at the body before the attendant closed the drawer. She wanted to commit to memory what he looked like after the murderers had been through with him. She would remember Kroslak and Gizela Dinova and the professor's nephew . . . and Peter. There were accounts to settle.

The attendant led them into the property office. A coroner's report had already been laid out for her. Nothing found by the coroner during the autopsy contradicted Jana's observations. She tucked the report into her shoulder bag, then gave her attention to the tray which held the property recovered from Kroslak: A wallet without cash, perhaps emptied to make it look like a robbery. Several coins. A cheap digital wristwatch, still running. Crumpled tissues; a cancelled tram ticket; reading glasses, which had been smashed; and a fountain pen. Jana fixed on the pen immediately. It was a sister to the pen that Kroslak used to leave with Willem Albert, the pen in which Kroslak left his love notes for the young man. She picked it up, opened the cap, and tested the nib on a piece of paper. No ink. She unscrewed the barrel of the pen, turned it upside down over the counter top, and shook it. A small roll of microfilm emerged. Jana felt a sudden sense of euphoria. Kroslak had left a posthumous "love" note for her.

Jana kept the microfilm and the pen. She and the professor then drove to the intersection where she had instructed the general to meet them. Jana parked, as the skies opened up and the rain began to pour down.

"The heavens are crying for us," observed the professor.

"No. Crying for the dead. The gods expect us to take care of ourselves."

She saw the general walk across the intersection, carrying a briefcase. He had brought an umbrella but the wind turned it inside out, and he was getting soaked. Following her instructions, he stopped at the corner and stood there for several minutes as the rain pelted down. Jana scanned the street where he'd come from. No car had slowed down or parked. She checked her watch once more. At the exact time she had given him, he began walking again. Jana waited, watching him, checking for anyone following him. She pulled her car out of its parking slot, passing the general, and parked a full block ahead. Again, she scanned the street.

It was time to make contact. She made a U-turn and parked facing in the opposite direction. Again, no one followed. As the general walked along the other side of the street, Jana beeped the car horn. He waved at her, then angled across the street to Jana's window.

"I'm going to die of pneumonia," he grumbled.

"Better than death from a bullet or strangulation."

He unsnapped his briefcase, pulled out a manila envelope, and handed it to her.

"Five photographs."

Jana took them out and examined them. She immediately picked out the man. He was smiling at the photographer as if he didn't have a care in the world.

"This is the man from the club." Jana handed the photograph to the general.

"You're sure."

"Very sure," she said.

The general cursed. "I'll stop by his apartment to pay my respects to the sick. Before I'm through, he will have an even bigger headache than the one you gave him when you pistol-whipped the son of a bitch."

The wind suddenly whipped the umbrella out of the general's hands, and he scurried after it, bending down at the rear of her car to retrieve it. He walked back to her, trying to straighten it out.

"They build them to break. That way, you have to buy another one." Jana put the car in gear. "I'll be in touch, General."

She pulled away from the curb, leaving him still standing in the rain.

Jana drove a circuitous route through the city, making doubly sure they weren't being followed, then headed for the highway that would take them on the road to the south.

"Where are we going?" the professor asked.

"Austria," Jana informed him.

"Why Austria?" the professor asked.

"Because I've always liked Vienna."

The professor grumbled. "I hoped we were going home."

"One more small stop, then maybe Bratislava."

"I don't like the word *maybe*."

"Professor, keep good thoughts in your mind and imagine yourself sitting in front of a fire, drinking a glass of warm plum brandy. If the elements are kind, we will be there before you know it."

Jana eased her foot down on the accelerator, the car surging forward.

Good-bye, Prague; hello, Vienna. She kept that thought in mind.

Chapter 36

They were on the road for an hour before the car appeared in the rearview mirror. It remained a substantial distance back in its lane. The car was pacing them, seemingly content to stay behind them at a certain distance. She would speed up; it would speed up. She would slow down; the car behind them followed suit. They were being shadowed.

The professor had produced a deck of cards from some hidden pocket and was now putting them through their paces, using a variety of shuffles which would warn any wary onlooker that this was not a person with whom one wanted to play cards. Every once in a while the professor would blunder, the cards would fall, or his shuffling was clumsy, but on the whole he was doing a very fine imitation of a card shark.

"Four aces," he said; and peeled four aces from the top of the deck. "Four kings," he intoned, peeling four kings off.

"Impressive," Jana complimented him, glancing nervously in the mirror.

"Not to another card man. My fingers are stiff, I have no touch, and my riffs are all rusty from disuse. As a magician, I am not up to showtime speed. It's all about age. You fumble."

"Did you do lots of card tricks in your act?" Jana eyed

the reflection in the mirror. The car was still pacing them. "I thought you did illusions."

"I did illusions, mind-reading, anything that I managed to fool myself into thinking the audience would appreciate. After all, that's what it's all about, making the public like you. Singer, dancer, acrobat, magician, all the acts are the same. We need to please the people who pay the money and fill the seats. No different than good bacon. If the customer likes the way you smoke the bacon, they tell other people, who also buy the bacon. It was the same with us: we please them, they buy, their relatives buy, their friends buy, and pretty soon everybody's eating your bacon."

"I'm not sure I like your comparison."

"Good. I didn't actually like comparing myself to bacon. Who wants to be a piece of fat in a bad stew?"

He dropped a card, made a rude noise, stopped, then tried again.

"I retired. Then, suddenly, bang! I was no longer a Clown Professor of Magic. It was time to take off the makeup." He did a particularly complex shuffle, and the cards flowed in and out of each other. "Not bad," he complimented himself. "Some of the skill is still there, peeking out."

"We're being followed, Professor."

He continued playing with the cards.

"Aren't you bothered with the fact that we're being followed, Professor?"

"Not yet."

"Why not?"

"You don't have that particular note of urgency in your voice that signifies that someone is about to try to kill us."

She flicked a glance at the mirror. The car following was still there. A road sign flashed past overhead, listing the cities and towns coming up in the next stretch of highway. Jana glanced at the fuel gauge. They would need to make a stop soon.

"I'm glad to hear that you have such trust in my ability to sense danger. Unfortunately, that doesn't mean that I can save us."

The professor shrugged. "If you can't, then I can't, so what would be the purpose of my wasting time by worrying?"

They drove on in silence for a number of kilometers.

"Are they still there?" he inquired.

"Still there," she confirmed.

The professor finally put the pack of cards away. A coin appeared in his hands. He began playing with it, making it disappear, reappear, roll through his fingers. As with the cards, he would make the occasional mistake, mumble his disappointment at his clumsiness, then rework the trick.

"Professor, all magic is deception and artifice, correct?"

"All of it, although I once met a man on the Island of Malta who could do a few things I never figured out, so I'm cautious in my answer. Never make a final judgment. It saves you grief in the long run." He let out a staccato laugh. "I do have one question, though: why are they content to stay behind us, Commander Matinova?"

"I don't know. There's another question, even more intriguing: how did they find us? I used all the right techniques. I doubled back, watched for all the signs to indicate that we were under surveillance, and then, despite my precautions, that pest suddenly appears, crawling along behind us. One would think it's magic, except we both concur there is no such thing as real magic . . . with the exclusion, perhaps of the man on Malta."

"Agreed."

An ornate road sign announced their imminent arrival in "Ceske Budejovice, the Crown of South Bohemia" in five kilometers.

"They make Budvar there. It's a good beer," the professor said.

"We have to stop for benzene, not beer."

"Why not get both?" The professor licked his lips in anticipation. "Thirst has to be quenched."

"And curiosity has to be satisfied," Jana responded. The off-road ramp was coming up. "There is an answer to everything," Jana declared rather cryptically. "Even to magic." Jana turned onto the ramp. A short distance from the E49, Jana pulled in to a large service station. She got out of the car with her bag hanging from her shoulder, her automatic easily accessible, and checked the surrounding area.

They were near a confluence of rivers, the water flowing past a conglomeration of Gothic buildings fringing the gas station, a clear contrast between their decaying elegance and the grime of the modern benzene station. Jana tried to block out the concrete of the station for the moment, focusing on the adjacent century-old buildings. They projected a sense of peace which, unfortunately, did not match Jana's need for readiness. Something was coming down the road after them, and she had no time to enjoy the scenery.

Jana stationed herself at the rear of their car, waiting for the following vehicle to pull off after them. After a few minutes, Jana realized the vehicle hadn't turned off the highway. Perhaps she had been wrong about it?

No, everything told her that the auto that had been behind them was intentionally following them. Jana waited a few more seconds, then pulled the pump handle from its hanger, filled the tank of the BMW, and went into the office to pay, keeping a close watch on the service area of the station through the plate-glass window. She also picked up some packaged sandwiches, candy bars, and two large bottles of water. Jana paid the cashier, then walked back to the BMW. No cars had driven in from the highway. Jana dropped the package of food in the professor's lap.

"I thought we were going to get a beer."

"It's not time to celebrate just yet, Professor."

Jana walked to the rear of the driver's side and leaned down to feel around the wheel well of the tire. Almost immediately she felt the small protrusion and pulled it away from the metal.

"I found the secret to their magic trick." She dropped the metal disc she'd removed from the wheel well into his lap. "A transponder. This little object has been transmitting our location to the ladies or gentlemen who have been following us. It was inside the tire well."

The professor examined it with an expression of distaste, then handed it back to her.

"How could they have put the miserable little creature in the well? They had no opportunity."

"What's the secret of all good magic, professor? Misdirection. Think back. What was the one moment when I could have been misdirected enough for someone to place a bug on the car while we were in the vehicle?"

The professor thought for a moment.

"Of course!" The professor slapped himself on the forehead. "I should have seen it."

"We only see when we look, Professor."

"The police general!"

"When he *lost* his umbrella in the rain, it blew to the rear of the car, and he went back and picked it up . . . at the same time planting the bug. Voila!"

"Not too professional, was he?" the professor growled.

"He almost fooled us."

"*Almost* is not good enough." He wagged his finger in the air, looking grim. "He's one of them!"

"Probably."

"We have proof positive."

"Conceivably his men are following us to give us protection."

"I don't believe it."

"Good," Jana nodded her approval. "Trusting people may be good; mistrusting them is even better."

She saw a vehicle drive up the pumps next to them. Jana tensed, then relaxed when the driver got out of his car and walked into the office. Jana toyed with the idea of placing the transponder inside the wheel well of the other vehicle to lead their "followers" onto a false trail, then decided against it. The professor could see what she was thinking.

"Why not?" he asked.

"They'd quickly find out. If they think their bug is still safely hidden in the BMW, they'll be content to follow where it leads."

"They could try to kill us at any time."

"They haven't, though. Why? They're herding us. I think they want us to lead them to someone. Someone they want perhaps more than us."

"Who?"

"I'm going to meet Colonel Trokan in Vienna. They know that. They just don't know where. Trokan is the key man running the investigation against them. He's supervised the whole thing: me, Peter, Kroslak. So they want to get Trokan. They're looking for that one unguarded moment on Trokan's part in which to kill him. I think they're depending on me to lead them to him."

She turned on the ignition, pulling out of the station onto the highway.

"So, what are we going to do?"

"Lead them to him."

Jana checked the rearview mirror. The same car was back in position. It had pulled off the highway and waited for Jana to get on with her journey so they could continue their game of follow-the-leader to Vienna.

Jana settled back in her seat, focusing on the road ahead.

Chapter 37

They rolled into Vienna with the professor asleep in the front seat. He was gently snoring, and Jana thought he looked cute curled up in the seat, so relaxed that she hesitated to wake him. She drove through the streets, eventually realizing that she would have to rouse him as they approached the Ringstrasse, the demarcation line between the outskirts and the inner ring of the once-fabled capital of the Hapsburg Empire. She shook him, and he sat upright, blinking at the sight of the buildings, realizing that they were in *Wien*.

"Very nice driving," he complimented. "Quick."

"It's always quick from Prague."

He swiveled to look through the rear window. "Too many cars. I don't know which is theirs."

"We'll find out soon enough. However, we have to lose them to find them."

He blinked, not understanding.

"Are you fully awake?" Jana asked.

He shook himself for a few seconds, then smoothed his hair back from the tangle he had created. "My blood has been fully energized, and I am now completely alert and ready to take on the world. What do I have to do?"

"I want you to collapse, Professor."

"Collapse?"

"Yes. You're going to have a fit on the street. I want

you to rant, rave, whatever one does when they are having a fit. You are going to drop to the sidewalk, frothing at the mouth, while a crowd gathers and the police and the emergency medical people arrive. They are then going to cart you off to a hospital, where they will put you under observation for the next ten or twelve hours."

He stared at her, his jaw open with surprise. "You want me to . . . perform?"

"A good word for it, Professor."

"And what do you do?"

"I escape."

"Leaving me behind?"

"I need a distraction, Professor. No, I need misdirection," she said, putting it in his terms so he'd see what she meant. "We've talked about it enough. They look at you and I identify them, and then I use the commotion to get away so I can meet Trokan. It's not healthy for Colonel Trokan to have them peering over my shoulder, taking aim at him. After the meeting, I'll come for you at the hospital."

"I don't like it!"

"Professor, we have to find a way to give them pause, even for a few seconds. That's all I'll need. You're the one who has to do this; I have no one else. Besides, you're the performer. I'm not."

He mulled it over. "I used to perform for pay." He looked at her meaningfully, a sly smile eventually appearing. He presented his cheek, pointing at it. "So, I'm waiting."

She kissed him on the cheek.

"One more," he insisted.

Jana kissed him again.

"I told you that old men like younger women. What I didn't tell you was that once in a while they also like to be kissed." He sat back in his seat, a satisfied look on his face. "Having been paid, I am now ready to perform."

Jana smiled. The professor was a very nice man.

She looked for a parking space on the street, then saw one marked NO PARKING. They were not going to need the car, now that they'd reached Vienna; so Jana surveyed the street, saw the requisite number of pedestrians, then parked in the prohibited zone.

"Performance time, Professor. Wait for me to cue you." They both got out of their automobile, Jana leaving the key in the ignition to make it easier for the police when they came to impound it.

The professor began rubbing his hands. "I always do this before a presentation. The heart pumps faster, the nerves become acute, all the senses are poised."

"Stop walking for a moment, but keep talking."

They stopped, Jana moving to face him, looking over his shoulder to see what their trackers were doing. A vehicle had stopped behind them. Three people were getting out. They were close enough to identify. Ryan, the Irishman whom Aidan Walsh despised, was first out of the vehicle, followed by Walsh himself. So much for their dislike of one another. A charade. They were close enough now to suggest they didn't mind committing murder together.

The third person out of the car was Paola Rossi.

Jana had known that Paola was one of them since their visit to the archives, but had hoped against hope that she was not. So much for "hopes" and "wishes." Paola was ready to commit murder with the others.

Their car continued up the street, passing Jana and the professor. Gyorgi Ilica was the driver. The pack that stays together murders together, Jana thought.

The professor was gabbling something that Jana could not understand.

"Esperanto," he explained, seeing her lack of comprehension. "You said keep talking. I couldn't think of what to say. That was Lesson One of Esperanto, or at least a part of it. It's how to order a kidney pie. I learned it in England."

"A man of many talents."

"Many," the professor agreed.

She and the professor began strolling again.

"Take a few more steps, stagger, then go into your act. Don't be surprised when I scream."

"Do you scream loudly, Commander Matinova?"

"Loud enough, Professor."

He took a breath, preparing. "Be well, Jana Matinova."

"The same to you, Professor."

The professor abruptly gasped, clutched at his throat, and moaned, the volume gradually increasing. Suddenly he collapsed, his body going into spasms, his eyes fluttering, spittle coming out of his mouth. Jana screamed as loudly as she could. The passersby anxiously looked around for the danger. Almost immediately they realized that the professor was on the pavement, shuddering, having what appeared to be a grand mal seizure. One or two of them tried to aid the sick man. Jana shouted in German for someone to call an ambulance, then immediately pushed her way through the circle of onlookers to the doorway of a shop. The people who had gathered around the professor effectively blocked her trackers from seeing Jana dart inside. She ran past the clerks who had come to the front of the store, through the back door, and into an alley. She hopped on a streetcar before the people who were following her even realized she was gone.

Within ten minutes, the Austrians, who have the most efficient medical services in Europe, had an ambulance at the site. They quickly loaded the professor onto a stretcher and had him in the ambulance within moments, sirening their way through the streets to Allgemeines Krankenhaus, the largest hospital on the continent. There was no question that he was going to get superlative treatment.

As for Jana, she took the tram all the way to Lerchenfelder Strasse, at the opposite edge of the Ring. She jumped off the tram when she spotted a large photography store that advertised reproductions. She checked the street to make sure that the car carrying the thugs, as she now thought of them, had not been able to follow her, and then walked inside.

The clerk she was served by officiously explained that the microfilm that Jana showed him would take some time to reproduce, going into a long technical explanation, only running down when Jana held up her hand and asked him to stop. "What's the quickest way to reproduce enlarged copies from microfilm? I want them on a standard-size sheet of Xerox paper."

"I can project and scan it. That should take only a few minutes, but will cost more, and that type of reproduction is not the best, so I can't guarantee—"

Jana slapped the counter top. "Do it!"

The clerk ran to the back where his equipment was. In ten minutes, he reappeared with the microfilm in one hand and the Xerox-size copies in the other. He put them in an envelope, quoting the cost. Jana threw enough money on the counter top to cover it and jogged out of the store.

She walked to a small green area just off Lange Gasse and, perhaps to spite the Austrian dislike of anyone sitting on their park grass, or in response to her own need to relax in the simplest way possible, she sat on the lawn with her back against a lamp post and read the pages. She read them several times to make sure she had digested everything, then put all the paperwork back into the envelope and into her purse. She looked at her hand when she tucked the envelope away. It had a slight tremor. What she had learned over the past few days was so dreadful that it made her feel sick. It was truly bad, ugly to such a degree that Jana knew it would affect the way she looked at her world from now on.

Policemen learn not to trust. They learn that lesson over and over. It's part of the bad side of being a police officer. This was one of those times for her.

Chapter 38

Jana called the Post Hotel, where she knew the colonel was staying, leaving a message for "Mr. Palicka" to meet her in an hour in the Schwedenplatz—Swedish Square—on the bank of the Danube Canal. She walked there at a brisk pace, glad to be able to engage in physical activity after so many hours of being cooped up in the car. The air was still crisp, perfect weather for striding through the city. The swarms of tourists were smaller then those in Prague, and less pushy, but the crowds on streets still provided anonymity. and she was at the square in less than a half-hour, giving her time to kill. Jana purchased an ice cream cone from an Italian ice cream parlor that advertised, both in German and English, the best ice cream in Austria, and slowly savored the cone while looking over the edge of the canal, watching people board a riverboat that gradually filled up and finally set sail down the Danube's concrete tributary.

As the time for the colonel's arrival approached, Jana surveyed the square, looking for any possible stalkers lurking in the nooks and crannies of the buildings, wondering, as well, what kind of problems the colonel was going to bring with him. She was carrying a very disturbing message for him in her handbag. The colonel knew that there was trouble with Europol, but he had no idea of the extent of the problem.

The hour she had given the colonel came and went. Jana waited for an additional thirty minutes. She was preparing to give up when she saw Trokan enter the square. He was hurrying, with two other men, one on either side of him, alertly scanning the people they were passing. They were bodyguards. Jana recognized both men immediately, Benco and Elias, both of them officers from her division. Not Elias, she reminded herself. He was now "temporarily" assigned to the anti-corruption group investigating the deaths of Peter and the professor's nephew. For the colonel to choose them to be his personal guards meant that he was now keenly aware of his danger. What Jana had to tell him would raise the threat level even further.

She watched the men walk to Laurenzberg, on one side of the square, then go down the steps and into the Griechenbeisi, a small Greek bar. Jana waited for a few more minutes to make sure they'd not been followed, then went after them, pausing only to follow the custom of throwing a coin down an open cellar door for good luck before she entered the bar proper. The colonel was sitting in the back of the bar, the two officers closer to the entrance, watching for any intruder.

Jana gave each man a brief nod and walked back to the colonel, sat next to him, and ordered a glass of wine.

"How are things at home, Mr. Palicka?"

"Not so well, thank you."

"I'm glad you remembered the name. I was worried."

"Palicka was my father-in-law. Hard to forget him. I remember when we came here with him. All he did was lecture me on why I should be nicer to his youngest daughter, ignoring the fact that she had begun the now long-standing habit of bombarding me with whatever was handy for her to throw."

"Are the demonstrations in Bratislava ending?"

"The furor about the nationalization of the oil field is fading away. Everybody is now counting the money that they think will be coming directly into the nation's pockets instead of the oil company's. The prime minister and the minister of economics are being beatified as national heroes." He took a sip of his beer. "It's good to see you still in one piece, Jana."

Their conversation took on a jocular tone, one they practiced when events were becoming grave, a buffer against their rising uncertainties.

"And I'm glad to see you without any unexpected marks of recent medical treatment, Colonel. I assume the two gentlemen are guarding you as a result of a threat or an actual attempt to kill you?"

"A bomb. Why is it that when assassins go after a high official, they invariably try to kill him with explosives rather than shoot him?"

"I hadn't realized that." Jana very carefully kept her shock at the news of the attempted bomb attack off her face, only a raised eyebrow signaling her concern.

"Maybe they don't use explosives with everybody. But whenever some individual comes after me, he tries to blow me up.

"My driver took the car to run an errand for me. Boom! His wife was very upset."

"Reasonable that his wife would be upset."

"He was a nice young man." Trokan took a sip of his drink, his tone changing. "The word on the street is that I am a dead man walking. My wife is now living at her mother's, and I'm moving from place to place to make it harder for them, whoever they are. I was hoping that you might have information that might save your colonel's body from being mutilated."

Jana pulled the papers out of her purse and laid them in front of him.

"Kroslak found that they have committed a total of at least twenty-eight murders to date. There are probably more that he did not find. He is now one of the dead, so there are at least twenty-nine homicides."

"They found him in Prague?"

"Yes."

"I'm sorry for him."

"Feeling sorrow is the least we can do."

"The very least."

He began reading, suddenly sucking in a breath from the shock of what he was reading on the first sheet of paper. "From what I understand," Jana continued, "they killed individuals in a number of countries in Europe and Africa, and two in Brazil, one in Argentina and, for good measure, one in Washington. A rather odd assemblage of numbers for a group of police officers who are charged with keeping everyone safe. It appears that a part of Europol has become a corporate conglomerate whose main product is murder."

The colonel went on to the next sheet of paper, as Jana continued her narrative.

"According to the figures that Kroslak discovered, they have earned a total of approximately nine million euros for the murders they've carried out. Not a bad return for their time. And no taxes to pay. A very successful business venture, which is a good reason for them to want us dead. Who knows, perhaps they're considering expanding? That's what a good businessman does."

The colonel angrily went on to the next page, reading it

with a restless energy, his tension apparent in slight body movements.

"You're squirming, Colonel."

"I'm upset."

"So am I."

"It gets worse with every page I read."

"I know." Jana felt her own anger beginning to build. She forced herself to remain calm, to keep her voice steady. "Most of the people they killed were either corporate or government officials. There are also three police officers on the roll of the dead."

"Maly from the Czech Republic. I knew him well. A good man. The Englishman, Abbot, was an expert in corporate fraud. I attended a seminar he gave. A very bright person. The third one, the American police officer, I know nothing about."

"The Americans will tell us."

"Then they'll demand that we take immediate action, probably forgetting to thank us for discovering the crimes at the risk of our own lives."

He turned back a page to note the payment for the particular killing. "Two hundred and twenty-five thousand dollars to kill the American. A bargain at twice the price," he noted sarcastically.

"Your name is listed."

"I saw. Not a great deal of money for the killers to murder me. I'm embarrassed that I'm worth so little. At least I'm worth more than the American."

"Something to be proud of. When this is over, I'll have to remember to tell all the troops."

He made a rude noise, then continued to read.

"The killings of the university student and your friend Peter are not listed."

"Kroslak went on the run. There was no time left for him to investigate those murders. My name isn't on the list, but they're after me as well."

More paper rattled as the colonel read through the last of the pages.

"Titans of business, political leaders. Paymasters for the killings." Jana leaned back in her seat. "Who better to hire to do your dirty work than the police who either will be called on to investigate the crime or have access to the information about the progress of the investigation of the crime? If the investigators are the killers, that's the end of the investigation." Jana sipped her wine. "They didn't count on Kroslak and his computer."

"How did he learn about them?"

"I think they tried to recruit him. They revealed information to bring him on board. He would have gone along with them, all the while looking for the evidence that could hang them. The information they gave him led to other information, other killings, other paymasters, until he put the package together for us."

The colonel leafed back to one of the prior pages he'd read.

"There is no paymaster listed for my killing."

"Kroslak ran out of time. He was still searching, which is why he went to Prague. They got him before he could come up with all the answers."

"He was a good cop."

"And a good man," Jana added.

"Can you pick up the investigation?" he asked.

Jana thought about her answer. "In Slovakia, you said I wasn't the appropriate person for the job."

"I also said that if we didn't get anywhere, I'd come back to you."

"I take it that Elias hasn't come up with anything?"

"Nothing."

"I can pick up the investigation," she assured him. "Actually, I never stopped."

"I assumed you wouldn't." He riffled through the papers. "I'd like your promise not to get killed."

"My promise won't be worth much if I'm dead."

"Take Elias with you. Brief him. The insurance man, Fico, is in Vienna. Elias was going to interview him. I've already told Elias you're back on the case."

"Good."

The colonel looked at the papers remaining in his hand.

"I don't understand this document."

"It's in Romanian. Peter had it."

"From Kroslak as well?"

"Kroslak had a copy."

"Get it translated."

"I've been trying."

"Try harder. I don't want to give them too much time to come after me again."

"Or me."

"Naturally."

He got up, scooping up most of the papers, leaving just the Romanian report, dropping money on the table for the drinks.

"My treat."

"This must be an unusual occasion."

He grimaced, then walked over to Elias, said a few words to him, and walked out. Benco gulped down the rest of his beer and trailed after him.

Chapter 39

They went to the address that Elias had for Fico, Suite 2 in a corner building on Gumpendorferstrasse. It took up the entire floor, a crisp, modern office that projected efficiency and prosperity. Except, surprisingly, at ten in the morning the office was absolutely empty of people, apart from a sallow young man with a thin moustache and a very small chin sitting at a front desk. A family photo on the edge of the desk indicated that he was at least temporarily trying to make himself at home. Reluctantly, he put down the book he'd been reading.

"What can I do for you?" The young man smiled half-heartedly. "No one else is in the office."

"I had an appointment with Mr. Fico," Elias told him as he handed him his card. "I made it two days ago."

The young man examined the card for a long moment, then handed it back to Elias. "We were bought out. There's no one else here," he repeated.

"Bought out by whom?" Jana asked.

"Another insurance-investigation group. I think they're Swiss. All I know is that they gave everyone five days off until the new management team arrives, except for me and my relief. We're supposed to look after the place, kind of. The phones have been rerouted, so they're dead, and I don't even have to answer them. I just sit."

"Fico?" Jana reminded him.

"He was a vice president of the old company. I'm not sure he'll be back. I heard the executives received bonuses to ensure their cooperation. None of the rest of us were given any extra pay. Which, I guess, is what happens in these things. The word is that there are going to be staff layoffs. So who knows who'll be back?"

"Mr. Fico was supposed to leave some material for us." Jana showed him her police badge. "We need it for an investigation we're conducting. It's imperative that we get it."

"I don't know how to get in touch with him."

"He does keep an office here, right?"

"Right." He pointed to the rear. "Back there. It has his name and title on the door. He got the office with the big window." He snickered. "He *used* to be an important man."

Jana began walking; Elias followed her.

"I'm not sure I'm supposed to let you go into his office," the young man called after them. He watched them continue toward the rear, shrugged, then went back to his reading.

Jana and Elias easily found Fico's office. It was locked. Jana nodded to Elias, who put his shoulder to the door and snapped the lock. They walked inside. A large picture window faced the street. A big wooden desk, plush executive chair, leather visitors' chairs in front of the desk, a hand-woven rug on the floor, and two very large oil paintings on the wall depicting famous Austrian battle scenes proclaimed executive importance. There were no papers on the desk or in the matching credenza and its wastebasket. The floor not covered by the rug had been recently waxed. The office and furniture were so clean, it looked as if it had been wiped down with an antiseptic. It was all ready for its new occupant.

"I talked to Fico yesterday," Elias confirmed. "He said nothing about the sale of the business, and confirmed our appointment to meet here."

"My thought is that the gentleman had no intention of keeping his appointment with you." Jana finished examining the desk, checking the computer as the last item on her list, turning it over, opening the bottom and looking inside. "No hard drive. It's been taken. They wanted to make sure there were no stray pieces of information left. Just like The Hague." She looked over the office. "I smell fear. The place is too well scrubbed. They even cleaned the walls."

"Your friends from The Hague?"

"It has to be. They came here and took the hard drive, and maybe Fico."

"They have him?"

"Perhaps," Jana said. "Or he's afraid of them and went on the run." She thought about what had happened to Kroslak when he was on the run, silently hoping the same thing hadn't happened to Fico. "You checked on the firm before you called Fico?"

"Of course. It's an independent insurance-investigation firm specializing in major cases on an international level, working for major insurers. They've been around for about ten years. From what I've been able to find out, they had a good reputation. In the comments I read, there were no rumors about the firm being up for sale."

"Our focus has to be Fico right now." She thought for a second. "There's another source of information. Firms keep a record of business trips executives take, with explanations of their expenses so they can bill for them. Fico will have left a paper trail in the accounting section. They'll also have a home address and phone number for him."

The two found the accounting section, then began going through the paperwork referring to Fico, finding his home address and phone number in Vienna. Then they began the much longer search for his caseload, his business trips and expenses. After a half-hour, the young man from the front desk appeared.

"I'll have to ask you to stop. I don't believe you're authorized to do this."

The two continued without pausing.

"If you don't stop, I'll have to call the police."

"Call Johann Swartzkopf at the *polizeiwache*. Ask for a direct line to him. He'll verify who we are," Jana told him. "Tell him it's Commander Jana Matinova." She continued with her search.

"I really think you have to stop until I get authorization."

Jana's voice became sharper. "You're interfering with a police investigation. Unless you want to be arrested, leave. *Schnell!*"

The young man ran out of the area.

"Who is Swartzkopf?" asked Elias.

"I've never heard of him," Jana admitted. "By the time the Austrian police give up on their search for a policeman named Swartzkopf, and by the time the young man comes back in here to face us with the fearsome fact that the police can't find a Johann Swartzkopf and he asks us to spell the name to make sure he got it right, we'll be through. So search."

They finished their search of the records and walked out, carrying several manila folders. The young man was on the phone. He set it down on its cradle as if afraid they might snatch if from his hands as they walked by. He glanced at the folders they were taking, but was too fearful to say anything about them.

Jana thanked him. "We appreciate your assistance."

"Have a good day," said Elias.

When they left the building, they walked several blocks, then stepped into a small *Imbiss-Stube* outside the Ring, ordered plates of rustic-style pumpkin soup and a glass of cheap Austrian white wine, then ate as they went over the papers they'd acquired.

Jana found ten locations in Fico's expense accounts that corresponded to sites where killings had taken place as indicated in the microfilmed Kroslak papers. The trips Fico had taken occurred at about the time of the killings. On a number of occasions, there had been multiple visits for "investigative purposes." On seven of those occasions, at different locations, the names of the victims listed on the Kroslak papers were mentioned. It was enough of a correlation for them to be certain that there was a connection between the killings and the insurance investigations. There was also a reference to Slovakia and to the approval of an insurance investigation, but there was no mention of the people who had been killed in Bratislava, or of the attempted murder of Colonel Trokan.

Perhaps Fico had not yet submitted his latest expense reimbursement request along with reasons for the expenses.

They took a taxi to Fico's home. If they were lucky, and Fico was cooperative, they might be able to put the whole scheme together, utilizing his information in conjunction with theirs.

They arrived just as the fire department finished putting out a blaze that had gutted Fico's apartment, but before the coroner's office carted off Fico's badly burned body.

The murderers were still one step ahead of them.

Chapter 40

Jana and Elias went to the hospital in a privately hired ambulance so they could get inside without being noticed if the public entrances were being watched. At the emergency area, the two of them hopped out, then slipped into a staff elevator, which took them up to the observation ward where the professor was being kept. The ward nurse informed them that the professor was in the children's ward. Jana guessed what he was doing.

There was the professor, powdered, charcoaled, and lipsticked in a makeshift clown's face, tripping himself up, accidentally getting stuck to the floor, doing pratfalls, juggling glasses, trays, and everything else that was handy, and, of course, doing magic tricks for the kids. Much to the dismay of the children and the professor, Jana and Elias dragged the reluctant man away from the performance and down the elevator back to the emergency area and out to the waiting ambulance. They didn't even give him time to remove his makeup.

The ambulance let them off at the Sudbahnhof station, where they caught the train for the sixty-kilometer trip across the Austrian border to Bratislava. There were a few stops in between the two cities for the hour-long run to Slovakia, but, at least for the moment, they could relax. The other passengers stared at the professor, still wearing his clown face, his arms folded in disapproval, sulkily refusing to talk to either police officer because they had interrupted his performance. Jana used the time to catch up on the information Elias had acquired with respect to the murders of Peter and the professor's nephew in Bratislava.

"Did you review of all of Peter Saris's . . . ?" Jana stopped herself. She felt a surge of depression when she mentioned Peter's name. Be professional, she reminded herself. "You reviewed the cases the prosecutor was investigating when he was murdered?"

"All the cases we knew about. There was one missing, the one he'd informed the attorney general was 'hot.' There was nothing left with respect to it, not a scrap, not even a case file name."

"He must have told the attorney general something about it."

"Just enough to get permission to open a John Doe file. He told him that the case might involve high members of the government and that he wanted to keep it all quiet. He said they needed to be assured that there would be no leaks until he was far enough along to brief the attorney general without compromising the case. They'd become aware that their office had a leak, either the police or their own people. That's the reason the attorney general gave me for agreeing to follow the prosecutor's suggestion."

"It sounds like the attorney general didn't want to know anything until he could be sure he'd be able to cover himself if anything went wrong with the inquiry. He wanted to 'Hear no evil' until Peter was absolutely sure."

Elias shrugged. "I think so. All politicians are alike. Nobody takes chances."

"It was likely to be connected to one of the other cases that the prosecutor was investigating. How else would he have come upon it? You're sure you checked through all of them, to see if a government minister or anyone else high up in the government was involved?"

"The only one that came close was the oil-equipment matter."

"What about it?"

"The oil company that was developing the new oil field complained that they were being taxed at the price of new equipment by Customs and Excise for used equipment they were importing. The oil company appealed and won. One of the customs officials disputed the ruling and sent a letter to the Anti-Corruption Section. So the prosecutor opened a file. From what I could determine, the company's appeal was correct. In any case, the original contract the government made with the oil company said that any equipment they brought in for the purpose of developing the field would be free of import duties, so I was surprised that the oil company agreed to pay any taxes at all. But they did, so what's the harm?"

"They paid the lesser amount?"

"Yup. I didn't see corruption there. If anything, they paid more than they had to. And they've taken an even bigger loss, now that the oil field has been nationalized."

"And no other case he was handling came close to involving major government officials?"

"The case files for his other assignments were all there. I didn't see anything suspicious."

Jana was beginning to seethe. One case or another of Peter's had to have led to his death. As yet, they were all isolated instances that did not cohere. Her frustration was beginning to choke her. She turned to Elias. "Did you get the chance to talk to Fico about his work in Slovakia?"

"He left Bratislava and was on the move until I reached

him by phone and arranged the meeting in Austria. You know what happened then."

"Did you find out what type of investigations he specialized in?"

"From what I learned, he focused on large-scale investigations, all insurance-related, everything from heavy construction overruns to oil spills to bankruptcy frauds. Nothing small. Almost all of them involved millions of rupees, dollars, pounds, or euros. The man was supposed to be very good at what he did."

"He was killed because he was on to something in Slovakia."

"Maybe they just caught up with him in Slovakia about a case from another country? So they tried to kill him at the hotel and got the kid instead?"

"You're convinced they tried to kill *him* and killed the student by mistake?"

The professor began focusing on the conversation when he heard his nephew mentioned.

"Fico was supposed to be sitting there," Jana said.

"But it wasn't Fico. Maybe they didn't know what he looked like?"

"Even odder, how would they know Fico was supposed to be sitting *there*? Could the killer have heard the student tell the maitre d' he was Fico? Perhaps somebody inside the restaurant signaled to the murderer? Seats for breakfast are not preassigned. Someone had to point him out when he sat down."

She pondered the issue. "It had to be the maitre d'. He checked the boy in. All he knew was that he was given the name Fico by the student. He would have been told by the killer to signal when and where Fico sat. We need to re-interview him."

Elias nodded.

The professor finally spoke up.

"I think they wanted to kill both this man Fico and my nephew." His words were forced out from deep inside. "And it's my fault."

"Professor, why is it your fault?" Jana kept her voice gentle. "Tell us about it. I know that whatever you did was not done with the intent to injure your nephew."

"I told him to do it!"

"To do what, Professor?"

"He brought it to me."

"What did he bring you, Professor?" Jana made sure her voice remained soft and nonjudgmental.

"The papers you showed me."

"The Romanian report?"

"Yes." His eyes had filled with tears, his voice husky with pain. "He showed it to me."

"Why did he show it to you, Professor?"

"He told me that in the course of his research he'd discovered this report. He said he thought it showed some kind of corruption. He wanted to know who he should send it to. I encouraged him. I told him that he was a good man, and good men have to act or bad ones will prevail. I saw the swastika on the report. They were bad men. We had to stamp them out." He stopped, the tears streaming down his face, streaking his clown make-up.

"I know it hurts, Professor." Jana's voice became even gentler. "You have to go on and tell us the rest."

"Yes." He composed himself. "When I was a very young boy, we fought against the Nazis to take back our homeland. Forty thousand Slovaks were killed by them during the revolt." He moaned. "I told him to send the report, despite the fact that I knew it might be dangerous."

He looked at her, his eyes pleading. "I never supposed it meant *that* kind of danger; I never thought he might be killed."

"I'm sure you didn't."

"So he sent it. We found the name of the prosecutor in charge of the anti-corruption investigations and sent it to him. He read the report."

"How do you know he read it?"

"He contacted my nephew."

More surprises, Jana thought.

"What did your nephew tell Prosecutor Saris?"

The professor shook his head. "I don't know. The prosecutor told him to keep their talk to themselves. My nephew honored the request."

"Professor, Prosecutor Saris would not have talked about the report to anyone else. He wouldn't even tell the attorney general about it. He would never have talked about your nephew to anyone. He knew better. It follows that there is no way you can hold yourself responsible for your nephew's death."

The professor bowed his head, then looked directly at Jana. His voice was almost inaudible, Jana having to strain to hear him.

"I told him to make sure that it was read by a person of authority, not ignored. That he should send it to at least one more person in the upper tier of government. So he sent it to one other person."

"Who?" Jana asked, almost afraid to hear the answer. Not another police officer, she hoped. Not Colonel Trokan. She said a silent prayer.

"The minister of economics."

Elias let out an audible gasp.

"So, you see," whispered the professor, "I helped kill my nephew."

Jana took a second to reply. "No," she said. "But I suspect that the minister probably did."

The train rolled on. Jana finally broke the silence.

"Professor, when I let you see the report, you didn't tell me then that your nephew had shown it to you. Why?"

He looked wretched. "I didn't want to admit my own guilt in placing him in a position of such danger." He stuttered to a halt, then started again. "He was my nephew. My advice killed him. I couldn't say the words that would describe what I had done. I was the one who killed him, just as surely as if I had put the bullets into him."

The train began to slow down for a stop.

Chapter 41

Just before the last stop, on the outskirts of Bratislava, at the Petržalka station, Jana saw them. There were six in all on the platform. She recognized them immediately: Gyorgi Ilica, the Romanian; Gabi Laszlo, the Hungarian who had brought Jana "greetings" from her friend on the Hungarian police; Zimmer, the tall Prussian with the bad teeth; Peete, the English cop who kept looking at his shoes during the party; Camille Grosjean, the Belgian who was the assistant director's favorite in SC 4; and Ryan, the man who had done the bump-and-grind on stage with the phallus. Ryan, Laszlo, and Zimmer headed for the rear of the train, the rest of them toward the engine, evidently planning to sandwich Jana and Elias between them. No more charades. It was now to be a direct frontal assault.

"They're here," Jana said matter-of-factly, pointing them out to Elias. "Time for us to pretend we're great marksmen."

"I had the momentarily pleasant thought that we were in the clear," Elias said.

"Too many of them; too much access to information. There are so many ways to track an individual today, even God would have trouble hiding."

They both stood. The professor stared first at the Europol men on the platform, then at Jana and Elias, and started to rise. Jana pushed him back into his seat.

"Not you, Professor. You don't have a gun. We'll be better off without you. Stay in your seat. My guess is that they probably won't even recognize you. They're here for us." She turned to Elias. "We go to the front of the train on the double. If we can surprise them, it will raise our odds. Hopefully, we hit them first before they even know we're there."

The professor stayed in his seat, helpless, watching them go.

Jana and Elias jacked shells into the chambers of their automatics, keeping the weapons tight at their sides to minimize passenger panic. Running through the cars was going to create enough of a stir. They reached the juncture of the first and second cars before spotting the first group of thugs through the window in the upper half of the door. The two paused, readying themselves.

"Take a breath; be careful and accurate. Not too fast," Jana cautioned Elias. "And please, don't kill any civilians."

"I'll try not to," Elias promised.

They took deep breaths, then opened the door to the next compartment, aimed and began shooting even as the three men saw them. It was, in fact, brutally quick. The gunmen got off two quick shots that went nowhere near the two detectives before they were hit. First Ilica and Peete; then Grosjean, who took a bullet in his shoulder and tried to run for it. Elias calmly put a last bullet in him just before he made it out of the door.

The few passengers were as startled as the three dead men had been by the sudden gunfight, cringing in their seats, aghast, cowering away from the two police officers as they quickly checked the bodies.

"Police officers," Jana repeated over and over, in both German and Slovak, as they passed through the car trying to calm the shocked travelers.

Jana kicked the weapons away from the men lying on the train floor. Elias stood at the ready in case one of them was faking.

"All dead," Jana announced.

"Three up; three down," Elias added.

"And three to go," reminded Jana.

"The odds are better now."

They quickly reloaded, then began running toward the rear of the train, Jana yelling for everyone to remain seated, that they were in no immediate danger. As they raced by, the passengers stirred uneasily, already frightened by the sound of the gunfire, now even more disturbed by the sight of two police officers running back through the car with their weapons at the ready.

"The train doors are open for loading. The Europol people will have heard the shots," Jana warned Elias. "We no longer have the advantage of surprise."

"Maybe they'll think their friends have killed *us*," Elias suggested.

"In any case, they'll be coming."

As they passed the conductor, Jana barked at him, "There are three dead men in the first car. Get the police!"

They ran to the next car, passing the professor, who stood and trotted after them.

"Professor, go back," Jana shouted at him.

He stopped for a moment, then began very deliberately walking after them.

Elias was in the lead now because Jana had paused to warn the professor. Both of them again began urging the passengers to stay in their seats, trying to calm them with the usual "everything is under control" and "none of the passengers have been hurt." They had reached the middle of the next car when Zimmer began shooting. Elias was struck by the first bullet and dropped like a stone. Jana squeezed off a rapid shot that caught Zimmer in the shoulder, throwing him up against a seat. Her next shot dropped him. She caught sight of Laszlo through the glass partition of the next car. She darted after him, but the distance was too great for accuracy with a pistol.

A panicked passenger blocked the aisle in front of Laszlo; Laszlo clubbed the man out of the way. This delay allowed Jana to close the distance between them. She took careful aim and squeezed off her shot. It caught Laszlo squarely between the shoulders, propelling him forward, splaying him in a grotesque posture over the back of a train seat. Jana ran back to aid Elias.

She crouched next to him. It was quickly apparent that the investigator was dead. "I'm sorry, Elias," Jana said. "You did well."

Abruptly, Ryan appeared from behind one of the seats, his gun at her head. He had managed to get behind her by simply taking a window seat, his head turned away, letting them run past him.

"There's no need to get up, Matinova. Put your gun on the floor."

She hesitated, then placed her gun on the center aisle carpet.

"I truly admire you, Commander. You're a good cop. With big balls. I've always admired good cops."

Ryan cocked the hammer of his gun . . . just as the professor hit him with a suitcase he'd grabbed from the overhead racks, knocking the gunman off balance. Ryan righted himself and fired at the old man. The slug propelled the professor down the aisle. The momentary diversion allowed Jana to pick up her weapon. She emptied it into Ryan. Jana continued trying to shoot the man even after she had run out of ammunition, ultimately stopping herself when she realized her gun was no longer firing.

She ran to the professor, kneeling down next to him. His eyes were open; he was fighting shock. Eventually, he managed to focus on her.

"You see, I'm truly invaluable."

"Yes, you are, Professor."

"Forgive me for not telling you about my nephew's report?"

"I forgive you, Professor."

"Was that the last of them?"

"The last of them on the train. Not to worry. We'll have the others soon."

He smiled.

"I told you that I could help you," he reminded her.

"You did, Professor."

"I hope I made it up to my nephew."

"He would thank you, Professor."

A number of Slovak police scrambled onto the train and into their car, their guns at the ready. One of them reached down and took Jana's gun from her hand.

"This man needs medical help. Quickly!" she said, in Slovak.

"One more thing," the professor managed to get out.

"Yes, Professor."

"That young man will break Marketa's heart. She should have stayed with me."

"There is no question about that, Professor. You are obviously the better man."

"Obviously," he repeated, closing his eyes.

Chapter 42

Trokan insisted Jana stay at a safe house while she wrote her report. Then they would decide what their next move should be. The place he chose was her warrant officer's home. He brought in a number of young officers from the hinterlands who had not been involved in major investigations and, therefore, were less likely to be tainted by contact with the murder group. They were to be body-guards for Jana. They were also to make sure that the Seges' apartment was secure.

Jana sent him a first draft of the report which Trokan immediately took to the minister of the interior. The two of them then took it to the prime minister. The information that Jana had brought back from The Hague and Prague, and the international implications of what had happened, were so large that they had to bring the prime minister in. The three of them then mutually agreed to send out a press release "explaining" the shootings on the train, an explanation that would be vague and obscure enough to confuse even the most astute reader. Everything else was to be stonewalled. The dead had been carted away in body bags, so there were no photographs, and the prime minister had even authorized fostering a rumor that the dead men were rival victims in a Russian mafia war. Everyone was now waiting for the prime minister's further orders.

Seges was not happy. It was not that his wife had complained. To the contrary, she had welcomed the opportunity to take her children off to see her mother. It was just that he did not appreciate having his commander sleep in his other bedroom, then waking up in the morning to see her already awake, dressed to go out, and facing her irritation at being housebound. It was all very uncomfortable.

Jana soon determined that sitting in the Seges' apartment was not her cup of tea either. After vegetating on the sofa, feeling ineffectual, she'd had enough of staring at the walls, so she swung into action. Jana contacted the courts and was referred to a translator. Despite the colonel's express order, she decided to go out. Seges did not try to dissuade her, hoping she'd leave him at home, trying to lag behind, only to be told to come with her. She also took an officer, a large man named Vesely who looked like he could take care of himself in a fight. There was some safety in numbers, and she wanted her bodyguards to look formidable.

They went to an office on Obchodna shared by a number of translators who served the courts. An expert in Romanian was waiting for her. She had a pleasant but neutral smile on her face. It was the same with all translators. They cultivated a nice but neutered quality that would convey objectivity to anyone who utilized their services within the court system.

Jana pulled out the last copy she had of the report that Peter Saris had hidden in her closet. She told the translator that she wanted it translated immediately. The translator balked. The woman insisted she would require at least a half-day to make sure all the nuances were correct. Jana assured the woman that a quick, reasonably accurate translation was all that was needed, adding that it was a matter of national importance.

Nervous, but afraid to say no, the translator scanned the report, made a few notes, then proffered a reasonably complete rendition in Slovak.

The report was a geological analysis of the exploration and testing of an area in Slovakia. The evaluation was based on a search for oil deposits conducted by Romanian geologists and petroleum engineers during the Second World War. The experts, men brought in from the Ploesti oil fields in Romania, had decided, based on the test drilling they had done, along with other studies, that the area of exploration was not a potential oil field of any consequence. They concluded that there was therefore no justification for further exploration and consequent exploitation. The Germans had signed off on this conclusion. Later, so had the Soviets.

When the translator finished, she looked up with her neutral smile, waiting for any questions. Jana tried to understand the implications of the report. Why was there so much concern over a report that had been written so long ago? Why had so many killings resulted from its being brought to light? Jana added the fatalities up: Peter's death from a phone bomb, the student's murder at the hotel, Kroslak's subsequent murder, as well as those of Dinova and Fico. Then there was the death of Elias and her own near-assassination. Murder after murder, for no apparent reason.

Break the whole down and examine the parts, Jana told herself. She now knew what the young Denis had done when he'd found the report. She understood the part that Peter had played. Jana also comprehended what Kroslak had been investigating. The only question that remained unanswered was Fico's role in these events. She needed to know that to complete the picture. No, there was one more question: what part had the minister of economics played in this? The leak had probably come from his department, the leak which led to the student's death, and Peter's death, and set this whole series of events into motion.

The insurance investigator, Fico, was the key.

Jana asked the translator to identify the area of land in the Tatras which the geologists had described. The woman very carefully printed the land description on a piece of paper giving plat descriptions and longitude and latitude, with two nearby city references to make it even clearer. Jana had a vague idea of the area they were talking about, but she would have to go to a map of Slovakia to further clarify it.

Jana thanked the woman, telling her to write up a full translation and send the bill to her office.

Seges looked hopeful.

"Back to the house?" Seges asked, a wistful quality to his voice.

"The attorney general's office is next."

"The colonel is going to get mad at me for letting you leave the house."

"You weren't designated as my jailer."

"He will say that I should have been more vigorous in my opposition."

"I'll tell them you put up an argument which was so intense that we almost came to blows."

"He won't believe that," Seges moaned.

"Then I'll tell him I overpowered you."

Seges liked that even less.

They were at the attorney general's office within ten minutes. This was where Peter had died. She controlled her emotions by focusing on her objective: finding out how the killer had planted the bomb. They went up to the third floor and walked down the corridor to Peter's work area, where his secretary sat in the outer office. Through the open door, Jana could see that the furniture had been removed and that painters were working on the walls. They were still cleaning up the scars left by the bombing.

The secretary looked up from her work.

"Commander Matinova, how are you?"

"As well as can be expected, Angelika: surviving."

"It's been a hard few weeks," Angelika looked sympathetic. "I understood that the police had taken you off the case?"

"I've been placed back in charge of the investigation by Colonel Trokan."

The secretary looked skeptical. "Oh?"

Jana decided not to waste any time. She took the desk phone and dialed Trokan, handing the receiver back to Angelika.

"Ask him."

The secretary spoke to Trokan, still trying to be delicate, mentioning that Commander Matinova was in her office and she seemed to be there investigating the explosion. She stayed on the phone for a while longer than seemed necessary, and when she finally put the receiver down she looked slightly shocked.

"He was angry, and used profanity." She was annoyed. "He said that, yes, you were back on the case, but to get your. . . ." She hesitated, trying to find a nice word. "You are to get your posterior back to the house. He doesn't want another murder on his hands. There were other things he said, which are unnecessary to repeat."

"I'll stay here just long enough to get the answers that I need. You know why I'm here?"

"About the phone bomb that killed Peter Saris?"

"I have a few questions for you."

"I talked to Investigator Elias."

"And you were very cooperative. Unfortunately, he's not here to fill in the gaps in his reports. The morning the bomb went off, were you here at your regular time?"

"Yes."

"Did anyone visit him that morning?"

"The attorney general, but very briefly."

"How briefly?"

"No more than five minutes. They didn't need me, so I stayed at my desk. They talked, and then the attorney general left."

"It seemed like it was a cordial conversation?"

"They were even laughing at one point."

"The night before, when you left, was the office locked up?"

"I didn't have to lock the inner office. Mr. Saris was still here. I did lock the outer door. We kept even the janitors out because of the sensitive nature of the reports we had in the inner office. He could open both doors from the inside if he had to. He told me he had worked all night when I came back in the morning."

"The outer door was still locked when you came in the next morning?"

"Absolutely. As you know, he spent the night in his office sometimes. And he did so that evening. He hadn't even shaved yet when I came in."

"Let's talk about the afternoon before the day of the bombing. I assume there were visitors?"

Angelika reviewed a desk ledger, then swiveled it around for Jana to read.

"All visitors have to sign in."

Jana examined the book. Three police officers had come in together, and apparently left together. Jana knew all of them. Nothing that she knew about them would cause her to suspect that they had planted the phone bomb. Their conference with Peter had lasted approximately two hours. There was only one other entry, immediately after the officers had left. The scrawled signature was undecipherable. So was the address and phone number. The agency the man was representing was also scrawled on the page, but had been made legible by a ballpoint overwrite. It said "Europol." Jana now knew where the bomb had come from.

"Do you know who overwrote the word 'Europol' on this entry?" Jana asked.

"I did. I knew he came from Europol. When I saw the scrawl, I felt we should at least be able to tell what agency he came from by looking at it. I wrote 'Europol' over his scrawl. It would be illegal to overwrite his signature. I left it alone."

"Did the man give you a name?"

"He said it very fast, and my English is very bad, so I can't even guess at what he said. Mr. Saris came out and took him into the inner office as soon as he came in, so I never was able to get him to rewrite the name."

"Peter was expecting him?"

"He appeared to be."

"Did Peter ever leave his office while the man was still inside?"

"For a short while. Peter had been drinking coffee with the officers for two hours and, you know, coffee goes right through you, so. . . ."

"He went to the toilet?"

"Yes."

"Leaving his visitor alone in the office?"

"Yes."

"Just one more question: can you describe the man who came to the office?"

"I told you he spoke English. He was broadly built. A little bit too heavy, his belly getting too big for his belt."

A picture of Aidan Walsh began to materialize for Jana.

"The only other thing I can think of was that he was eating a candy bar when he came into the office."

Aidan Walsh.

He had killed Peter.

Chapter 43

"Oil" plus "insurance" were the two words that kept popping up in her analysis. Jana didn't yet know the questions to ask about oil, so she focused on insurance. Despite the fact that Fico's insurance-investigation firm was international in scope, it was headquartered in Vienna. Austrian firms also handled a lot of the big-money insurance transactions in Bratislava, with the biggest of them headquartered on Hlavne Namestie near the Japanese embassy, so Jana headed in that direction, with Seges protesting all the way.

"Do you have insurance?" she eventually asked him.

"I'll get it when I'm older."

"You need it now to take care of your wife and children in case the colonel kills you. The Austrians will come up with a good policy. Think of the security your wife will have. Then again, if you complain to her like you complain to me, maybe having insurance will be another reason for her to get rid of you."

"That's not funny, Commander."

"It's not meant to be."

They parked near Hlavne Namestie, walked past the embassy, then went into the building that had a gold plate on the side of the door advertising "Hayden-Schoenbrun-Weyl" with no other explanation. The organization evidently had the hubris to believe that if you came to them, you already knew what they did. Jana and Seges left Vesely at the front door looking formidable, then took the stairs up one flight to the first of the firm's two floors. The receptionist hesitated about announcing them. But a police commander demanded respect, and, at Jana's request, she called one of the senior agents to the front. His name was Ernst, a very polite middle-aged man, balding, patting his vanished hair into place, but still with a bit of salesman's charm. He led them back into his office, where the main feature was a huge antique desk which Ernst sat behind, relieved to have a barrier between himself and the police. Jana explained they were there to obtain information which might aid in an investigation.

Ernst spoke Slovak with only a slight accent. "We always cooperate with the police, if we can, so it's a pleasure having you here. How can I help?"

"I need to know about insurance."

Ernst looked a little amused. "We rarely insure private individuals; only on occasion, as a favor to corporate client executives, so if that's why you've come, we can't help you."

"I'm not interested in insuring myself."

"Yes?"

"Did you know a man named Fico?"

He looked surprised at the mention of the name.

"I've just this morning heard that he had died. Murdered. Horrible. Mr. Fico was well known in the business. Very well thought of. A good investigator. We used him and his firm a number of times. They did good work. Is his murder the reason you're here?"

"Mr. Fico was in Slovakia recently. Did you know why he was here?"

"Not on our business. And we're not personal friends, so he didn't contact me when he came to Slovakia."

"Can you find out which firm he was working for when he came to Slovakia the last time?"

Ernst shrugged. "I prefer not to. We're not supposed to track the business of rival firms, Commander. It might look like we're trying to undercut them or to steal their customers. We take pride in our own ability to service our clients without having to poach on other firms. Our clients come to us."

"I'm happy to hear that. However, I'm not concerned about the fees or profits or incentives to sign with any given insurance company: I'm just interested in the names of the companies he was here on business for. So, it's just a small favor that the police are asking of Hayden-Schoenbrun-Weyl. Surely you can accommodate us. And if and when you need the help of the police, well, you will have built up a reservoir of good will which you can call on. We remember favors owed."

He looked at her a long moment, then smiled broadly.

"We have had long, good relations with the police in Slovakia. And we do try to keep track of trends," he said vaguely. "So, perhaps this one time I can get you the information you need."

"I'd appreciate that, Mr. Ernst."

He stood up, bowed, and walked out of the office.

Seges eyed the office fixtures, then the antique desk.

"I should have been an insurance salesman instead of a police officer."

"I agree with that, Seges. You might even have made money." Jana could not resist the jibe. "Although I doubt it."

"Why not?"

"You need a little charm to succeed in business."

"My wife thinks I'm charming."

"No, she doesn't."

"She's told me that I'm charming."

"All wives lie to their men."

The two of them sat in silence until Ernst returned. For a man who claimed that his firm did not track other insurance companies' business, he was back very quickly, a few sheets of paper in his hands.

"I seem to have been lucky," he announced. "One of my associates has been researching the area of reinsurance in Slovakia and, it so happens, Fico was in the country investigating a number of policies that my associate was aware of. We don't know the purpose of the investigation. However, I brought a list of the companies." He handed the papers to Jana. "You can keep these."

"Thank you, Mr. Ernst." She skim-read the list, then looked up, puzzled. "Can you explain what reinsurance is?"

"Of course." He steepled his hands, preparing his lecture. "Reinsurance is a means by which an insurance company can protect itself against the risk of losses by sharing the risk with other insurance providers. It allows the company to assume greater individual risk than its own assets would safely allow. It's a hedge strategy. Most of the time it's a strategy of surplus relief reinsurance, generally on a quota share basis, with many other insurance companies covering fractions of the loss over and above what the main insurer is covering."

Jana leaned forward, nodding her head. "So, if an insurance company can only afford to pay out, let's say, a hundred million euros on a policy, it reinsures for the surplus that may have to be paid over that to cover the complete loss."

Ernst beamed. His pupil had understood his explanation.

"And is that what happened here?" Jana prodded.

"I would think so, because of the multiple insurance companies involved."

Jana ran her eyes over the sheets of paper Ernst had given her. The main policy was for 50,000,000 euros. She did a rapid computation. The sum total of all the insurance policies was 180,000,000 euros.

"A large sum of money," Jana hazarded.

"For some things; not for others," he agreed, pride in his voice at being in a business that dealt with such huge sums.

"What kinds of things would they insure?"

"Loss from earthquake, hurricane, flood, fire, this kind of thing. It's really for catastrophic events that are going to completely or substantially destroy the item being insured; a building project of huge proportions, for example."

She checked the pages Ernst had given her.

"There's nothing on here to indicate what is insured, just the sums of the policies and the insurers. What was insured?"

"My colleague didn't have that information. You can find out, once you get through their red tape, by asking the insurance companies that are listed. Given the position you occupy on the police force, I assume they would check with their upper management and, if the policies are not on a confidential list, you could probably find out in a few days."

"A good idea," suggested Seges.

"Not such a good idea," Jana countered. "There are still people out there trying to kill our illustrious Colonel Trokan, trying to kill me, and kill anyone else that they think may be trying to stop them from whatever it is that they're doing. I'm not sure I have a few days."

Ernst looked shocked.

"Someone is trying to kill you? The mafia people on the train?"

Jana didn't answer, countering with another question.

"Some insurance companies specialize in insurance for certain industries. Do any of the ones on this list focus on certain events or certain goods, or crops, or buildings; or the like?"

She handed back the list. He went over the names of the insurers. She got up, going behind him to look over his shoulder as he ticked them off.

"Earthquake for this one, so they're into structure insurance. This one also. That one also insures against earthquakes, generally focusing on geographic areas that are high-risk. They can charge exorbitant premiums that way. These two write petroleum insurance; for example, if an oil field catches fire and burns up. The other three are generalists. They all seem to specialize in reinsurance, which is less risk for them because they bet that the prime coverage has covered enough of the risk so that their liability will not be involved. And they all handle types of insurance other than those I've indicated when it's profitable; we all do." He handed the papers back to Jana.

"Thank you, Mr. Ernst. You've been very helpful."

"My pleasure, Commander."

Jana shook Ernst's hand, and he walked them to the door of his office. He waved before closing his door behind them.

"Did we get anything?" Seges asked.

"Not enough." They passed the front desk and began walking down the stairs. "Peter got on to whatever it was, and so did Kroslak. The student who was killed understood it based on the old report that he found." She lightly slapped the side of her head. "But nothing is coming to this *brilliant* mind of mine." Vesely fell in behind them as they walked to the corner, turning in the direction of their parked car.

Jana saw a small magazine/newspaper store across the street. The owners had pasted news headlines cut out from old newspapers in an artistic pattern in the window to call attention to their business. One of the headlines, almost dead-center in the window, proclaimed the nationalization of the oil field in the Tatras. The headline reminded Jana of the report the customs man had sent to Peter about the oil company shipping used equipment into Slovakia for work on the oil field, and then settling the complaint when they probably could have avoided any taxes if they'd fought.

A drawer in her mind suddenly opened up to disclose its contents. She knew the answer.

"Keep walking to the car. I'll catch up with you!" she yelled at Seges. She jogged back around the corner, running even faster to the building housing Hayden-Schoenbrun-Weyl. Inside, she took the stairs two at a time, running past the startled receptionist and down the corridor to Ernst's office, plunging inside without knocking. Ernst looked up, startled.

"Mr. Ernst, would any of the insurance companies cover the loss by the company which had been awarded the contract to develop an oil field—I mean the total cost of development—if the field was nationalized? The prime minister has just nationalized the oil deposits in the Tatras and taken them away from an American oil company. Would insurance policies cover the loss to that company?"

He was still gaping at her.

"Can you answer the question, Mr. Ernst?"

"Insurance can cover anything, Commander."

Jana smiled. She had reason to smile.

The pieces had come together.

Chapter 44

Jana was surprised. She and Seges were getting along better, like two old people who had fought their way through life's wars and were now, at least, acceptant of each other's idiosyncrasies, tolerating each other's ways with minor irritation rather than anger. Sitting around a small apartment, waiting for the telephone call that never comes, is hard, but there was no alternative. So they each selected one half of the living room and stayed there, staring at the ceiling, making small talk only when required by some exigency like eating or sharing the newspaper. Silence was golden.

In the early afternoon, Jana's cell phone rang, jerking them both to attention. It was Trokan. Thirty minutes later, they were all in the central city area walking a wide circular route east on Panska and then Laurenska, turning right at its end onto Gorkeho and then west back to Rybne Namesti, and then around the circuit again. The procession was strung out, with Seges, Vesely and Trokan's bodyguards stretched out behind them like a comet's tail. A light snow was falling, gradually getting heavier. Their footprints started to remain on the street when they passed. All of them were in uniform, wearing their greatcoats, looking faintly sinister to the pedestrians who increased their pace as they went by. The public had not lost its fear of the police, the dread still clinging from the communist era, although it had diminished slightly in the past few years.

A car splashed by, spraying slush on the sidewalk, causing Trokan and Jana, to jump out of the way. "That man has no consideration for pedestrians." They walked on. "I hate the snow. Too many accidents," a dour Trokan announced. "People ought to stop using cars."

"Would you give up your vehicle if it snowed?" Jana asked, knowing what the answer would be.

"Of course not. I'm only talking about stupid drivers who have suicidal impulses, which means most people. I'm different."

"How are you different?"

"Haven't you noticed the insignia of my rank on my shoulder? I have been declared superior to everyone else. This is an apparent fact of which the Gods of Winter take notice. So, I would be exempted."

"I hadn't heard of that. Did they hand down a decree?"

"They talked to me directly."

"Perhaps you could put in a good word for me."

"I'll think about it."

"Tell me what the interior minister said when you briefed him."

"I think he was struck speechless. For a while, I think he believed that I had gone quite insane."

"You convinced him otherwise."

"It took me a while. He read your report over and over again, just to make sure that the words would remain the same. I showed him the microfilm copies, the Romanian report, your narrative of the events, including the shootings on the train and all the other killings which your friends from The Hague seemed to be involved in. When I was sure he had completely digested everything, I told him about your 'suspicion' that the minister of economics was involved. That was when he started to choke."

"When he had his breath back, what did he say?"

"That there was not enough proof against the man." He kicked at a small ball of snow, the ball immediately becoming a puff of white powder. "I agreed with him."

"So do I, at present. Will he talk to the prime minister?"

"Not for the moment."

"And my other suggestion?"

"I thought about it."

"Yes?"

"You know if you do what you say you want to, then we are both in for it if it goes bad."

"I will take full responsibility."

"Naturally, and I will take full credit."

"Of course."

"Except, this time, I will have to share accountability. I've already started. No one would do what I wanted unless I gave them my personal word that it was a matter of state, and that I took absolute responsibility. One of them even demanded a personal letter to that effect."

"Which you gave him?"

"I had to. Of course, when this is over I'm going to ship him to the other side of the country. Revenge will be sweet."

"So we're ready."

He checked his watch. "Just to make sure everyone has finished, call the minister of economics in an hour. He'll want to see you right away." They walked on in silence; the snow came down even harder. "I keep thinking of accidents in the snow. Don't be one of the accidents, Jana. We're both on the line for this."

"The Winter Spirits also talked to me. They informed

me that they were going to give me a favorable assist on this one."

"Don't trust them. The Spirits are very fickle."

"Thank you for the reminder."

They finally stopped walking. Trokan signaled to the men following them, and the officers formed a small, irregular circle around them. Trokan saluted her, Jana returned the salute; then Trokan stamped his feet several times trying to clear his soles of the snow.

"Hard to walk on this damned stuff."

He turned and strode away, followed by his bodyguards. Jana watched him go. Seges, feeling the cold, slapped at his arms.

"Time to go inside," he suggested.

"Go home," she said. "Call your wife and tell her she can come back."

"You're sure?"

"Just do it. Bring my things to the office. I'll be back there tomorrow."

"The colonel said to guard you," he reminded her.

"Not any more."

Seges stood there; Jana became impatient.

"I said to go. So, go!"

Seges wavered, threw her a salute, and walked away without looking back. Jana went to a small café, ordered a hot chocolate, and sat at the table until it was time to make the call, which was patched through only after she had waded through a series of self-important aides determined to display their authority, eventually reaching the minister of economics through sheer tenacity.

"Minister, thank you for taking my call." She put the right note of deference in her voice. "But it's a matter of the utmost importance that we talk in private."

He agreed to meet her in his office.

Chapter 45

The minister was a tall, obviously once-athletic individual who was still vaguely handsome even though jowls were making their appearance. His hair was receding and had become sparse in back; the once-firm body had begun to bloat from too many noon drinks and nighttime banquets. He gave her his flashing political smile in greeting, gestured for her to take a chair, and waved his aide out. The aide closed the office door behind him.

"We've never had the pleasure of a formal meeting, Commander. All the same, your reputation precedes you, so I'm glad to finally meet you in the flesh." He flashed her another smile, then leaned back in his chair, putting on his "paying intense attention" look. "You said that it was extremely important that we meet. I'm always all ears when a person of respect says that."

"I hate to bother you, Minister. But, for the country's sake, it's a matter of the utmost importance for you to maintain your appearance of integrity. That meant that I had to speak to you as quickly as possible."

"My 'appearance' of integrity?" He moved uneasily in his chair. "I take it that someone has accused me of chicanery, of malfeasance in office?"

"We try to guard the reputations of high public officials, particularly those whom we see are responsive to the needs of the public and the future of our country. I thought it was necessary that you be apprised of the facts in a case that has developed so that you can marshal your defenses. The media raptors make scurrilous accusations all the time, and will almost assuredly do so again when we are required to file charges against the other defendants."

He sat, blinking at her, his ruddy complexion slightly paler now.

"What 'other defendants'? What are the charges against them?"

"Multiple murders, attempted murders, grand theft, corruption, bribery of public officials, conspiracy to commit these acts. We have them rounded up and the cases against them are documented. In one of those cases, perhaps the principal one, several defendants have accused you of being a participant."

The minister laughed, a derisive comment on the accusation. "That kind of person will make up all kinds of stories to save himself. If anyone has accused me of any type of corrupt activity, then it's a huge lie."

"That's just what I said, Minister. I feel that the men accusing you are trying to save themselves by pointing to a bigger fish, trying to make some kind of bargain in order to save themselves. So I thought it advisable to come here to warn you."

"Which I appreciate, Commander." He flashed his smile again. "Perhaps you could tell me what they're saying?"

"They claim that there is a plot to fake the presence of oil in Slovakia when there is no oil. They claim that the oil field in the Tatras that we have nationalized—I understand at your urging to the prime minister—never existed."

The minister looked frightened; for the first time he betrayed a real emotion.

"Why would I ask that we nationalize an oil field that

doesn't exist? Incredible, to claim a field doesn't exist when we know it does."

"It doesn't exist."

Jana placed the Romanian report on the desk in front of him. He made no effort to read it.

"The Nazis and the Soviets both explored the area, concluding that there was no oil there. It's the same area that the American oil company leased, the same area that was nationalized. The criminals claim that the oil company used false data as the basis for beginning its fraud on the public. After they had gone through some initial steps to create the illusion of development of the project, they *wanted* the government to nationalize the field."

The minister slapped the top of his desk to emphasize his disbelief. "This is absurd. What would they have to gain? What would *I* have to gain?"

"Gain? A share in the 185,000,000 euros the oil company is going to collect from the insurance companies that underwrote the project. The companies will indemnify them for the company's losses: all their exploratory activities, all the tanks they set up, their rigs, the hugely expensive drilling bits, the operating machinery, the man-hours involved, the power lines they laid but which the state paid for, et cetera, et cetera. As for their claim about you, a share in that kind of pot is going to tempt even the most scrupulous of men. Of course, I realize you had no knowledge of this."

"I'm shocked and bewildered," he said. His face was now extremely pale and there was a line of sweat on his forehead. "Of course, there's no truth to any of this."

"I'm sure there is none. Once more, I believe you. I just wanted to warn you of what was coming, to make sure that you were not overwhelmed by the media frenzy that we expect. The news will probably go out to the public in the morning, so if you . . . well, I'm sure the oil company didn't pay you any money, so you have nothing to worry about when the search begins of the accounts of everyone concerned."

She stood.

"Odd how we catch up with these people. Just a little event triggered the whole investigation. The company brought in used equipment from outside the country. Obsolete stuff. Useless, really. Customs wanted to levy an import tax on the equipment. The company initially fought it, and won. Then, even though they probably had the right to bring the equipment into the country free of any tariff, they backed down. Why? Because they didn't want to spotlight the fact that they were bringing old equipment into the country. When they claimed their insurance compensation, they wanted to be paid for new equipment.

"It caught the attention of a lawyer in the prosecutor's office. You know, the one who was murdered. I wonder who ordered his killing? Whoever he is, he is at the top of the list for retribution, wouldn't you agree?"

"I certainly would."

Jana walked to the door.

"I'm so sorry that the days ahead may be somewhat rocky for you. You'll pull through. You're one of the most promising political lights of this country." She paused just before she opened the door. "And perhaps you will remember to put in a good word for me when a colonel's slot comes vacant. Maybe even the head of the police. I'm thinking of applying for it."

"I certainly will, Commander; and many thanks."

"Good-bye, Minister."

Jana walked out.

An hour later, she called Trokan.

"What happened when I left?"

"As predicted, he began making telephone calls. The taps worked perfectly. The Americans loaned us wonderful equipment; good sound recordings. He's still making calls as we speak. We have his bank accounts now. Several are in his wife's name. And his lawyer's, as well as his. Stupid, scared men. Lots of incriminating statements. We even have him calling the oil company president. So we have the head of the company in the mix, too."

"Panicked people do stupid things."

"You did a good job."

"It wasn't hard."

"They thought they were going to make a huge profit. Small outlay; big return."

"Anything else?"

"The bug in his office worked so well that I could swear you said you wanted to be the next head of police."

"Not a bad thought."

"I'd better keep a closer watch on you."

"No need." She paused, hesitating. "Peter thanks you."

"He should thank *you*."

"A kiss from him would be better."

". . . Sorry, Jana."

"It can't be helped."

They hung up.

Chapter 46

It didn't take Jana long to get to the Carleton Savoy. She walked into the lobby, then looked through the entrance of the restaurant to her right, observing the maitre d', who recognized her at the same time, giving her a curt nod in greeting. She swiveled around to check the desk. The manager was talking to a guest. Maria handed a guest a note that had been left with the hotel's answering service. Jana walked to the desk, first nodding at Maria, then greeting the manager. The manager finished with the guest, then came over to Jana.

"Hello, Commander."

"Good afternoon. I see that everything is back to normal. Your dining room is busy. You have guests filling the lobby. Everyone has forgotten about the murder, as I predicted they would."

The manager tried to smile, but the ends of her mouth barely twitched. "It took us a while, but everything seems to be normal again."

"Excellent. I thought I might talk to you for a few minutes, just to straighten out a loose end."

The manager lost even the semblance of a smile.

"I'm very busy, Commander."

"You have Maria on the desk, and we both know how competent she is, so I'm sure she can handle the traffic." Jana glanced at Maria, who was looking concerned.

"You can handle the desk for a minute or two, can't you, Maria?"

Maria checked with the manager before she answered; the manager reluctantly nodded.

"I guess I can."

"Good." Jana smiled.

The manager joined Jana, who gave her a reassuring pat on the shoulder. "Thank you for your cooperation. I'll make sure upper management hears about it." She began walking toward the restaurant. "A cup of coffee with conversation is always more pleasant, don't you think?" She ambled into the restaurant, followed by the manager. The maitre d' again nodded at Jana, then at the manager, escorting them to an empty table. Jana noticed that the table at the window where Denis Macek had been killed was vacant.

"How about over there? I prefer a window seat."

"As you wish," the maitre d' murmured.

"Coffee for us both, please," the manager requested.

As the maitre d' started to leave, Jana put her hand on his arm, stopping him.

"Join us."

"I'm on duty, Commander."

"I said, 'Join us.' It's not a request: it's an order."

He hesitated, looked to the manager for guidance, then sat next to her, calling for coffee from a passing waiter.

Jana ran her hand over the window glass. "No more bullet holes." She looked at the two sitting across from her. "Everything repaired. It is as if it never happened. Humanity just goes on, forgetting what came before . . . except for police officers. We're required to remember."

The waiter placed three cups in front of them, pouring coffee from a silver pitcher.

"Take the front while I'm here," the maitre d' ordered him. The waiter nodded and moved away.

"A good staff here. Experienced. Always ready, no matter what they're called on to do." Jana voiced approvingly. "The hotel deserves the reputation it has as the best in Bratislava."

"Thank you," the manager said grudgingly.

"I wanted to talk to you together, because my conversation with you after the young student was killed left questions that won't go away." Jana's voice took on a note of steel. "Not that I believe you were knowing conspirators in a murder, but because I'm aware that you were unwittingly complicit by not telling me everything that you knew. That's your sin, one of omission. That's the sin I'm here to face you with."

"I . . . don't . . . know . . . how you can say that. We've been completely cooperative," the manager said. "We have done everything we've been told to do, readily answered each and every question."

The maitre d' just gaped.

Jana continued as if she had not heard the manager.

"I kept asking myself, after looking at the body of Denis Macek, seeing his young face, how anyone could have believed he was a hotel guest arriving on a Friday morning to have the Royal Breakfast." Jana focused on the maitre d'. "An experienced maitre d' would have spotted him immediately as a fraud, no matter how dressed-up he was. His suit, which he had worn for the occasion so he could pass muster, was clean and pressed, but old, not to speak of his worn tie and ineptly ironed white shirt." Each of Jana's words was now very distinct, hard-edged. Jana let her words sink in. The maitre d' looked down at the table, frightened at what he saw in Jana's eyes.

"I didn't like a young student being killed. I've always felt that you don't just murder one young person when you kill. You also destroy all the children they might have had in the future, and their children's children. I have to say good-bye to all of them. I don't like it. So I'm impelled by all those deaths to press on, to get all the answers to his murder. And I want those answers now, do you understand?"

Jana waited, the maitre d' finally looking up.

"Yes."

"Maria, the desk girl, talked to you, didn't she? About the student?"

"Yes. She asked me to let him into the dining room if he gave me Fico's name. She knew Fico rarely had breakfast when he was a guest at the hotel. She wanted to make sure there were no problems when he came in, so she told me he was a starving student . . . and I agreed to let him have breakfast."

"If you allowed anyone into the dining area who was not entitled to the Royal Breakfast, you'd be jeopardizing your job, wouldn't you?"

"I guess so."

"That would be a big risk for you to take. You are well respected and have a well-paying lifetime job in the best hotel in Slovakia. Would you risk your livelihood to help a young woman and her student friend? I don't think so. You had your family to take care of, after all, didn't you?"

"It was a big risk," he acknowledged.

"There was a way. You went to your friend, the lady sitting next to you here. And you said, Madam Manager, we throw out lots of food that hasn't even been touched at the end of the day. That is a sin against heaven. We both remember the food we didn't get to eat, because our parents couldn't afford it, when we were children. Madam Manager, Maria has asked me to let a student into the breakfast area. It will never be discovered by higher management. He's going to use the name of one of our guests, Fico. So, can I do it? And, surprise of surprises, she agreed. Right?"

"Not true!" the manager yelped. "I would never agree to such a thing!"

The maitre d' gave the manager a quick look, his lips suddenly tight with anger.

"It's the truth," the maitre d' confirmed.

"It's a lie," the manager insisted.

Jana turned her focus to the manager.

"Have you heard of the crime in the Penal Code called 'Lying to a Police Officer,' Madam Manager? If you persist in lying, I will have the pleasure of arresting you in front of your entire staff, cuffing you with your hands behind your back, and marching you off to jail. Understood?"

The manager was breathing hard, her eyes blinking.

"Do you understand, Madam Manager?" Jana repeated.

The manager eventually managed to get out a "yes."

"Good." Jana softened her tone. "The request from your compatriot fit with something else you'd been asked to do, didn't it?"

The manager forced out another "Yes." Her face revealed her internal struggle. Eventually she admitted, "I thought it was part of the other Fico plan."

Jana waited. "You had been asked by someone else about Fico?"

"Yes."

Jana thought about the "other" Fico, the *real* Fico. It was becoming clear. She now knew why the shooter had come to the window when he had.

Jana encouraged the manager to go on. "You were asked

to make a call, give a signal, when the real Fico was either eating breakfast in the breakfast area or leaving the hotel to start his day. A man paid you to do this, didn't he? So you agreed."

The manager sat mute.

"This is my last warning. The truth, or you go to prison. No more manager's job. However, if you tell me the truth, nothing happens to you. It's your choice. Make it quickly."

"I won't go to prison if I answer you?" the manager whispered.

"No problem," Jana assured her.

The manager didn't need any more prompting. "A man said that he wanted to proposition Fico about a business project and that Fico wouldn't talk to him. He just wanted five minutes with him. That's all. A few minutes. And he offered me so much money to do it, I couldn't turn him down. So I agreed."

"What happened?"

"That morning, Fico came striding out. I was going over receipts at the desk and looked up just in time to see him going out of the front doors. I dialed the man who had asked me to signal him about Fico to tell him that I was late with my call. Then I saw the student going into the dining room. When the man answered, all I could think about was I'd missed the signal and dialed him too late. So I said the maitre d' had just checked Fico into the dining room. If the man was angry, I could point to the maitre d'. He had checked the name off. To all appearances, Fico had arrived, and I had fulfilled my agreement."

"Describe the man who paid you."

The manager gave Jana a description. Her word portrait fit Aidan Walsh.

"You didn't know he was going to kill anyone?"

"Never." The manager began to cry. "How could I know?"

"How could you know," Jana assured her. "And how could you know that he was also after the student?"

Jana got up, putting a small bill down on the table top for a tip.

When she got outside, she called Trokan on her cell phone and told him that she was on her way to her house. Trokan tried to talk her out of it; Jana insisted.

"I'm ready," she told him.

"You're stepping into it," he warned. "I don't endorse your adventure."

"We know that."

Eventually he gave in, advising her to take her time. Jana agreed, and put her phone away.

Jana walked over to the window that had been replaced and faced the table where the student had been sitting when he was killed. The manager and the maitre d' were gone; the waiter was cleaning up the coffee cups no one had touched. He saw Jana through the window and, picking up the tip she had left, mouthed a thank-you.

Jana turned away, strolling in the direction of her neighborhood, taking her time as the colonel had suggested. She thought of Denis Macek, the young student, sitting in the booth ready to enjoy his breakfast, not knowing that the killer who had been assigned to assassinate Fico was as ready to kill him. The killer didn't make a mistake, Jana silently told the student. He was in the city to kill you; he was in the city to kill Fico. The fates had placed you in the booth instead of the real Fico. The killer was expecting to find the real Fico at the table; but he also had your photograph as someone else he was supposed to take care of. He recognized you and made a quick adjustment to his plans, really no adjustment at all: he shot you.

Jana had heard that there was such a thing as black magic. If there was, it had certainly been present that morning. "I'm sorry, Denis," she murmured. "I know: magic has a way of going badly. Very badly. When it does, there's nothing we can do about it."

The snow, which had stopped falling, began again. It would soon cover the city in white.

Perhaps Bratislava would look better to her then.

Chapter 47

Jana walked the last hundred meters through the blowing snow dragging her feet, trying to postpone the confrontation. This time her spirits were not going to soar when she saw her familiar house. Instead, she would look for violations to her sanctuary, bruises on its walls, a cracked or broken window, splintered wood. Unfortunately, there was no way to delay further.

Jana turned onto her walkway. Her tension increased as she walked up the steps to the front door. The entry was unlocked. As she had thought so many times, "Who would be stupid enough to break into a police commander's house?" Today was different. She had to force herself to grasp the door handle, then urge herself to turn the knob. The door swung open and she walked inside.

Standing next to the door, gun in hand, was Aidan Walsh. Sitting on the living room couch was Assistant Director Mazur. A few meters away from him was Paola Rossi, a cigarette in one hand, her automatic in the other. Odd, Jana thought. She had never realized that Paola smoked.

"Good afternoon, everyone," Jana managed, keeping her voice steady. "Always good to see old friends."

Walsh closed the door behind her, then shoved her into the living room, following closely behind her. He quickly patted her down, removed her gun from its holster, and tossed it on the couch next to Mazur.

"Eat any candy today, Walsh? You should take the wrappers with you the next time you search a place. They're incriminating."

"Fuck you," he muttered.

"Paola, you should stop smoking. Its bad for your health."

"Shut your mouth, Matinova."

Walsh propelled her toward a chair. "Sit down."

"Kind of you to offer me a chair." Jana sat. "I would make you all something to eat or drink, but my sense is that you're only here for a brief time and would rather I dispense with a hospitable welcome."

Mazur sat on the couch, a slight smile on his face. "I warned you against doing stupid things when you first came on board," the assistant director reminded her. "Everything has its order, its place. Right from the beginning, you ignored this. So here we are, not a place I wanted to be. Your fault. You kept forcing the issue, blindly pushing ahead despite everything."

"I'm just your average police officer," she reminded him. "That's what *we* do. Or have you erased that, along with everything else that a police officer is supposed to be, from your memory?" She took in the other two with a quick glance. "When did you all decide to kill people for a living? What prompted you to steal, to cheat, to band together into a murder machine? Who made the first suggestion? Who thought it was a good idea?"

Paola walked over to her and hit her across the head with the barrel of her gun. The blow knocked Jana off her chair. Blood ran down the side of Jana's face from the gash above her hairline. She lay on the floor, oddly enough, despite her daze, noticing that her boots still had snow on them. Jana forced herself into a sitting position, then, with more effort, up into the chair. She eyed Paola.

"Are we going to play 'Beat the Police Officer to Death' like you did to Kroslak? Or 'Shoot the Victim' like you did with the student?"

"Kroslak was an informant," Paola muttered. "He deserved every kick we gave him. It should have lasted longer."

"He was a policeman," Jana corrected.

Mazur held his hand up for silence. "Matinova, we believe you have some material of ours. Kroslak had it. We think it's now in your possession."

"What would that be?"

"The microfilm. The Romanian report."

"Very good reading," Jana affirmed. "I'd want it too, if I were you. Unfortunately for you, even as we speak, it's being forwarded to police agencies in all the appropriate jurisdictions. We're even sending a copy to your superiors, Assistant Director. I don't think you're going to be an assistant director much longer."

"Too bad," Mazur said.

"Just shoot the bitch," suggested Walsh.

"Like you did the boy in the hotel, Walsh? And the phone bomb that killed the prosecutor? That was yours as well. The prosecutor's secretary has identified you. You're going down for that one, Walsh. And the others as well. Which one of you likes to use a garrote? Mazur, I'll bet that if we examine their past, we'll find Walsh had training in explosives. Maybe Paola likes a garrote?"

"She hasn't got the papers we want. Let's just do it and get the hell out of here." Paola took a deep inhale of her cigarette. "We shouldn't have come in the first place."

"We couldn't let her go." Mazur shook his head. "A bad precedent if we let her walk. We had to finish the business."

"So get on with it."

Jana brushed blood from her eye, then wagged a bloody finger at them. "Kill me and it's your heads that will roll. Look out the window."

They stared at her, not quite comprehending.

"Look out the window!" Jana's voice was stronger. "You can, from time to time, see unusual things in the snow."

They continued to stare at her.

"The window! I brought you a present."

Walsh walked to the window. Outside, in the swirling snow, was a skirmish line of police officers carrying assault weapons, some behind cars, others kneeling in the snow, all of them focused on the house.

Paola saw Walsh's face change. She went to the window herself, looked out, then ran to the back of the house and peered through the kitchen window. More police officers. She ran back to the living room, walked up to Jana and put the barrel of her gun to Jana's head.

"You won't live to see it."

She started to squeeze the trigger. Walsh pushed the gun aside before she got the shot off. He looked over to Mazur, asking for direction. Mazur went to the window to check out the line of police.

"Give the commander a towel," Mazur said. "We don't want her comrades to think we've been abusing her."

"What?" Paola spit out.

"Paola, we can still walk on the other matters. If we kill their commander, we won't crawl out of here alive. You know how police officers are when you kill one of their own."

"He's right," Walsh agreed.

Jana slowly rose to her feet. Unhurriedly, she walked to the front door, still a little unsteady on her feet from the blow.

"I'd better let my colleagues in before they get impatient. We don't want that, do we?"

She opened the door, took a last look back at them, then stepped out. Trokan was standing to the side of the front door. As she walked over to him, he signaled his men. Slovak police officers poured into the house. Trokan saw Jana's scalp wound, his face becoming grim.

"We should have done without all of this and killed them when they first went into the house."

"That's not our way. It's theirs."

"I suppose. All the same, it would have been satisfying."

"Did you get everything?"

"Everything. Electronics are a wonderful thing."

"We needed their statements. What hard evidence do we have on Paola, Walsh, and the assistant director? They might have walked away from court without this. Now we can be sure."

"Yes." They walked toward the police vehicles. "A short time ago, they arrested the general in Prague. He claims that he was only thinking of your security when he put the tracking device in your car."

"Maybe he was."

"I don't think so." Trokan's anger showed. "I always liked him." He shrugged. "I suppose that reveals that my judgment is fallible."

"No, it doesn't. I have absolute trust in the colonel's infallibility."

"Are you making fun of me again, Commander?"

"Never, Colonel."

They reached the vehicles. Jana looked back; her three colleagues from The Hague were being taken out of the house in handcuffs.

"I'm tired." She relaxed against Trokan. Jana was more than tired. She felt drained.

Chapter 48

After they stitched up her scalp at the hospital, Jana went to the professor's room. He was out of intensive care and Jana had arranged for him to have a private room, but it was empty. She asked the floor nurse where he was. The nurse pointed down the hall to one of the other wards. Before Jana reached it, she could hear the peal of children's laughter. Jana knew what he was doing.

Not just the "Clown Professor of Magic," as he had titled himself, but the "Crown Prince of Magic," as she now thought of him. The prince was again in his kingdom.